PRAISE FOR *WHITE TOMBS*

Named Best Mystery of 2008 by Reader Views
Winner of the Garcia Award for Best Fiction of 2008

"After the owner of *El Dia*, the foremost Hispanic newspaper in St. Paul, Minnesota, is killed in his home, homicide detective John Santana must solve this high-profile case in spite of the community's unwillingness to help and pressure from the mayor to make a speedy arrest. He is also at odds with the detective from the mayor's office, who is doing his best to make Santana look incompetent. Valen's debut police procedural provides enough plot twists to keep readers engrossed and paints a clear picture of the Hispanic community in St. Paul."

—*Library Journal*

"Christopher Valen addresses a very wide range of extremely relevant social issues in *White Tombs*, and this book goes well beyond being just a detective story. The characters are fantastically well developed, and finding more of their layers gradually through the developing story makes them particularly fascinating. Just like in real life, there is more to every character than what first meets the eye. Mr. Valen deftly shows the influence of one's surroundings as well as past events on a person's life. The writing is solid an elegant without unnecessary detours. Any lover of solid writing should enjoy it greatly. White Tombs also screams out for a sequel—or better yet sequels."

—Olivera Baumgartner-Jackson for Reader Views

"John Santana of the St. Paul Police Department is a man you will not soon forget. The book is a great read, and Santana is destined to become one of my favorite detectives. Truly a five-star read from this author."

—Patricia Reid for Armchair Interviews

"Fast-paced, suspense-filled and packed with accurate detail. A gripping story of revenge, murder, and official corruption."

—Brian Lutterman, Author of *Bound to Die* and *Poised to Kill*

"Santana is an intriguing character. St. Paul readers will enjoy Valen's sense of place."

—Mary Ann Grossman, *St. Paul Pioneer Press*

"In this page turner, Christopher Valen presents a clear picture of a modern, urban Hispanic community—plus the horrible Minnesota winter weather."

—*The Poisoned Pen*

"*White Tombs* is a superb police procedural starring a fascinating lead detective. Santana is a wonderful new addition to the sub-genre."

—Harriet Klausner for *Midwest Book Review*

"*White Tombs* is a well crafted who dun it I enjoyed immensely. It's action packed. On a scale of 1-5, I give it a 5."

—Cynthia Lea Clark for
Futures Mystery Anthology Magazine

"*White Tombs* is a promising start to a detective series. I thoroughly enjoyed reading it and look forward to future novels with John Santana."

—Cindy Koppinger for the *Bismarck Tribune*

To Dan,
Thanks for your help
& support.

The Black Minute

A Novel by

Christopher Valen

NORTH STAR PRESS OF ST. CLOUD, INC.
St. Cloud Minnesota

Cover art: Jeff Holmes

"If You Forget Me" by Pablo Neruda, translated by Donald D. Walsh, from *The Captain's Verses*, copyright © 1972 by Pablo Neruda and Donald D. Walsh. Reprinted by permission of New Directions Publishing Corp.

Copyright © 2009 Christopher Valen

ISBN: 0-87839-332-3
ISBN-13: 978-0-87839-332-9

First Edition, September 1, 2009

Printed in the United States of America

Published by
North Star Press of St. Cloud, Inc.
P.O. Box 451
St. Cloud, Minnesota 56302

northstarpress.com

Dedication

For Pat Frovarp and Gary Shulze

"A female blowfly's eyes are widely set. The male's eyes are so close together they almost touch. Bitches will quit flying once the temperature drops below fifty degrees." She was examining the fly as if it were a rare, fine diamond, not one of a million similar insects.

A gust of wind shook the trees surrounding the park. The leaves were turning yellow and red now. They rattled more than summer leaves. Some were floating on wind currents like sailboats on a wavy sea.

Yellow crime scene tape encircled the area. Three forensic techs dressed in white jumpsuits had examined the ground near the body, looking for matted grass, broken twigs, indistinct footprints, and vehicle tracks, but had found nothing. Now they were fanning out, widening the search area.

"Probably some fresh flies here as well," Tanabe said, tipping the tiny wings at an angle. "Species can be distinguished by color, size, and appearance, or by examining the rows of hairs that appear on every one. Different species. Different hair. All ninety of them."

"Any idea as to time of death, Reiko?"

Tanabe considered the question. Santana knew it was because she wanted the answer she gave to be as precise as possible under the circumstances, and not because she was unsure of herself.

"Rigor's complete and the body's cold and stiff. But there's no discoloration of the skin in the lower abdomen and groin. No signs of bloating." She pointed with an index finger toward the body. "The first maggot instar begins anywhere from eleven to thirty-eight hours after eggs are laid depending on the fly species. Given they're blue bottles, I'd say we're looking at twenty-four to thirty-six hours."

Santana was as familiar with the progression of decomposition as a geriatrist was with aging. The type of insects found on and around the body would determine where in the decomposition cycle they had entered the picture. The earlier in the process the body was discovered, the more accurate the establishment of approximate time of death. Accuracy dropped as the body moved through the five stages of decomposition from fresh to bloat to decay to dry to skeletal.

"I'll take a look at the small intestine when I cut her," Tanabe said.

Since a light meal took approximately two hours to digest, and a heavy meal from four to six hours, Santana knew the stomach would be empty and wouldn't tell Tanabe what the dead woman had last eaten. "Any idea how she died, Reiko?"

Tanabe shook her head and unconsciously touched the café au lait mark just below her right ear; a habit Santana had noticed when he first began working homicide cases with her. "There's no apparent evidence of trauma, John. Could be drugs. I'll run some tests." She held up something in her gloved hand. "I found this underneath the body."

"Looks like a small piece of duct tape."

"I'll bag it," she said. "Did you find any ID?"

"Nothing. No purse. No cell phone. No high school or college graduation ring. No watch. But looking at the line on her wrist, I'd say her watch may have been removed."

"I don't see any tats or outstanding characteristics. Maybe someone didn't want us to know who she was."

"Could be. Or the perp didn't want us to know the exact time she died if the watch had stopped."

"I'll collect some maggots. They have to be raised until adulthood to be certain of the species identification. I'll need to catch a few of the adults as well. There's a professor of entomology at the university I've worked with before."

Blowflies were the first colonizers and feeders feasting on bodies left outdoors. In summer, carrion beetles, ants, and wasps would soon follow, feeding on the blowfly eggs and maggots. Forensic entomologists called it insect succession, a process that followed a continuum that began the moment death occurred and enzymes in the digestive system started eating the tissue.

"Make sure you get some nail scrapings and hair samples, Reiko. I'm going to need prints."

Santana could see that rigor had bent the dead woman's fingers toward the palm of her hand. There was no point in attempting to extend a finger. It was too stiff to be straightened.

Tanabe seemed to know what he was thinking. "I could cut the tendons in the fingers, John, so they can be straightened. It's effective, but I'd rather not do it. It's simpler just to bend the hand backward at the wrist."

3

Santana had seen it done before. Once the hand was bent backward it was possible to hold a finger firmly and lift it up to make the print. "Whatever you need to do, Reiko, do it quickly. Rain's coming."

He stood when he saw his partner, Kacie Hawkins, striding toward him. Hawkins was a fitness fanatic, and her lean body was as dark and hard as ebony.

Over her shoulder, the park spread out like a large grassy mat toward the Clarence Wigington pavilion and the Target stage band shell. Two tall towers, one on each side of the band shell, held up a roof that looked like the wing of a giant prehistoric bird. Farther west, the Minnesota Centennial Showboat was anchored at the Padelford Landing. During the summer, the University of Minnesota theatre department presented period musicals and melodramas on the turn-of-the-century-style riverboat.

The park was nearly deserted at this time of the morning except for two men from the city water department who had been marking the underground irrigation system with blue chalk lines, and were now standing just beyond the yellow crime scene tape, trying to get a closer look at the dead woman lying among the weeds.

"Tanabe give you anything?" Hawkins asked.

"She figures the vic's been dead at least twenty-four hours."

"Usually busy around here during the weekend, John. But people walking from the parking lot toward the promenade wouldn't see the body in the tall weeds."

"I agree."

Santana watched Reiko Tanabe as she made several rapid, back-and-forth sweeping motions with a collapsible aerial insect net, reversing it on each pass, like a martial arts master performing an intricate *kata* with a Bo Staff. The net had an attachable handle, which increased the working distance as well as the speed at which the net could be manipulated. On the final pass, Tanabe brought the open portion of the net up to chest level while rotating the opening 180 degrees to trap the bugs.

She placed the end of the net containing the blowflies directly into the wide mouth of a killing jar that contained several cotton balls soaked with fresh ethyl acetate. Once it was capped, the flies would die in two to five minutes. Tanabe would then give the jar to a University of Minnesota entomologist.

4

With any luck, Santana thought, he would find witnesses who had seen or been with the victim before she died and wouldn't need to rely solely on the ME and a university entomologist to pinpoint the time of death.

"What do you want me to do?" Hawkins asked.

"It's going to rain soon, Kacie. Get a crime scene tent set up over the body. Then run the description of the dead woman through the Missing-Person database and her fingerprints through AFIS. See if we come up with anything. Also check NCIC. And have some officers search all the garbage bins in the parking lot. Someone could have dumped her purse and ID there."

"I located the woman who found the body. She lives on her houseboat just through Gate F over there." Hawkins gestured toward the river. "Third boat down on your right. Name is Grace Chandler."

As Santana headed across the parking lot, he focused on the main walkway that continued west past a 1946 vintage towboat, the *MV Covington*, which was outfitted with rooms for guests and parties. The main walkway continued west, running parallel to the Mississippi, to a broad, twenty-foot-wide promenade opposite the Clarence Wigington pavilion. Here, red tiles embedded in the promenade memorialized dead St. Paul firefighters, and a large set of stairs led down to a public dock that extended 800 feet into the river. A sidewalk that split off at a twenty-degree angle from the main walkway led to the Mississippi River and to the houseboats moored at the docks in the lower harbor.

Santana walked past a set of *Pioneer Press* delivery boxes and went down a set of steps and through an open gate. People stood on the decks of their houseboats and along the dock, their necks craning as they observed the crime scene, their voices at first low and then turning to whispers when Santana approached, as though they feared any noise might disturb the investigation or somehow wake the dead.

From the deck of Grace Chandler's houseboat, Santana could see mallards swimming in the river and the sweeping panorama of the city's skyline. The clouds were darker and lower over the city now, their underbellies swollen with rain.

An open sliding glass door on the houseboat led into a living room that was submerged in shadow. Before entering, Santana flipped open his badge wallet and held it up so the slim woman standing behind a center island in a U-shaped galley could clearly see it.

"I'm Detective Santana, Ms. Chandler, from the St. Paul Police Department."

The woman remained silent and motioned with her hand for him to enter and be seated.

He stepped into the room and looked quickly but carefully at the spacious interior of the houseboat. It was decorated with a rich-brown carpet and wood paneling that matched the wooden blinds on the starboard windows, the couch, and reclining chair. A coffee table made out of a ship's wheel stood in front of the couch. Directly to his left was the ship's instrument panel. A built-in fireplace and bookshelf filled with hard covers, paperbacks, and a CD player covered the portside wall.

Grace Chandler came around the galley island and sat in the recliner.

Santana sat down on the coffee-colored leather couch and took a pen and a small spiral notebook from the inner pocket of his sport coat. "I like your boat," he said, trying to ease into the conversation.

He held his eyes on her pretty oval face and pale complexion, which was as smooth and clear as ivory.

"Are you at all familiar with boats, Detective?"

"Some. How big is it?"

"It's a sixty-five-foot aluminum hulled Skipperliner with a fifteen foot beam."

Santana nodded. "Seems to have plenty of room." He looked around. Many boats had tiny little box refrigerators. This one had a full-sized one. He also saw an oven and stove, a trash compactor and microwave in the galley. It didn't have the compact, sometimes cramped feel of other houseboats he'd seen. "How many square feet does this place have?" he asked, curious.

"The main deck has about nine hundred square feet and the open-air upper deck about five hundred."

"It seems well-appointed for a houseboat."

The woman shrugged. "All the comforts I need," she said, her tone deadpan.

"With the blinds closed, it's easy to imagine this is a house rather than a boat."

"That's the general idea." She spoke softly but with a trace of sarcasm.

"Seems a shame to miss the view though."

"I much prefer the shadows and solitude. I can still feel and hear the water."

Her shoulder-length, dark-brown hair was tousled and damp, as though she had used a towel instead of a comb after stepping out of the shower.

"How long have you lived on the river, Ms. Chandler?"

"Nearly three years."

"Less expensive than owning a home?"

She frowned slightly. "Well, owning a home is more of an investment. This is like owning a car—it depreciates in value. Living like this isn't as cheap as most people think. I've got boat payments plus a slip fee to the marina. And insurance is expensive."

"Why do it then? Why not live in a house or apartment?"

She gently rubbed her palms on her faded blue jeans and then tugged at her denim shirt, the tails of which hung casually over her waist. "I'm pretty handy. I like being on the water and the freedom that comes from pulling up anchor and heading somewhere else, though not all marinas allow full-time liveaboards."

"Where did you live before you bought the boat?"

"Minneapolis."

"Do you work there?"

"I'm . . . self-employed."

Santana waited, hoping she might offer something more substantive, but apparently she was used to silence and comfortable with it. Not necessarily a bad habit, he thought, unless it hindered a homicide investigation. "I understand you found the young woman's body this morning."

"Yes."

"About what time?"

"I usually get up early and go for a walk," she said.

"How early?" He waited patiently as she contemplated his question, listened to the mallards in the river quacking at one another, watched as a ray of sunshine seeped through the blinds and lit the carpet before the light faded away.

"I left here a little after seven-fifteen. I saw the flies on my way back to the boat."

"What time was that?"

"Around eight o'clock. I thought an animal had died. Happens quite a bit around here." She leaned forward and propped her arms on her knees. "Did you or someone you know ever get a strong feeling about something, Detective Santana? Like maybe something isn't right?"

Santana remembered when he was in high school. He and his friends would save their allowances. On Fridays they would visit the witch who lived in the poor neighborhood of Manizales, Colombia. She would read the tealeaves and tarot cards, or the cigarettes of those who smoked, and predict the future.

"Sometimes," he said.

"Well, I had this feeling. And then I saw the woman, and I knew."

"Knew what?"

"I knew she was dead."

A stiff breeze suddenly blew through the open sliding door.

"Did you see anyone near the body or in the park?"

"It's pretty dead at that time of the morning." She immediately caught the double-entendre and her hand went to her mouth, briefly covering the slight dimple on her chin. "Sorry. I didn't mean to say that."

"You never told me what you do for a living, Ms. Chandler."

"You never asked, Detective Santana." The corners of her mouth drew back in a slight smile.

He waited again, hoping that the momentary lag in the conversation would prove too uncomfortable for her and she would offer more information. But he was as wrong this time as before. "Would you like to tell me?"

"What does my occupation have to do with the investigation?"

"Maybe nothing. Maybe something."

Outside, thunder rumbled like a heavy weight rolling across a hardwood floor. Murder, Santana thought, was like a change in the weather, inevitable yet unpredictable.

"I'm an artist," she said at last. "Water color mostly. I've had a few shows. I rent a small studio in downtown St. Paul."

"That one of your paintings above the fireplace?"

"No. It's a reproduction of the Legend of the Grateful Dead. Are you familiar with it?"

"No, I'm not."

"The original fresco was painted on an ossuary wall in Baar, Switzerland. The man kneeling in the cemetery is being chased by a band of thieves and is praying for help. Grateful for the man's prayers so their souls can rest in peace, the dead rise up out of their graves to protect him, some with scythes, others with sticks. It's actually a twist on the usual macabre genre of the time. Instead of being a menace, the fleshless corpses lend a hand to the people crying out in fear. The message being that we should pray in memory of the ones we loved."

Santana remembered the earlier breeze on his neck, how it felt like the cold hand of death. "You must get paid rather handsomely," he said, nodding at the surroundings.

"There's a price to pay for everything, Detective Santana. But I suspect you already know that."

"I'd like to think so, Ms. Chandler. But there are some people in this world who do a great deal of harm and don't appear to pay much of a price for the decisions they make. Usually, it's the poor and uneducated who end up paying, and often with their lives."

"You're quite the cynic," she said with a little smile.

"An occupational hazard."

Raindrops began hammering the roof. He could feel the houseboat shift underneath him as if the earth were moving. It reminded him of the earthquake that had hit Manizales when he was fourteen. Only five houses had collapsed in the quake. All five were designed and built by an American company for their employees.

"You're the detective whose partner was killed eight months ago, aren't you?" she said.

Her words jolted him, as if the dead had suddenly begun walking out of the painting on the wall. "How did you know that?"

She smiled in amusement. "I read it in the newspaper."

He thought that she had a good smile, a warm smile, a smile that added some color to her complexion and some life to the blank canvas that was her face.

9

Santana could hear the river lapping at the dock pilings and the rain pounding the roof of the houseboat. Thick clouds had eclipsed the sun and turned the dark, lavender sky the color of a decomposing body. He thought of Reiko Tanabe, the forensic crew, and of all the evidence outside the tent that would be washed away in the pouring rain. And he wondered again if the dead women's watch had been taken. Wondered if Grace Chandler knew something about it.

"Is there anything you can tell me about the young woman you found this morning?" he asked.

Her gaze never wavered as she reached into the pocket of her denim shirt and took out a woman's silver watch. She held it out in front of her like a worm.

"Why did you take her watch?"

"I didn't take anything," she said. "I found the watch near the parking lot when I returned from my walk. I thought it might belong to the dead woman, but I wasn't sure. I wanted to ask at the yacht club first. See if anyone was missing a watch." She tilted her head to the left and to the right, peering at the watch, as though she wanted to get a different perspective. Then she set it delicately on the table in front of her. "It's made by Citizen," she said. "There are no identifying initials or markings. I just wanted to double-check."

If she was being honest about the watch, Santana thought, then the perp might have taken it as a trophy and lost it on the way to the parking lot. Then again, Grace Chandler might be correct. The watch could belong to someone else.

He took an evidence envelope out of an inner pocket, unfolded it, and lifted the watch off the coffee table with his pen and dropped it into the envelope.

"I'd rather not get involved with any of this," she said.

"You already are, Ms. Chandler. You found the body."

"As far as I'm concerned, that's the extent of my involvement."

"Is it?"

Grace Chandler blew out a long breath. "I'm sorry if I caused a problem. Are you going to arrest me for picking up the watch?"

He took out a business card and set it on the coffee table. "I don't think so."

She picked up his card, glanced at it, and then appeared to come to a decision. "Ever do any boating, Detective John Santana?" Her pale-blue eyes shimmered with energy, like a patch of water lit by an underwater light.

He knew that she was inquiring about more than his interest in boating. "Once in a while."

She smiled. "I could use a good deck hand."

A single framed photo stood on a shelf. The man in the photo had thick, blond hair and resembled a model. Santana wondered if it was her boyfriend or her husband. "You know where you can reach me."

"Yes," she said, waving the card at him, "I certainly do." She stood and walked away, disappearing into what he assumed was a bedroom in the stern of the boat.

Santana stared for a time at the empty space she had inhabited and then peered down at the spiral notebook in his hand. He hadn't written a word.

Chapter 2

Clouds spit scattered drops of rain on the hood of Santana's white Crown Victoria as he drove out of the parking lot on Harriet Island.

He had spent two hours talking with the yacht club members who lived on their houseboats in the marina, hoping he might find someone who had seen the Asian woman before she died, someone who might own the watch, someone who might offer some clues that could help solve the mystery of her death, but he had come up empty. He had spent another forty-five minutes completing an initial crime scene report on his laptop as he sat in the front seat of his car. Since the department had begun providing portable laptops for detectives, he was able to complete his paper work nearly anywhere besides headquarters.

It had taken him longer than expected to finish the report because Grace Chandler kept intruding on his thoughts. He found himself drawn to her. But she had discovered the body. She could be considered a suspect if it turned out that the woman had been murdered. Still, he found her interesting and very attractive.

Kacie Hawkins called him on his cell just after he completed the report. A latent print taken from the dead woman had been matched in the AFIS database. The victim had been identified as Mai Yang. She and a woman named Jenna Jones ran an in-call/out-call service out of an apartment in the Battle Creek neighborhood. They both had been arrested for prostitution a year ago and fingerprinted.

Santana remembered a time not long ago when searching for a match between a latent print at the crime scene with a criminal fingerprint database was virtually impossible. Now, with the development of the Automated Fingerprint Identification System, it could be done in about ten minutes. The only drawback to the AFIS system was that one state's database could not be searched by a system sold by another vendor.

The address Hawkins gave Santana was in a two-story brick apartment building near Lower Afton Road in Battle Creek, a neighborhood south of Interstate 94 and west of McKnight Road.

In 1975 when St. Paul had first formed community councils in the seventeen districts that encompassed the city, it was decided that boundaries would be set based on neighborhood identities rather than by population. Battle Creek was the oldest settlement within the city limits. The Kaposia band of Dakota Sioux had lived in the area until the 1830s. It had remained primarily farmland until after World War II when the first Baby Boomers were born and the housing explosion of the 1950s began. Still, many of the houses in Battle Creek had been built after 1970. The neighborhood was mostly white with a small percentage of blacks and Asians.

Santana parked the Crown Vic in the apartment lot off Hillsdale. The rain had stopped, but the leaves were still dripping water, and the asphalt was slick and shining like a polished floor in the headlights. A large crow sitting high up on an oak branch near the trunk of the tree called out as Santana walked into a small lobby. He remembered learning as a child that a single crow over a house meant death was near, particularly if the crow cawed.

He used a security phone to ring an apartment on the second floor.

Someone said, "Come on up," without asking his name. The security system buzzed, and he went up a short set of stairs to the apartment and knocked on the door.

"Jenna Jones?" he said when the apartment door swung open.

"You're early," she said, giving him a rehearsed smile. "But I like what I see. Tall, dark and handsome."

The smile was supposed to be sexy with a hint of pleasures to come, but sadness lingered behind the glossy red lips. Jenna Jones wore a white, low-cut halter-top that showed off her ample breasts, tight pink slacks and white sandals. He could smell the vanilla in her perfume and the cigarette smoke in her bleached blonde hair. He estimated she was about twenty-three, though her face was beginning to wear like a tire driven hard and for a long time.

Santana showed her his badge. "I think you have me confused with someone else."

She stopped chewing her gum, and a momentary flicker of concern showed in her brown eyes. Then, it was gone.

"I'm Detective John Santana. St. Paul PD."

She nodded hesitantly.

"Expecting someone?"

"Just a friend."

"I'm not here to bust you."

"Bust me for what?"

Santana had hoped he could avoid the quick denial by letting her know where he was coming from, but she was still putting up a front. Having no desire to argue with her, he said, "I want to talk to you about your roommate, Mai Yang."

"What about Mai? Is she in trouble?"

"Why don't we sit down?"

Jenna Jones stood perfectly still, fearing perhaps that the glamorous world of fancy cars and clothes, expensive jewelry and rich men she still imagined was about to end. Santana had seen it all before. The dreams never died, only the young women.

He stepped into the apartment and shut the door behind him.

That seemed to snap her out of the trance. She turned and walked over to a futon with light-blue cushions and sat down.

It was a standard two-bedroom apartment with a small living room, dining room and kitchen. The only pieces of furniture in the living room, besides the futon, were a cheap coffee table, an overstuffed chair and entertainment center. Nothing matched.

It reminded Santana of his first apartment. After he had fled Colombia at sixteen, he had lived with a St. Paul detective and his wife. At eighteen, he had gone off to the University of Minnesota and into his first apartment with the couple's secondhand furniture and pots and pans.

Santana sat down in the overstuffed chair.

A solitary glass of wine stood on the coffee table beside a LeAnn Rimes CD sleeve. The volume wasn't loud, but Jenna Jones picked up a remote lying next to her on the futon and turned off the music.

"What about Mai?" Jenna Jones asked again.

"We found her body this morning on Harriet Island. I'm sorry."

Jenna Jones's bottom lip quivered, and her brown eyes glistened. But she held herself together by crossing her arms tightly across her chest, refusing to let even the death of her friend light an emotional fire. "What happened?"

"We don't know yet."

Santana took out his pen and spiral notebook. This time, he promised himself, he would write something down. "When was the last time you saw or spoke with Mai?"

"Saturday night."

"Was it unusual for her to be gone for a day and a half?"

"Not really."

"Was Mai with someone on Saturday night, Ms. Jones?"

"She got a call just as I was going out."

"Where might Mai go when she's out for the evening?"

Jenna Jones thought about it. Then she said, "Probably the Myth nightclub. I went there with Mai quite a bit. A lot of the Hmong go there."

"So she's Hmong."

"Yes."

"Did Mai have a cell phone?"

"You didn't find it in her purse?"

"Both the phone and purse are missing. I'll need the cell number."

Jenna Jones told him, and he wrote it down.

"Did Mai wear a watch?"

"Yes."

"Gold or silver band?"

"I believe it was silver."

"Do you know what kind of watch she wore?"

Jenna Jones shook her head.

Santana dumped the watch out of the evidence envelope and onto the coffee table. "Does this look like her watch?"

"Yes."

He used his pen again to place the watch back in the envelope. "Do you keep any kind of records?"

"Records?"

"A client list."

"I don't know what you mean?"

"Sure you do."

He could see she wanted to protest, that it was important for her to continue the illusion she had created for herself. But she knew that he knew what she did for a living, and it would be futile to deny it.

"I never kept any list," she said. "I don't think Mai did either." She reached for the cigarette burning in an ashtray next to a roam phone and a *TV Guide* on the coffee table, picked it up, knocked a long ash off the end of it and took a small hit.

Santana had never smoked, but he had been around a lot of people who did. Jenna Jones handled a cigarette as if it were a stick of dynamite about to explode. "Did Mai take any drugs?"

"No."

"You're sure?"

"I'm sure."

"You'd know?"

"Of course I would."

He could tell by the way her eyes darted back and forth that she was already thinking about how to answer his next logical question. He decided to reassure her once again. "Like I said before, Ms. Jones. I'm not here to bust you. I just need answers, truthful answers, if I'm going to find out what happened to Mai."

She nodded and set her cigarette on the edge of the ashtray.

"Do you use?" he asked.

She kept her eyes on the trail of smoke that rose from the ashtray. "I've done a little pot, a little coke, but nothing more."

"Then how can you be so sure Mai wasn't using?"

When her eyes met his again, he saw that there was something wistful and remorseful in them now. "Mai wasn't like that," she said. "I'm not like that."

Santana imagined that under the dark eye shadow and heavy makeup Jenna Jones was a girl who might have grown up on a farm. Maybe she had been a homecoming queen or maybe as a young girl she had belonged to 4H and had brought a calf that she loved to the state fair. Perhaps sometime in her teens she had taken a closer look at her boyfriend and decided that she could do much better, that being a farmer's wife in a small Minnesota town was more confining than a straightjacket. Like many young girls with dreams of modeling and acting, she figured her face was her ticket out of town. But she soon discovered there were lots of young women who had come to the same conclusion, and many of them were prettier and more talented.

Modeling jobs in the city were hard to come by, especially if you were a few inches under five-foot-ten and were more than just skin and bone. Money had probably become tight. She had to eat and pay the rent. She couldn't go back home and admit to her family and friends that she had been wrong, that the stable future she had once rejected now seemed more appealing than the one she had chosen for herself. So when someone she thought was a friend had suggested there were easier ways to make money and that the profits outweighed the costs, she decided to use the last asset she had, a decision worse than all the bad decisions that had preceded it.

"What can you tell me about Mai?" he asked.

"Her parents live in Highland Park. Her father was a general or something during the Vietnam War."

"Was Mai a refugee?"

"No. She was born here."

"Any other family you know of?"

"I think she has a brother."

"Do you have an address for her parents?"

17

Jenna Jones shook her head, ran a hand through her shoulder-length hair. "There might be something in Mai's bedroom."

"Mind if I take a look?"

"I don't think Mai would like . . ." she paused, and then gestured toward the hallway. Her brown eyes appeared as vacant as an abandoned barn on the prairie. "It's the room on the right."

Santana filled out a Consent to Search form and had Jenna Jones sign it. Then he got up and went into the first bedroom.

The room had a double bed with no headboard. The wall just above the bed was stained blue where pillows with blue cases had rested against the wall. The spread was folded back to reveal rumpled sheets. On one side of the bed was a nightstand on which were a phone and a *Glamour* magazine. Along the wall on the other side of the bed was a dresser and large mirror. The top of the dresser was filled with perfumes, hand lotions, a brush, and comb. A large poster of Brittney Spears was taped to the wall. He went through the dresser drawers and the closet, empty hangers clanging as he checked coat pockets. The clothes were provocative and smelled strongly of a perfume he didn't recognize.

Santana had spent many hours as a homicide detective rummaging through the belongings of the dead, not knowing precisely what he was looking for, only that he would recognize it if he found it. At first it had bothered him. But he soon came to realize that the dead could speak to him through their personal effects. The victim was what homicide detectives called the silent witness. And so he ignored the little voice in his head that told him sometimes to rush it, that told him the odds were against him, and there was nothing in this room that would tell him whether Mai Yang had been murdered or who the murderer might be. He took his time, searched carefully, and listened intently for something to speak to him, as Mai Yang could not.

When he came out of the bedroom, the wine glass on the coffee table in front of Jenna Jones had been refilled.

"Did you find anything?" she asked.

"At this stage of the investigation, I don't know exactly what I'm looking for." He sat down on the chair across from her again and said, "How does someone go about contacting you?"

"We run ads on Craigslist."

"You run your own ads?"

"Yes."

Santana set a business card on the coffee table. The name on the card read, KAREN WONG, PSYCHOLOGIST. An appointment was written on the back along with the next day's date and a time of 1:00 p.m.

"Where did you find the card?"

"In the nightstand next to the bed. Did you know Mai was seeing a therapist?"

She shook her head.

"Did Mai's parents know what she did for a living?"

"I think so. But Mai's mother died recently. She hadn't spoken to her father for a long time."

"What about your parents? Do they know what you do for a living?"

Jenna Jones averted her eyes and stared out a window at the large crow still sitting on a branch in the oak tree near the front entrance. It had begun to rain again, and drops splattered against the glass like bugs on a windshield.

"My name isn't really Jenna Jones. It's Carol. Carol Baumgartner." A black wing of sadness suddenly appeared to envelop Jenna Jones, as though in changing her name, she had lost her identity. "I changed it to Jenna because it's the first name of a famous porn actress. Jones seemed to go with Jenna. And if I was ever arrested, my real name wouldn't appear in the paper."

Santana had changed his name from Juan Carlos Gutierrez Arángo when he came to the States at sixteen. He thought that changing it would help protect him from the long reach of the Cali cartel. But he had been mistaken. "Did you ever consider going home?"

"St. Paul is my home," she said.

"I don't think so."

She looked at him. "Do you think I'm in danger?"

"Until I know how Mai died, you could be."

Her gaze shifted to the dead ash hanging from the cigarette and then toward the bare, white walls of the living room. There was a distant look in Jenna Jones's eyes now, as if she were seeing a vast expanse of wheat fields on a farm in western Minnesota instead of the narrow horizons of her apartment.

The phone rang and she nearly jumped out of her sandals.

"Answer it," Santana said. "Tell him to come up."

"How do you know it's a him?"

"You were expecting a client when I arrived."

She nodded reluctantly and did as she was told.

After she hung up, Santana said, "What's his name?"

"He calls himself Thomas Carlson. He called Saturday and set up an appointment with Mai for today."

"He asked specifically for Mai and not you."

"Yes. But since she wasn't here, I thought he might like . . ." She shrugged.

"You don't think Thomas Carlson is his real name?"

"Most men, especially if they're married, use phony names."

"How do they pay you?"

She hesitated, obviously uncomfortable with the tacit admission of her profession, before she said, "Cash."

"You ever met Carlson before?"

"No."

Santana got up and went to a spot against the wall where he would be behind the door when it swung open.

Someone knocked.

Jenna Jones regarded Santana as though she needed reassurance.

"Invite him in," he mouthed.

She drank the rest of her wine in one swallow, stood, and walked unsteadily to the door.

She opened the apartment door and a man came in.

Santana pushed the door shut behind him.

Chapter 3

The man had an olive complexion and a lean, muscular physique. He wore black-framed glasses, a green polo shirt, khaki pants, and brown loafers with tassels. His black hair was cut short and combed straight forward. He had the small, dark eyes of a bird, and they flicked warily from Santana to Jenna Jones and then back to Santana again. Santana made him for forty, but if his name was Thomas Carlson, then Santana was Ole Swenson.

"What's going on?" the man asked with a heavy accent Santana guessed was Indian or Pakistani.

Santana held up his badge wallet.

The man looked as if he was about to faint. "I don't want any trouble, please."

"You have an ID?"

His head went up and down quickly. As the man reached a shaky hand into his back pocket, Santana noticed he had long, thin fingers. He handed Santana the wallet, which contained two hundred dollars in cash, an AT&T calling card, a photo of a woman and young girl, and a Minnesota driver's license with the man's picture. The name on the driver's license was Rashid Hassan.

"This your real name and correct address?" Santana said, holding the driver's license.

"Yes."

Santana motioned toward the futon. "Why don't you sit down?"

"Of course." He brushed past Jenna Jones as if she were invisible and sat down on the futon.

Santana asked Jenna to sit next to Hassan, then took a seat in the over-stuffed chair again and took out his notebook and copied the information from Hassan's driver's license. Then he said, "What do you do for a living, Mr. Hassan?"

"I am working for 3M."

"And what is it you do there?"

"I am an environmental engineer."

"How long have you been in this country?"

"Two years."

"You here on a work visa?"

He nodded.

"From where?"

"Pakistan."

"You married?"

"Yes."

"Kids?"

"A girl. Safia."

"I'm sure you wouldn't want your family to find out about this."

"Oh, no. I am truly sorry for my behavior." Hassan cast his eyes on Jenna Jones and shrugged his shoulders, as though he thought he had insulted her by apologizing.

"You really haven't done anything," she said to him. "Isn't that right, Detective Santana?"

"Technically, yes."

Hassan held his hands between his knees and rubbed them together as though he were trying to get them clean. "I have never done this before. I know you hear this statement many times in your line of work, Detective."

"More than once. Where were you Saturday night, Mr. Hassan?"

"I was at home."

"Can anyone verify that?"

22

His dark brows knitted. "My wife. Why do you ask?"

"Mai Yang was found dead on Harriet Island this morning," Santana said.

Hassan's hand went to his mouth, and he began to rock slowly back and forth. "Oh, my goodness."

"Are you all right, Mr. Hassan?" Jenna Jones asked.

"This is terrible," he said, coughing. "I knew I should not have made this call. I knew it." He coughed again.

"Would you like some water?"

"Yes. That would be most helpful."

She got up and went into the kitchen.

Hassan took a handkerchief from a front pants pocket, removed his glasses and began wiping the lenses so hard Santana thought they might shatter.

He seemed genuinely frightened and embarrassed, as most men would if caught in similar circumstances. Having to explain his actions to a wife or an employer could certainly cause Hassan the kind of stress Santana was seeing. Still, Santana was skeptical. It was his nature. Having spent the last five years in homicide only increased his level of skepticism and his ability to detect false mannerisms. "Have you ever been to this apartment before, Mr. Hassan?"

"Oh, no. Never."

"How did you get this number?"

"It was advertised on the Internet."

"Lots of ads like the one you called?"

"Oh, yes," he said, putting on his glasses again.

"Why did you ask specifically for Mai Yang?"

"I wanted an Asian woman."

"Is your wife Asian?"

"No," he said, looking away.

Jenna Jones came back into the living room with a cup filled with water and set it on the coffee table.

Hassan coughed, wiped his forehead with the handkerchief, and then picked up the cup.

"I'm going to walk you out to your car, now, Mr. Hassan," Santana said.

Hassan abruptly stopped drinking the water but kept his eyes on Santana. "I am free to go?"

"For now."

"Oh, thank you, Detective," he said with a relieved smile. "Thank you so very much."

"You might want to find something else to do in your free time, Mr. Hassan."

"That is most certainly good advice. I will follow it."

"See that you do."

* * *

On the way to Highland Park, Santana called the communications center and got General Yang's address. He tried Mai Yang's cell phone number, hoping that whoever took her phone might answer, but all he got was her voice mail. Then he called Kacie Hawkins on her cell, gave her the address in Highland Park, and told her to meet him there. When informing the family of the death of a loved one, it was standard procedure to have two detectives deliver the news.

Highland Park was a mostly residential area located in the southwestern corner of St. Paul. Bound on the north by Randolph Avenue, on the east by Interstate 35E and on the south and west by the Mississippi River, it was the home of several well-known private schools and the College of St. Catherine. The area also included the large Ford Motor Company plant at Mississippi River Boulevard and Ford Parkway. It had been in operation since 1926, but was now in danger of closing because the light trucks made there were selling about as well as sun tan oil during a Minnesota winter.

Santana took 94W downtown where he caught Shepard Road west, which he followed to Mississippi River Boulevard, the last street before the winding river divided St. Paul from Minneapolis. The rain had ceased once again, but heavy gray clouds still rolled like billowing smoke across the sky.

About half a mile from the Ford Assembly Plant, he saw Kacie Hawkins's Crown Vic parked on the shoulder of the boulevard in front of a large, white, two-story house with black shutters. With its circular driveway, three colossal columns, and second floor balcony and railing that extended over the front entrance, the house appeared out of place among the predominately ranch-style homes in the neighborhood. Apparently, the general had done very well for himself after the war.

Santana parked on the east side of the boulevard directly behind Hawkins. On the opposite side of the road, a tar walking path followed the curve of the tree-lined boulevard, and a black, wrought-iron railing kept children from falling down the steep bank and into the river far below.

Hawkins got out of her car, taking long strides with her muscular legs, and met him as he got out of his. She wore jeans and a white cotton pullover under a light-blue blazer. At twenty-eight, she was seven years younger and a half-foot shorter than Santana's six-foot-one. She was the only African American and the youngest detective in the homicide unit, but she was street wise and tough, having grown up in Chicago before moving to Minnesota to attend college. She had made a name for herself on the sex-crimes unit two years ago busting johns before transferring to homicide. She was known as "Designer" around headquarters not because of her penchant for expensive clothes but because of her perfectly shaped ass. Rita Gamboni, the homicide commander, had asked Santana to work with Hawkins after his last partner had been killed.

Santana briefed Hawkins about his conversations with Carol Baumgartner, a.k.a. Jenna Jones and Rashid Hassan a.k.a. Thomas Carlson, before they began walking up the driveway toward the house.

"You think the two of them were being truthful?" she asked.

"Maybe. Get a warrant for Mai Yang's phone records and do a background check on Rashid Hassan."

Santana pushed the doorbell and heard chimes ringing inside the house. He imagined if General Yang sat on the balcony, he could see the houses on the high bank across the river once the leaves had fallen from the trees.

The man in the perfectly creased black pants and matching knit pullover who answered the door stood about five-foot-seven thanks to the thick-heeled boots he wore. His dark, crewcut hair was graying at the temples, though his face looked considerably younger than his age, which Santana guessed was at least sixty. Only a thin, jagged scar, which began just below his left ear lobe and ran down his neck, marred his smooth skin.

"Can I help you?" he asked. His dark, hooded eyes calmly surveyed Santana and then Hawkins. He appeared as relaxed as a cobra just before it struck.

Santana figured Yang was a man accustomed to commanding respect, a man who feared little and had seen his share of death, a man who would appreciate being addressed by his former military rank. "General Yang?" he said.

"Yes?"

"I'm Detective John Santana with the Saint Paul Police Department. This is my partner, Detective Kacie Hawkins. We'd like to talk to you about your daughter, Mai." Santana held out his badge wallet.

Yang ignored it. Instead, he gave a nod, stepped back from the door, and gestured toward a pair of open-paneled doors to the right of the staircase in the foyer.

Santana followed Hawkins into the foyer and through the paneled doors that opened into a small study. There were four red high-back wing chairs with brass nail heads that formed a U around a coffee table in front of the fireplace. The general closed the paneled doors and sat in one of the chairs to the left of the table. Santana sat in a chair next to Hawkins, facing the general.

From where he sat, Santana could see that the floor-to-ceiling bookshelves on one wall held the six volumes of Jules Michelet's, *L' Histoirie de France*, Jean Paul Sartre's existentialist classic *Being and Nothingness*, and tactical classics like *The Art of War* by Sun Tzu, *Instructions to His Generals* by Frederick the Great, and *On War* by Karl Von Clausewitz.

"You would not be here, Detective, unless my daughter was in trouble. What has she done this time?"

Telling parents they had lost a child was always the toughest part of the job. Santana had never found an easy way to say it, and so he used as few words as possible. "A body was found this morning on Harriet Island. We believe it's your daughter. I'm very sorry."

The general showed no reaction other than a nearly imperceptible nod, as if Santana had told him he had just been given a parking ticket. "Was she murdered?"

The question was unusual but not unprecedented. Perhaps the general had suspected the worst, given his previous comment concerning his daughter's propensity for trouble.

"We don't know yet. We're merely conducting an investigation at this point. Your daughter's body was taken to the medical examiner's office at Regions Hospital. You'll have to identify the body. Once we have the autopsy report, we might be able to draw some conclusions." Santana placed a card on the table. "There are phone numbers on this card for a victim advocate, the medical examiner's office, and the Ramsey County Attorney's Office if you have questions."

Yang peered at the card but didn't pick it up.

"Have you spoken with your daughter recently?"

He shook his head. "Not since my wife's funeral."

"And how long ago was that?"

"Three months."

Santana glanced toward the coffee table and a framed photograph of Mai Yang in a mortarboard hat at her high school graduation.

The general pointed to a similar photo on the table of a young man who appeared to be a few years younger than Mai, and who looked like a clone of his father. "That is my son, Kou."

"And where is he?"

"Kou is at the University of St. Thomas. He is studying business."

Santana wanted to dig more into the family dynamics, but he sensed that he would get nothing from the general if he dug too quickly and too deeply.

The general must have guessed what Santana was feeling because he said, "Unfortunately, my daughter chose to destroy herself and her reputation. This is not something that is acceptable in Hmong society. We act as a group, not as individuals. Respect for your elders is very important."

"How do mean your daughter chose to destroy herself?" Hawkins asked.

"My daughter was a prostitute, Detective Hawkins."

"Is that why you haven't seen her for three months?"

Yang directed his eyes at Hawkins for a time without speaking. There was nothing overtly hostile in his expression, just a sinister feeling that surrounded him like an aura. Santana saw Hawkins draw back slightly and unconsciously touch her cheek with a hand, as though the general had reached out and slapped it.

The panel doors suddenly swung open, and the general's son marched into the study. He wore a short-sleeved cotton shirt open at the collar, stone-washed jeans, and a pair of athletic shoes. On his left forearm, there appeared to be two recent cigarette burns that had scabbed over.

"What are the police doing here?" he asked, pointing toward the boulevard where the two Crown Vics were parked. His tone was more accusatory than questioning.

As the general peered calmly up at his son, Santana could see the vertical wrinkles between the young man's eyes and his hard, penetrating stare.

"The detectives are here about your sister," the general said without emotion.

"What about her?"

"Your sister is dead."

Santana noticed an immediate change in the young man's expression as his eye lids rose and his mouth opened in a dumbfounded look. But it was the temporary expression of anger indicated by his lowered brows and the hard stare in his eyes that caught Santana's attention.

"Dead? How can she be dead?" Kou Yang's response sounded more like a statement than a question.

Santana glanced at Hawkins to see if she had noticed, but she was busy writing in her notebook. "We're not sure at this point. When was the last time you saw your sister?"

Kou shrugged his shoulders and then looked away.

"Was it a week ago? A month?"

"My son was not close to his sister," the general said.

The tears Santana saw in the young man's eyes seemed to indicate differently.

"What about your sister's friends?" Hawkins asked. "Would they be able to help us?"

"I didn't know any of her friends." His fists were balled tight, but the corners of his lips were drawn down in an expression of sadness rather than anger.

Santana was certain that the general had noticed the inconsistencies between his son's body language and his responses. Yet, he remained quiet. Kou was, after all, his son. But if the general was protecting him, Santana wanted to know from what or from whom. "Do you know anyone who might want to harm your sister?" Santana asked.

Kou shook his head stiffly, turned and stormed out of the room, slamming the front door closed behind him. A few moments later, a car engine roared and tires squealed on blacktop as the boy sped away.

"I apologize for my son," the general said. "He often gets emotional."

"Something wrong with that?" Hawkins said.

The general's expression appeared to remain the same, yet there was something cold and dead in the look he gave Hawkins. "I'm afraid my son is a product of the American system, unlike you, Detective Santana. You are not from this country."

The general was more perceptive than he let on.

"I think South America."

"I'm from Colombia originally."

General Yang nodded thoughtfully.

"What do you do for a living?" Santana asked.

"I own some rental property. I have some investments."

"Does your son live at home with you?"

"No. He lives in a house near the college."

"Could you give us the address?"

"My son can't help you."

"Why don't you let us determine that?"

The general smiled, but there was no warmth in it. It was the kind of a smile he might have given to a captured Viet Cong soldier he was about to interrogate.

General Yang told Santana the address, and he wrote it in his notebook.

"Is there anything more you can tell us about your daughter," Hawkins asked. "Friends she might've had? Boys she might've dated?"

"As I said before, I know little about my daughter's life and nothing about her death."

The general's tone was so cold Santana could almost see the condensation forming as he spoke. "Did Mai own a watch?"

29

"Yes. My wife bought her one for her last birthday."

Santana showed the general the watch with the silver band.

"Yes," he said. "That looks like the one my wife gave her."

"We'd like to borrow a photo of your daughter if you have one, General."

The general pushed himself effortlessly out of his chair. He slid the backing off a single four-by-six gold frame resting on a bookshelf and removed the photo of his daughter. He held it in his hand and gazed at it for a time before he gave it to Santana. "You will let me know the results of the investigation."

"Of course." Santana and Hawkins stood. He handed the general one of his business cards. "This is my number at the station. Also, my cell."

General Yang put the card in a pants pocket and led them out of the study to the front door.

When he opened it, Hawkins went out quickly.

"I have upset your partner," the general said. "She believes I did not love my daughter."

"It was easy to get that impression."

The general drew a long-stem rose out of a vase on a pedestal near the door and rotated it gently in his small hands. "Roses were my daughter's favorite flower. I used to buy them for her."

"Maybe when we talk again, General, you can tell me more about your daughter."

"You seem to believe I have not been completely honest with you, Detective Santana. Why is that?"

"We have a saying in Colombia, General. *Verdades y rosas tienen espinas*. Truth and roses have thorns."

"So they do."

Santana started out the door and then paused and looked back at the general. "I'm going to find out what happened to your daughter. And if she was murdered, I'm going to find out who's responsible."

The general fixed his eyes on Santana's. "Yes," he said at last. "I believe you will."

Chapter 4

"I'm sorry I lost it in there," Hawkins said. "But there's something about the general that made my skin crawl."

Hawkins was resting her designer ass against the hood of her Crown Vic. Her arms were crossed in front of her, and she wore a look that was a combination of anger and regret.

"You can't let a guy like Yang get to you," Santana said.

Hawkins looked at him but said nothing.

"What is it, Kacie?"

She kept her eyes on his and blew out a breath. "You don't have to be my guardian angel, John, just my partner."

"You think I'm being overly protective?"

"Like a mother hen."

"I don't see it that way."

"Think about it."

"I just don't want you to let some guy yank your chain so you miss the small details."

"Such as?"

"The kid's body language. While Kou was denying that he had seen his sister recently, his non-verbals were telling us he was lying."

31

"So was the general," she said. "He knows more about his daughter's life and death than he's telling us."

"Perhaps. But there are people you push and those you don't because they'll push back. Knowing the difference is important. The kid's the one we need to go after if we want the truth."

Hawkins gave a frustrated shake of her head. "I won't let it happen again. But I don't need a babysitter, John."

Santana was willing to cut her some slack as long as she learned from her mistakes. But maybe he had been overly protective, though he had a valid reason. He didn't want Hawkins to end up dead like his last partner. "The kid had two cigarette burns on his left forearm," he said. "It's a classic Asian gang sign."

"You think he knows more than he's telling us about his sister's death?"

"I'm sure of it. Check Kou Yang's house. If he's home, call me. I want to talk to him without his father present."

"What about you?"

Santana glanced at his watch. "I'm going to see Karen Wong."

Hawkins arched her eyebrows and long, horizontal wrinkles creased her forehead. She held the look for a few seconds before she said, "I thought you already met once with her after the shooting."

"I did. But I found this in Mai Yang's bedroom."

He showed Hawkins the business card he had found in the nightstand. "Maybe Karen Wong can tell us something about why Mai Yang died."

* * *

Police agencies around the country had different policies regarding officer-involved shootings. For some departments, a mandatory post-shooting intervention with a qualified mental-health professional was standard operating procedure. Mandatory interventions reduced the stigma of seeking help. For other departments, an intervention was voluntary. Making it voluntary usually helped reduce resentment and left the shooter feeling more in control at a time when everything could feel like it was spinning out of control. But many officers would refuse to participate if post-shooting interventions were strictly voluntary. Santana was no exception.

The SPPD chose a hybrid approach. Santana had been required to see Karen Wong once in order to obtain information on what resources were available to him. Because there were no further contacts after the first intervention, she had periodically left messages on his answering machine asking how he was. Her most recent call had come a week ago.

Santana hadn't returned any of the calls.

He stopped at a Chipotle Mexican grill where he ordered a burrito and Coke. Then he called ahead and alerted Wong he would like to see her.

Karen Wong lived in a nineteenth-century Brownstone in the Crocus Hill neighborhood of St. Paul. Clients used a separate entrance to her office.

"Good to see you again, Detective Santana," she said as she held open the side door.

The voice belonged to an attractive Asian woman with a heart-shaped face and soft, full black hair cut even with the nape of her neck. She wore it brushed across her forehead so that it drew attention to her large brown eyes.

Santana shook her small, delicate hand.

"I wasn't sure I'd hear from you after my last phone call. How are you doing, Detective?" Her smile had none of the artifice he had seen in Jenna Jones's smile.

"I'm doing fine. But I'm not here to talk about the shooting. I'm here to see you about Mai Yang." Santana pulled out Wong's business card and showed it to her. "I found this in Mai Yang's nightstand. Her body was discovered on Harriet Island this morning."

"My god! What happened?"

"I don't know. I thought maybe you could help me find out."

Karen Wong stared at the business card Santana held in his hand, as though the answer to Santana's question might be found in the lettering. Then her eyes met his again. "I only saw Mai twice."

"Twice might be enough."

She gestured for him to sit down in one of the two white upholstered chairs facing a black-lacquer claw-foot coffee table. On the opposite side of the coffee table was a matching white upholstered couch.

"Would you like some bottled water or tea? I'm sorry I don't have any hot chocolate," she said with a smile.

"You remembered."

"You're the only man I know who prefers hot chocolate over coffee."

"I'll take water."

She disappeared for a time and returned with a bottle of Dasani.

He twisted off the cap, took a long swallow of the cold liquid, and surveyed the living room as Karen Wong sat down on the couch.

Pagoda lamps rested on black-lacquer tables at each end of the couch. The end tables were inlaid with hand-carved mother-of-pearl birds and flowers. Hanging on the walls were a jade queen scroll, an oval-shaped, black calligraphy mirror, and framed paintings of pine trees and cranes and young Chinese women socializing in a garden. There were thick, hardcover books, small porcelain vases, and figurines of emperors on a bookshelf in one corner of the room. A black-lacquer screen stood in another corner.

"You were fortunate I was here. My husband and I were scheduled to attend a concert at the Ordway this evening, but he was called out of town on business at the last minute."

On one of the end tables stood a five-by-seven framed photograph of Karen Wong and her husband. He was Caucasian and appeared to be a good fifteen years older than his wife.

Santana set the bottle of water on a coaster made of a square tile with a red Chinese fan imprinted on it. He took out his notebook and pen and said, "How did Mai Yang end up with your business card?"

"I've done a few workshops with the students and staff in some of the St. Paul schools. Mai recognized my name in the phone book. I think she wanted someone who knew something about the Hmong culture, without actually seeing a Hmong therapist. Besides, there are very few Hmong therapists, though it's gradually changing."

Karen Wong's left hand tugged gently on the pearl necklace around her neck, the large diamond on the third finger sparkling in the lamplight. She looked both professional and elegant in her black alligator pumps, white knit top, black skirt, and two-button jacket with a notched collar. She also still appeared fresh, even after listening to her client's problems all day long.

"How do you know so much about her culture?"

"I was born in the Hunan region of China in the city of Changsha. The Hmong were originally from China. I believe there are approximately eight to twelve million of them still living in Hepeh and Hunan regions today. Changsha was the city where Mao Zedong grew up and went to school."

Santana let the information pass without comment. He had no reason to believe that Karen Wong was a communist and really didn't care. Most of the communists he had met in his youth in Colombia were university students, professors and labor organizers. He had learned then to keep his mouth shut when discussing politics. It wasn't until he came to the States that he realized disagreeing with someone politically wouldn't get you shot. Most of the time.

"Mao was actually born in a little town called Shaoshan, about one-hundred thirty kilometers southwest of Changsha. There are tours that take foreigners to his birthplace now."

Her tone was both wistful and nostalgic and led Santana to believe that she missed her country rather than its politics.

"Sorry for the digression," she said with an embarrassed smile. "But I haven't been home in a long time. How about you, Detective? Do you get home to Colombia often?"

"No," Santana said. "I'm afraid I don't." *I'd be dead within a day.*

"That's too bad."

Santana changed the subject. "Why were you seeing Mai?"

"It had to do with some poor choices Mai thought she'd made."

"Prostitution?"

"That and other issues having to do with her family."

"Such as?"

Karen Wong collected her thoughts before she replied. "It isn't easy adapting to another culture. I'm sure we've both experienced that, Detective Santana."

"From time to time."

"You have to understand. Hmong parents believe and often practice the concept of shame and honor as a way to discipline their children. This is different from the American parents who speak of unconditional love. Hmong parents believe if their children have good manners and behaviors, they will bring honor, pride and respect to their extended families and clans. But if their children grow up having poor manners and bad behavior, they will not only bring shame, disgrace,

35

and a loss of face to themselves, but also to their parents and clans. The clans are very important. There are eighteen of them. They provide material and spiritual support to their blood members from birth to death. Mai wanted to marry inside her clan."

"And that was a problem?"

"A big problem. Members of the same clans are prohibited from marrying each other even if they are not related through blood or marriage. The Hmong believe all members of the same clans were biologically related in the beginning of the creation and descended from the same ancestors. In both theory and practice, everyone is related to each other as brothers and sisters simply because they have the same surnames and belong to the same clans. They can only have courtship and marriage with those members who belong to different clans. In Mai's case, her parents spent most of their lives in the mountains of Laos immersed in traditional Hmong culture. It's not unusual for them to want to retain their cultural heritage, norms, and customs. The problem is that many Hmong children want to become Americanized. The family dynamic was ripe for generational conflict."

"Do you think Mai Yang became a prostitute because she couldn't marry someone from her clan?"

"I think that contributed to it."

"Did she ever say anything that led you to believe her life might be in danger?"

"No."

"Did she talk at all about her father?"

Karen Wong considered the question.

Santana drank some water.

"Have you met Mai's father?" she asked.

"Yes."

"What was your impression?"

Santana gestured with the bottle. "Colder than chilled water."

"That's similar to Mai's description. Mai's father was a general during the Vietnam War, fighting for the Americans. The general and many of the Hmong believed the U.S. would help them establish an independent homeland after the war if they joined in fighting against the North Vietnamese in Laos. But when the U.S. troops pulled out in 1975, the Hmong were left without a country. Thousands of them fled Laos, most of them to refugee camps in Thailand. They eventually filtered out to France, Australia, Canada, and the U.S. The last of the Hmong refugees recently arrived in St. Paul, thirty years after the Vietnam War ended. Though there are still reports of Hmong being hunted down by the communist government in Laos."

"Given what General Yang has lived through," Santana said, "what he's done to survive, to make sure his family is safe, I can understand why he might not be mister warmth."

"You sound like you can relate to the general, Detective Santana."

He drank more water.

She paused a beat and then continued. "I know you came here to talk about Mai's death. But I would like to talk with you more about the shooting. Perhaps help you get some closure."

"I have closure. The perp is dead. I'm not."

"The taking of a life is a traumatic experience, Detective Santana. It might help to talk about it."

"It might," he said. "Then again, it might not."

"Have you spoken with anyone from the EAP?'

"Briefly."

Some members of the St. Paul Police Department sarcastically called the Employee Assistance Program "the rubber gun squad." Santana understood the mission of the EAP and had no problem with the well-intentioned officers who ran it. Before the program was instituted, seventy-five percent of the cops involved in officer-involved shootings left the department within five years. Now the majority of them stayed. But Santana also understood that cops were allowed to cry only at funerals for fallen officers. Otherwise, they could show no sign of weakness. That included therapy. Everyone was expected to adhere to the rule, especially female officers.

"Do you experience any times of remorse or guilt, Detective Santana?"

"The perp killed my partner. He tried to kill me and was about to kill Angelina Torres."

"The woman you were trying to protect."

"Yes."

"Do you believe that taking his life was justified?"

"I do."

She regarded him without responding, without any expression of recrimination on her attractive face.

Maybe Karen Wong thought she knew more about him than she actually did. Maybe she thought she could read him like he could read a suspect.

"Have you been sleeping well, Detective Santana?"

"I never sleep well, but it has nothing to do with my killing anyone."

"There is, perhaps, something else troubling you?"

"Half the population of the country doesn't sleep well."

"And you're no different from them."

He knew that wasn't true. He was different from most. He had been different ever since he killed the Estrada brothers in Colombia when he was sixteen. And, like the perp who killed his partner, he believed that they deserved to die.

"I think you should talk about what's troubling you, Detective Santana."

Santana nearly said, "I don't care what you think," but he held his tongue. Took a deep breath.

"You are upset with me," she said.

"Look, if I ever feel the need to talk, you seem like someone worth talking to."

She blushed slightly. "That's a start."

"Is there anything else you can tell me about Mai Yang?"

Karen Wong remained silent and still for a time, in harmony with her surroundings and her thoughts. Finally she said, "There is something else."

He waited.

"I believe Mai Yang was raped when she was eighteen."

Santana leaned forward. "Did Mai Yang tell you she'd been raped?"

"Not directly. But I've seen young women like Mai before."

"Who's responsible?"

Karen Wong inhaled deeply and let out a slow rush of air, as if she had been down this road before and knew it would be an uncomfortable ride.

"I've heard stories of gang rapes, kidnappings, prostitution rings, and other violent sexual assaults involving Hmong gang members. Unfortunately, the majority of the victims in these incidents are juvenile Hmong females. In my experience the girls thought they were just going for a ride or to a party. Instead, gang members took them to an attic of a garage or a house, turned off the lights or put a blanket over their heads, and raped them. Gang members call this doing the Ninja because the victim can't identify who sexually assaulted her."

"And that's what happened to Mai?"

"Whether it happened that way or another, it happened. I'm nearly certain of it."

Santana wrote the information in his notebook. Then he said, "Did she talk much about her brother, Kou?"

"Some. From what I gathered, I believe she and her brother had drifted apart."

"Did she say what caused it?"

"No. But it could be he was ashamed that she had become a prostitute. Certainly her family and clan members would be upset."

"Do you know anything about the Hmong gangs in St. Paul?"

"Very little. Why are you interested in this?"

"I think Mai's brother is a gangbanger."

Her mouth opened slightly. "Mai never mentioned that."

"Maybe she chose not to."

"Maybe she didn't know."

"Possible," Santana said. "But, I think, unlikely."

"Do you think Kou knows what happened to his sister?"

"I intend to find out."

Chapter 5

Kou Yang lived in a dull gray house on Marshall Avenue in St. Paul, less than a mile from the University of St. Thomas campus. It had a screened-in front porch, a small living room, dining room, and kitchen downstairs, and was the type of inexpensive house that college students across the country rented.

The kid wasn't thrilled to see Santana and Hawkins but not many were.

The detectives sat on a couch that oozed stuffing next to a cheap coffee table stained with beverage rings and marred with scratches. Like most young men attending college and away from home for the first time, he didn't make cleanliness a priority.

Kou sat in a battered recliner opposite the detectives. A baseball glove lay on the floor beside a spiral notebook. The letters KY were inked across the strap and the numbers 1 and 3 were scribbled all over the notebook cover. He explained that he shared the house with two other students.

"If you're here to talk about my sister, I've already told you what I know." He spoke as though he was angry at the world and he wanted everyone to know it.

"We're here to talk about you," Santana said.

"Me? I'm not the one who's dead. You should be looking for the person who murdered my sister."

"Who said she was murdered?"

"You're homicide detectives aren't you?"

"We're trying to determine what happened to her."

"So, what are you doing here?"

"You know more than you've told us."

"Like what?"

"Like who raped her."

"How did you . . . ?" He stopped suddenly and averted his eyes, apparently realizing he had already said more than he should have. "I don't know what you're talking about."

"I think you do. Why don't you tell us about it?"

Kou Yang's gaze drifted to the window behind the couch, and out into the streets and back alleys where a wrong turn often led to a dead-end. Then he looked at Santana again. "It happened two years ago."

"Gangbangers?" Hawkins asked.

"That's right."

"What gang do you belong to?"

"I don't belong to any gang."

"Then tell us how you got those cigarette burns on your left forearm," Santana said.

Kou glanced at the burns that had scabbed over. "That was an accident."

"Funny how an accident formed that pattern."

"Hilarious."

"What gang was responsible for your sister's rape?"

"I have no idea."

Santana wasn't buying it. "Did you join a rival gang to get revenge for your sister's rape?"

"Why don't you spend your time finding out who killed her instead of wasting it on me."

"Did your sister use?"

Kou's eyes flared with anger. "No. Never."

"How do you know?"

"I knew my sister. She wasn't into drugs."

"When was the last time you spoke with her?"

"Just last week."

"So, you kept in touch."

Kou took his time before responding. "Mai was a good kid. Even if she got involved in prostitution."

"That was something your father couldn't accept."

"He pretty much cut her off."

"Did your two roommates know your sister?"

Yang shook his head. "They're white."

Santana knew what Yang meant. His roommates would never date Mai. He checked a page in his notebook. "When your father told you about your sister, you said, 'How can she be dead?'"

"So?"

"Most people would have asked *how* she died."

"I guess I'm not most people."

"Did you ever meet any of your sister's . . . dates?"

Kou pressed his lips together, tightly raised the corners of his mouth and wrinkled his nose in a look of contempt and disgust. "I never met any of them. And you don't have to call them dates. We both know what they were."

"You ever try and get her out of prostitution?" Hawkins asked.

"Sure. I wanted her to go back to school. Mai was smart, smarter than me. She could have been anything she wanted." Tears welled up in his eyes, and he balled his fists. "The last time I talked to her, she said she was going to get out. She was going to quit." He stood up. "I have to go."

Santana knew he'd get no answer if he asked Kou Yang where he was going. But he had a good idea. He offered Yang his card. "Call me if you think of something."

Yang hesitated and then reached out, took the card and stuffed it in a pants pocket. "You can let yourselves out," he said, and the front door slammed behind him.

Hawkins let out a sigh and turned her eyes on Santana. "What do you think the kid's going to do?"

"What would you do?"

"Go after whoever I believed killed my sister."

"That would be my guess. Follow him. See where it leads."

* * *

The Myth nightclub was located just north of St. Paul, in an area littered with fast-food restaurants and retail stores. The club sat behind a shopping center and across the road from a small strip mall. An LED message board near the entrance to the large asphalt lot announced the names of upcoming musicians. Neon lights lit the front of the building like a blue flame. Santana could hear and feel the pulse of hip-hop music thudding from car sound systems.

As he badged his way past the bouncer and entered the building, he realized why there was no line forming along the sidewalk leading to the front doors and no dance music blasting from the speakers. Instead of beams of colored light pooling on the smooth, gleaming dance floor, a large, octagonal ring plastered with local corporate ad logos stood in the middle of the huge floor encircled by a crowd of adrenaline-driven young men and screaming women seated in folding chairs. Some wore T-shirts emblazoned with the words Death Clutch.

Inside a chain-link cage, two muscular young men dressed only in trunks and leather half-gloves circled one another like bull elk in rut. The men's bodies glistened with sweat under the harsh white light streaming down from overhead spots. One of the men had a gash just below his right eye. Blood ran down his face and torso and splattered his white trunks.

Promoters called the battle inside the ring mixed martial arts, but it reminded Santana of the cockfighting he had seen as a child in Colombia.

He approached a bartender who was hanging clean glasses on a rack behind one of the numerous bars, showed him his badge and the photo of Mai Yang that the general had given him.

"You recall seeing this woman in here a couple nights ago?"

The bartender took the photo from him and scanned it quickly. "Not that I remember," he said, handing it back to Santana. "But I'm usually too busy making drinks to pay much attention to faces."

Santana found that hard to believe, especially if the woman was attractive. "This woman was a regular."

"Try Derek. If she's a regular, he'll know her. He's the manager." He gestured with the towel in his hand. "Upstairs."

Santana found Derek sitting with a woman at a black wrought-iron table on a roof-top patio. Neon lights strung along the top edge of the building shadowed the patio in a blue light. The night air felt unusually warm and thick. Santana could hear the echo of the crowd inside and the hiss of tires on the nearby freeway.

Derek and the woman appeared to be in their mid-thirties. But Santana doubted he had much in common with them besides his age, especially when it came to discussing a homicide.

He flipped open his badge wallet and said, "I'm Detective John Santana with the St. Paul Police Department. I'd like to ask you a few questions."

"About what?" Derek asked, his voice suddenly catching in his throat.

Like most law-abiding citizens, Derek saw the badge and immediately feared he had done something wrong. Santana imagined the rush of adrenaline and increased heart rate the man experienced was similar to what many drivers felt the second a siren wailed behind them.

Santana tried to calm Derek's nerves by showing him Mai Yang's photo. "I'm looking for someone who might've seen this woman here two nights ago. Her name was Mai Yang."

"Was?" the woman said. She leaned slowly back in her chair as if Derek had suddenly become radioactive.

Santana turned his attention to the woman now, and as he did, he felt a sudden chill, as though he had stepped into a freezer. The woman looked like his mother, Elena, and exactly how he imagined his younger sister, Natalia, might look in her twenties. The woman's auburn hair was the color of a maple leaf in autumn, her smooth, unmarked complexion deeply tanned and slightly freckled, her iridescent eyes seemingly changing from blue to green in the shifting light. Santana knew intuitively that the woman wasn't Natalia, yet he continued to stare without speaking.

The woman cast her eyes down at her dress, as if checking it for stains or spills. Then she looked at Santana again. "Is something wrong?"

"What's your name?" he asked.

"Brittany," she said, hesitantly. "Brittany Hayden."

His sister's face lingered before his eyes like the afterimage from a camera flash. Santana blinked twice, trying to erase the image. Then he took out his notebook and pen. Tried to refocus. "Mai Yang's body was found on Harriet Island this morning."

Derek let out a low whistle and peered up at Santana. "I don't remember seeing her here two nights ago."

"But you've seen her in the club before."

"I didn't say that."

"Let me see," Brittany said. "I was working on Saturday night."

She took the photo from Derek and immediately let out a gasp. "She was here two nights ago. I didn't know her name." Brittany's words were spoken like short bursts of gunfire.

"Mai Yang was with a man," Santana said.

"How do you know that?" Derek asked.

Santana stared at him but said nothing.

Derek reached for his glass and took a drink.

With his diamond-studded earrings, silk shirt, and expensive looking linen suit, Derek struck Santana as a man who had carefully constructed a slick façade that could shatter as easily as window glass struck by a bullet. "I need a description of the man," Santana said to Brittany. "Or even better, his name."

"I don't remember."

"You don't remember what he looked like or you don't remember his name?"

"Both," she said weakly.

"Was he Caucasian? Asian? Tall? Short?"

"I wish I could be more helpful," she said.

Santana noted that Brittany Hayden's hand trembled slightly as she returned the photo.

* * *

When Santana fled Colombia at the age of sixteen, he had left his sister, Natalia, behind. Father Gallego, Santana's favorite teacher at the Gemelli School in Manizales, had promised that he would keep Natalia safe and protect her from the long reach of the Cali cartel. Santana had changed his given name but Alejandro Estrada had never quit searching for the man who killed his twin sons, had not given up until he located Santana years later in Minnesota.

Soon, Estrada began sending assassins after Santana, one at a time. It had been Estrada's idea of a cruel joke. He wanted Santana to be constantly looking over his shoulder. Wanted him to live in fear for his life. Wanted him to know that assassins would keep coming until he was dead. But Santana had vowed long ago that if Estrada ever found him, he would stand his ground. He wouldn't run; he wouldn't become a victim; he wouldn't go easy. But if Estrada had found him in Minnesota, he could certainly find Natalia in Colombia.

Many nights over the past twenty years, Santana had experienced a haunting, recurring dream. He would see Natalia walking away from him along busy Avenida 12 de Octubre in Manizales, forever seven years old. He would call out, asking her to wait for him, running between and around people on the side-walk, trying to catch her. But she would keep walking until the crowd swallowed her. When he arrived at the place where he had last seen her, he would find noth-ing ahead of him but impenetrable blackness, blackness so cold and ominous that fear kept him from following.

Though he tried to remain optimistic, in his darkest hours Santana knew that what he most feared had possibly become a reality. But tonight, as he drift-ed into sleep, the dream was different. Tonight, as he stood in the place where he had last seen Natalia, he heard her calling his name.

"Juan."

Her voice resonated as though she were calling to him from the floor of a canyon.

"Juan."

He tried to move toward her, but his body was frozen, encased in cement.

"Juan."

He felt a cool breath against his cheek. Sensed that she was standing in the darkness just ahead of him. He struggled to reach out to her, struggled to free himself from the paralysis that held his body like a straightjacket.

"Juan."

Santana jerked himself awake, sat up in his bed. "Natalia."

He had heard her voice as clearly as he had heard his own. But all he saw as he surveyed the room was his golden retriever, Gitana. She was sitting on the floor near the foot of the bed where she slept, her head tilted slightly as she peered at him.

Sweat soaked his T-shirt and shorts, dampened the back of his neck. He felt his heart pounding in his chest. He knew that one part of his brain had been awake and one asleep, paralyzing his muscle control center, a system designed to prevent humans from reacting dangerously to dreams.

He remembered that Natalia's brain was wired differently. Often when they were children, he would wake in the middle of the night and find her standing beside his bed, completely unaware that she was sleepwalking. Gently, he would guide her back to her room. Tuck her in bed. In the morning she would have no recollection of her actions.

Now, Santana got up and walked barefoot across the cool, hardwood floor to a window where moonlight beamed through the glass. He stood in the ghostly, pale light wondering if Natalia was looking at the same moon, thinking about him.

Sometimes he wondered if she even wanted him to search for her. Maybe she was angry with him for leaving her behind. He hadn't taken her with him because she'd had no passport or papers and in the time it would have taken for her to get them, they would have both been dead. But leaving her behind in Colombia left a guilty hole in his heart, a hole that no amount of rationalization could repair.

Santana had learned as a child never to discount nor ignore the power and meaning of his dreams. Yet, without Ofir, the maid who had lived with his family in their home in Manizales, he had no one who could help interpret his dreams, no one who could explain why the dream had suddenly changed, and why he had heard Natalia calling out to him.

For a moment, Santana feared that she had been killed, and he felt a sickness in his stomach and weakness in his knees. Tears stung his eyes. He wiped them away on his T-shirt sleeve and returned to his bed and sat down.

His eyes were again drawn to the splash of moonlight on the bedroom floor and then to a book that had apparently fallen off a shelf in a corner. He went to pick it up.

It was a book of Pablo Neruda's poetry, and it had fallen open to a poem entitled, "If You Forget Me."

The first verse read:

> I want you to know one thing.
> You know how this is:
> if I look at the crystal moon,

at the red branch of the slow autumn at my window,
if I touch near the fire the impalpable ash
or the wrinkled body of the log,
everything carries me to you,
as if everything that exists,
aromas, light, metals,
were little boats that sail toward those isles
of yours that wait for me.

A rush of adrenaline shot through Santana's body and again he felt his heart thumping in his chest.

He turned slowly and gazed at the moon and the bright light beaming through the window. A bubble of emotion rose inside his body and burst out of his mouth, as if from beneath the surface of water. "Natalia."

And for the first time since he had fled Colombia twenty years ago, Santana was convinced that his sister had called to him, that she was still alive.

Chapter 6

The next morning, a thick layer of fog blanketed the lowlands and banks along the St. Croix River. It misted on Santana's face as he ran along a tar road beside Gitana.

The dog's previous owner had been killed during the same homicide investigation in which Santana's last partner had lost his life. Santana had elected to keep the dog rather than leave her in an animal shelter. It wasn't only guilt that led to this decision. Gitana offered him companionship. Something Santana had been without for what seemed like a long time, something he would never admit to needing.

He rarely kept Gitana on a leash since she never ventured far and always seemed to have him in her sights. She was still shy and timid around him, as if she feared any mistake would send her back to the shelter.

Last night's dream occupied Santana's thoughts. He saw the dream and the fallen book open to the Neruda poem as a hopeful sign, despite lingering worries that Natalia had called to him because she needed him now, needed him because she was no longer protected, no longer safe.

The image he had retained in his mind's eye of his sister kept melding with the image of Brittany Hayden, the woman he had questioned the previous evening at the Myth nightclub.

Santana didn't believe in coincidences. Something else was at work here, and he was determined to keep an open mind and to watch for additional signs.

49

He finished his two-mile run and returned to his house. The place sat on two heavily wooded acres of birch and pine on a secluded bluff overlooking the St. Croix River, which formed the east-west boundary between Minnesota and Wisconsin. The area along the river was cut by deep ravines and grassy ridge tops. He enjoyed the fresh scent of pine, the occasional sightings of deer and fox, the privacy and the scenic location the house afforded.

He did three sets of bench presses and curls in the downstairs bedroom he had converted into a gym, then took a hot shower. After dressing, he ate a breakfast of eggs, *arepas*, and hot chocolate.

His pager vibrated as he headed for the garage. It was the watch commander's office at headquarters. Santana dialed the number on his cell. "What have you got?" he asked when a sergeant named Brody answered.

"We got a DB behind a Thai restaurant in Frogtown."

"Hawkins and I just caught the last one yesterday on Harriet Island."

"I know that. But this one might be related."

"What makes you say that?"

"Both vics are Hmong."

* * *

The early morning fog had burned away, but a thin haze lingering in the metallic sky dimmed the sunlight as Santana drove to headquarters and signed out a Crown Vic. The white Crown Vics detectives drove were stripped down versions of patrol cars. But the new chief, Carl Ashford, had decided the department needed black and white patrol cars. No decision had been made yet regarding what detectives would eventually end up driving.

Rush hour on Interstate 94 was once confined to early morning and late afternoon. Now, traffic remained heavy all day as Santana nudged the Crown Vic slowly to the Dale Street exit just west of downtown. He crossed University Avenue and turned west on Minnehaha Avenue where he drove by the Oriental Market. Then he veered right on Pierce-Butler, which jogged north and then west again.

The landscape was a mixture of craftsman homes bunched closely together, small apartment complexes and cyclone-fenced warehouses with semi-trailers parked in dusty lots. The area of the city called Frogtown was fast becoming known as Hmongtown due to the grocery stores, pastry shops, bookstores, newspaper offices, and restaurants now run by Hmong business owners.

Santana pulled into a huge asphalt lot that fronted a bowling alley and forlorn-looking strip mall off Seminary. Spikes of grass and weeds grew between cracks. Potholes dented the asphalt surface, as if small bombs had fallen on it. Two large satellite dishes were attached to the roof of the bowling alley along with a chipped and faded neon sign advertising food, bowling, and cocktails. The mall featured a liquor store, a dry cleaning establishment, a beauty school, a chiropractic office, and a Thai restaurant with a KARAOKE DANCE banner in the window.

A grid search was already underway in the lot, patrolmen looking for evidence that might be connected to the crime.

Yellow plastic crime scene tape cordoned off the area behind the restaurant. Squad cars blocked access to the adjoining street. Uniformed officers kept traffic moving along Pierce-Butler Boulevard and the small crowd of neighborhood onlookers away from the crime scene.

Santana parked his Crown Vic behind a collection of departmental vehicles and got out. A uniformed officer in charge of the crime scene log took down his badge number. He saw Kacie Hawkins approach the yellow tape as he ducked underneath it. "What do we have?" he asked.

"The owner of the restaurant found Pao Yang next to the dumpster this morning when he took out the trash."

"Any relation to Mai Yang besides the clan affiliation?"

"I don't know."

Santana saw a sign on the wall above the dumpster.

NO PUBLIC DUMPING.
AREA UNDER VIDEO SURVEILLANCE.

"You ask the owner of the restaurant for a copy of the video surveillance tape?" he asked.

"He claims his system is broken."

"Any wits?"

"I've got officers canvassing the neighborhood."

"What did the owner have to say?"

"He doesn't remember seeing Pao Yang in the restaurant," Hawkins said. "I got a list of staff working last night. But they'll be reluctant to talk to us either out of fear or lack of trust."

Santana's attention was drawn to a petite, Asian woman in the midst of the forensic crew huddled around the dumpster. A detective shield hung from a chain around her neck. "What's Diana Lee doing here?"

"Gamboni sent her."

Diana Lee had recently transferred to Homicide from the department's gang unit as a replacement for the retiring Nick Baker. Santana had met her, but had never worked with her.

"Have you talked to her, Kacie?"

"I tried. But she would only speak with the lead investigator. That would be you." Hawkins smile couldn't disguise the sarcasm in her voice.

It was obvious that Lee's refusal to speak with her had made her angry. Santana would have felt the same as Hawkins had their roles been reversed. "The vic must've been a gangbanger," he said. "Otherwise, Lee wouldn't be here."

"If he's an Asian Crip, John, you and I both know Kou Yang has to be the prime suspect."

"Weren't you following him?"

"For a while."

"You lost him."

"I did. Sorry."

Santana wanted to give her some space after her angry outburst yesterday outside General Yang's house. "Let's hear what Lee and Tanabe have to say."

Diana Lee glanced at Hawkins and then shifted her attention on Santana as he neared the body.

"Detective Lee," he said.

She had copper skin and shiny black hair that glistened like wet asphalt.

Santana didn't offer a hand, and he knew Lee wasn't expecting a handshake at a crime scene. "What do you have Reiko?" he said to Tanabe, who was squatting beside the body.

"The vic's neck was cut," she said without looking up. "There are no hesitation marks, so I don't believe it was a suicide. No superficial incised wounds that would be caused by the vic struggling or the perp's hesitation to cut the throat. This happened quickly. The vic was approached from behind. His head was pulled back, exposing the neck, and the weapon was drawn across it. The wound has clean-cut straight edges. It's free of abrasions or contusions. He was most likely killed with a knife. But it could've been a razor or even a sharp piece of glass. No way to tell."

Santana could see the wound ran downward and medially at an angle, then straight across the midline of the neck, and then upward, ending on the opposite side of the neck, lower than its point of initiation. The cut was shallow at first, then deeper and shallow again as the blade was drawn across the neck.

"The wound starts just below the right ear," Tanabe said. "Means the perp was probably left-handed. I'd estimate the TOD between midnight and 3:00 a.m."

"Anyone locate a weapon?" Santana asked.

"We're working on it," Hawkins said.

"Find anything on him?"

"Just his wallet."

Santana looked at Lee. "What can you tell us about the vic?"

"Pao Yang belonged to the Asian Crips. He came here from Fresno, California, three years ago after he did a short stretch for assault. Like most gangbangers who do time, prison was like finishing school instead of punishment. We've had him under the magnifying glass, but he's slick. He was also twenty-four, which was older than most of the ACs. Any suspects?"

"Not that I know of." Santana could tell by the way Hawkins looked at him that she was wondering why he hadn't told Lee about Kou Yang.

"I heard you found the body of a young Hmong woman on Harriet Island yesterday," Lee said.

"We did."

"You think there's a relationship between the two killings?"

"Not at this time. The woman we found dead yesterday was a prostitute."

"Who's in charge of looking for wits?"

"I am," Hawkins said.

Santana noted the challenge in Hawkins voice, as if she were waiting for Lee to protest.

"Fine," Lee said.

"You want to tell us a little more about Pao Yang?" Santana said. "What he was into? It might help us figure out who killed him."

"Let's get out of the way, first. Let the ME do her job."

The three detectives walked away from the body and under the crime scene tape to Santana's Crown Vic.

Lee leaned against the driver's side door and folded her arms across her chest.

"There are four Hmong gangs that cause most of the problems in the city. The Oroville Mono Boys, the Purple Brothers, the Menace of Destruction, and the Asian Crips. The Crips are the most violent and usually stand against the other three gangs. They've also gotten their hands on lots of guns through the iron pipeline. But they don't control turf and aren't as organized as black and Hispanic gangs. There hasn't been a leadership structure. No one has to ask anyone for permission before committing a crime. But I think Pao Yang was trying to change all that."

"So how come someone with Yang's street smarts is out behind a restaurant without his gangbanger buddies for protection?" Santana asked.

"I don't know. Hard to believe he could be taken completely by surprise." Lee peered in the direction of the body, thinking. "The ACs are trying to control the meth and ecstasy business," she said, looking at Santana again. "The Latin Kings might have taken exception to that. If the Latin Kings green lighted his murder, there's going to be hell to pay. Although knife work this close suggests a crime of passion. I'll have the gang unit do some jump-outs. See if they can shake something loose."

Santana knew that jump-outs involved driving around in SUVs to areas where gang members gathered. The detectives would literally jump-out of the SUV and arrest gang members who had outstanding warrants.

"Minnesota has become a way station for gangbangers and guns from both coasts," Lee continued. "They come through here transporting guns to another state and commit crimes in transit."

"Did Yang have any family here?" Santana asked.

"Some aunts and uncles. His parents still live in California. I can make the phone call."

"Kacie, did you get an address on Pao Yang?"

Before she could respond, Lee said, "I know where he lives. Mind if I ride along?"

"Be my guest," Santana said.

Chapter 7

Pao Yang's address was off University Avenue in the Midway neighborhood, which derived its name from being midway between the downtowns of Minneapolis and Saint Paul. It was St. Paul's primary warehouse district and included the passenger rail terminal, Hamline University, and Concordia University, as well as Midway Center, one of Saint Paul's key shopping districts.

Santana could have asked Lee to drive her car, as Hawkins was doing, instead of agreeing to drive her back once they checked out Yang's place. Had Santana done so, he might have avoided the dirty looks he received from Hawkins.

But Santana wanted to get his own impression of Diana Lee. With just seven detectives, Homicide was a small department. He knew from his own experiences that she would be judged not just on the number of cases she closed, but how well the other detectives in the department respected her.

The SPPD was the closest Santana had ever come to joining a club or a team. He had always preferred to go his own way, to make his own decisions. He knew the other homicide detectives respected him for his abilities, but sometimes resented his aloofness, his unwillingness to be part of the club.

"Your partner's wound a little tight," Lee said.

"She just wants to be treated with respect."

"You don't think I respect her?"

"What I think doesn't matter."

56

"You're lead detective on the case. I thought I should talk directly to you." Lee fell silent for a time and peered out the passenger side window. "I understand you and Hawkins haven't been partners for long."

"What else have you heard?"

She gave him a sidelong glance. "Not much."

"Since we're working together, call me John."

"All right. I'm Diana."

"You've been to Yang's place before?"

"A couple of times."

"Know anything more about him?"

"The Crips were his family."

"Did he live alone?"

"Yang was never alone."

"Except when he got his throat slit," Santana said.

The house that Yang lived in was located on a corner lot opposite a small, rectangular, cinder-block office and metal warehouses encircled by a cyclone fence with coils of razor wire along the top. The road angled to the right at the end of the block where a late model, dark green, Mazda sports sedan sat beside the curb. Across the road from the car and behind a row of houses was a baseball diamond and tall, cyclone-fence backstop.

Santana parked the Crown Vic beneath a large oak whose roots had pierced the ground like bones washed out of a grave. Large drops of rain began falling, and he could hear them slap against the pavement and the car hood. The air felt as heavy as a damp coat, and it smelled of wet grass, soil, and the autumnal expectation of death.

He slipped off his sport coat and tossed it in the backseat. Then he moved to the trunk and got out two Kevlar vests. He put one over his shirt and handed Lee the vest she had placed in the trunk before leaving the crime scene. Hawkins, who'd parked right behind Santana, put on her vest and then they all slipped on dark-blue windbreakers or raid jackets with SPPD written in large yellow letters on the back.

The small, one-story craftsman with the chipped and sun-blistered clapboards appeared to sag in the middle as though it were sinking into earth softened by the rain. It had an unenclosed, partial porch and was set far back off the street, unlike the other houses on the block, leaving a long walk to the front door. The windows fronting the street were closed and the shades drawn. A six-foot-high evergreen hedge ran along the right side of the property. To his left, Santana could see the rusted bodies of two cars that had been stripped of their tires and most of their parts, laying in the overgrown grass and weeds beside the dilapidated garage in back of the house.

Hawkins headed for the front door without waiting for Santana and Lee.

"Hold up," Santana said.

She waited near an elm tree until Santana and Lee caught up.

They all went up a set of steps onto the porch and under an eave, sheltered from the rain.

Lee opened the screen door and rapped on the front door with her knuckles. "Police!" she said loudly.

Santana could hear no birds chirping or kids playing or traffic humming. Only the leaves rustling in a gust of wind and raindrops that sounded like small arms fire as they exploded against shingles, metal gutters, and cement.

"Give it another try," Hawkins said. "Only harder."

Lee cast a glance at Santana. Then she raised her fist and knocked again. Harder. "Police! Open up!"

No one came to the door. Nothing moved.

"I'll go around back," Santana said. "You check the garage, Diana." He looked at Hawkins. "Stay here, Kacie. Keep your eyes on the front door."

Santana and Lee walked along the left side of the house to the backyard. Lee headed for the garage facing an alley while Santana went up to the back door and knocked. The door was partially open, and it swung slowly into a small foyer and a set of stairs that led down to a dark cellar.

The floorboards creaked as Santana stepped into the foyer and then into a small kitchen to his right.

Two Hmong males who appeared to be in their late teens were seated in wooden chairs at each end of a rectangular table. The one to the left was slumped over the table, his face pressed in a plate of half-eaten noodles, an entry wound in the right side of his head. The one seated to the right had a look of fear frozen on his face and a bullet hole between his eyes. His head lay against the back of the chair and his eyes were staring blankly at the ceiling.

Santana drew his Glock smoothly out of the holster on his hip and cautiously approached the table.

It appeared that the vic on the left had taken the first shot. The star shaped pattern of torn skin radiating from the entrance wound, caused by gases from the barrel expanding between the skin and skull, indicated that the gun was a larger caliber, possibly a .38 Special, and that the muzzle was in contact with the head when it was fired. Blood spatter had misted on the wall near a kitchen window.

Urine had puddled underneath the vic seated to the right. He probably had a couple of terrified seconds to process the fact that he was about to die before a bullet scrambled his brains, exited out the back of his head, and lodged in the wall behind him, spattering it with a fine spray. The small size of the two blood spatters indicated the direction of travel prior to hitting the wall and suggested a high velocity impact.

Santana noted that several kitchen cabinets and drawers were open, as if someone had been searching for something.

He was wondering how someone could have gotten this close to the two vics without them noticing or without arousing suspicion when he heard Kacie Hawkins yell something that was lost in a gust of wind and pounding rain.

A moment later, gunfire erupted from the front of the house.

Santana moved quickly into a narrow, shadowed corridor with floorboards that creaked underneath him.

He had heard two shots in rapid succession. Then the gunfire had stopped. Now, all he heard were raindrops splattering hard against the roof.

He made his way past a small bathroom on his right until he had a clear view of the living room and the open front door.

He felt his heart sink like a stone dropped in water.

From where he stood, he could see the rain slanting down and Kacie Hawkins lying motionless on her back on the front lawn.

Chapter 8

Kacie Hawkins lay in a bed at Regions Hospital. An intravenous line hooked on a drip trolley fed antibiotics into a vein in her arm and another tube blew oxygen into her nose.

She had taken two bullets, one at chest level that had lodged in her Kevlar vest. A second bullet had struck her left shoulder, breaking her collarbone as it exited.

"If I hadn't lost Kou Yang the other night when you asked me to follow him," she said, "this wouldn't have happened." Her lips were parched, and her voice sounded like a soft breeze blowing through the dry, narrow slit that was her mouth.

"You don't know that, Kacie." Santana meant what he said, but he could tell by the frustration in her dark-brown eyes that she wasn't buying it.

"I didn't stay by the front door like you asked me to, John. I wanted to run the license number on the parked Mazda."

"If you had been on the porch, Kacie, it might've been worse."

"Is Yang in custody?"

"It won't be long."

"I didn't see the gun in his hand, John."

"Did you get a good look at him?"

Her face lit up with uncertain surprise, as though she were suddenly looking into a bright light. "The Mazda was registered to Kou Yang."

"That's not what I asked."

As she thought about his question again, he could imagine her rewinding the tape of yesterday's shooting in her mind, playing it over, wondering what she might have done differently.

"It was raining hard, John. Yang was running for the Mazda. He was wearing a windbreaker with a hood. I only saw his back. I yelled for him to stop and drew my Glock. But he turned quickly and got off two shots."

"So you didn't see his face."

"Not clearly." Her eyes were glassy, her eyelids heavy with sedation.

"How tall was he?"

"I'd say he was fairly tall. Not short."

Santana knew Hawkins was five-foot-seven. "Was he taller than you?"

"I think so."

"You're sure it was Kou Yang?"

"I'm only sure of one thing."

"What's that?"

"It was lucky I was wearing a vest." She gave him a weak smile.

"Not lucky," Santana said. "Prepared."

He felt responsible for her wound and for the pain the bullet had inflicted. He was the more experienced detective. He should have done more to protect her. As he held her small, nearly weightless hand in his and watched her drift off to sleep, he felt flames of anger burning his blood. Someone had attempted to kill his partner. Someone was going to pay.

He sat beside the bed until needles of sunlight punctured the dark clouds on the eastern horizon, and he was summoned to a morning meeting at headquarters with Rita Gamboni.

* * *

Santana went home, fed Gitana, showered, changed and grabbed a quick breakfast before driving to headquarters on Grove Street.

The SPPD had recently moved out of the Public Safety Building that had housed the department for seventy-three years and into the renovated six-story Griffin Building on St. Paul's east side just outside downtown.

The brick building previously had been a lab. It was now headquarters to the police administration, detectives and support staff, the crime lab, training and workout facilities, and the Central Team district office. It sat on a campus adjacent to the Ramsey County Law Enforcement Center, which was the new home of the Ramsey County Sheriff's Department. The two buildings were connected by a skyway.

The original design had placed the communication and call center for the city and county on the fifth floor of the SPPD, but it was moved across the street and connected to the SPPD and LEC by a skyway after the Ramsey County Sheriff's Department won a turf battle for control of the center. The large room on the fifth floor was now vacant.

Santana took an elevator up to the second floor where he used his card key to enter the Homicide Unit. Interior security in the new building prevented anyone from gaining access to the offices and departments without a card key or escort.

Sound partitions sectioned the room, as they had in the old headquarters, but the new Homicide Unit was more spacious. Each of the seven detectives assigned to Homicide had a desk, though they shared a common work area.

The three detectives who were at their desks when Santana entered spoke in hushed voices as they asked about Kacie. They nodded solemnly and patted Santana on the shoulder and promised to do what they could. No one would rest until the perp was caught.

Rita Gamboni, the senior commander, held regularly scheduled murder meetings with all the detectives at a rectangular table set up in the work area. At these meetings each detective shared information regarding the case he or she was working.

Gamboni believed the group IQ was higher than an individual IQ when it came to solving a case. She had been Homicide commander for a year, and the framed 100% Clearance Citation hanging in the standing glass case outside her office was a testament to the correctness of her thinking.

"Sorry I'm late," Santana said, as he entered Gamboni's office.

Gamboni sat on the corner of her desk, her long legs stretched out in front of her.

Outside of a new desk and chairs, this office looked much the same as her old one. A framed FBI certificate signifying a course she had completed in

Behavioral Sciences at Quantico hung on the wall behind her along with a framed picture of her SPPD academy graduating class and one of her in uniform. A cluster of gold-framed photos of her two elementary-age nieces was arranged on the corner of her desk along with a hardcover book entitled *Conflicts of Integrity*.

Diana Lee occupied one of the two chairs in front of the desk.

"I asked Detective Lee to be here because you're going to need a partner while Kacie recovers," Gamboni said. "How's she doing?"

Santana sat next to Lee. "The bullet passed through her shoulder. She'll be okay once the break in her collarbone heals."

"That's good news. Did you talk with the OIS team?"

"Briefly. I've got to meet with them again later."

"Good. As you know, Detective Lee has experience with the Gang Strike Force. She gave me some background on Pao Yang. I'm aware that Kou Yang owns the same make and model Mazda that was at the crime scene. An APB has been issued." Gamboni brushed a strand of white blonde hair off her forehead. "Why don't you bring us up to speed, John?"

Santana began with the discovery of Mai Yang's body on Harriet Island and finished with the interview he and Hawkins had conducted with Kou Yang.

Lee glanced at him as he told Gamboni about the interview with Kou Yang. But she remained quiet and raised no concerns that he had withheld this information from her at the Pao Yang crime scene.

Gamboni must have picked up on Lee's body language because when Santana finished, she said, "Did you inform Detective Lee about your discussion with Kou Yang?"

Before he could respond, Lee said, "Detective Santana told me everything I needed to know."

"Really?"

The hard stare Gamboni gave Lee caused her to momentarily avert her eyes.

"What's your version of the shooting, Detective Lee?" Gamboni asked.

"When I heard the shots, I ran to the front yard. Hawkins was down, and the perp was running toward the car. My line of fire was directly into the houses across the street when he drove off. I didn't want to risk a shot."

Gamboni shifted her tall frame on the corner of the desk and looked at Santana. "So the evidence suggests that Kou Yang killed Pao Yang and the two vics in Yang's house."

"It does." Santana knew that if Gamboni had continued her first line of questioning, he would either have had to lie to her in order to support Lee, or come clean and hang Lee out to dry. Now, he felt relieved and somewhat surprised he didn't have to make that uncomfortable choice.

Gamboni focused her gaze on Lee again. "What do you know about Kou Yang?"

"He wasn't on the Strike Force's radar screen as a known gangbanger. I ran his name. His record is clean. It's possible the Latin Kings could've green lighted the Pao Yang killing. They've been fighting over the meth and ecstasy business. But if the Asian Crips think the LKs killed Pao Yang, they're going to be looking for payback."

Gamboni let out a sigh of frustration and shook her head slowly in anticipation of the shit-storm that was about to rain down on St. Paul. "Jesus. And the president will be here in a week for a fundraiser and a tour of the new Federal Courthouse. We need to get this cleaned up soon."

"Do we have IDs on the two vics in Yang's house?" Santana asked.

"They were cousins of Pao Yang and members of the ACs. They had priors for burglary and auto theft. This probably goes without saying, but I want you both to turn over every rock until we find Kou Yang. I want him in custody as of yesterday."

Gamboni stood up. "That'll be all for now. I'd like you to stay, Detective Santana." She waited until Lee left the office before she went behind her desk and sat down.

Santana noted that she had put a barrier between the two of them.

"I need you to work together with Lee on this case, John."

"What makes you think I won't?" He kept his face blank.

Gamboni shook her head. "Don't play me, John. We've got a cop shooting, and the primary suspect has disappeared."

The tide of adrenaline that had heightened his senses and kept him alert at the crime scene and awake at the hospital had receded. His muscles ached now as if he had been swimming against a strong current all night. He had no desire to argue with Gamboni, but he felt there was something else bothering her, something beneath the surface he knew was there yet couldn't see. "You angry with me?"

Gamboni held her eyes on his for a time before speaking. "I just want you to do your job."

"I'm not talking about the job."

A moment of silence hung between them, as though Santana had hollered an epithet in a heated moment.

"Quit flattering yourself, Detective Santana." She leaned forward and pushed a piece of paper across the desk to him.

He picked it up and read the name on the phone message. "David Chandler? That name sounds familiar."

"It should. He's one of Minnesota's two senators."

"What does he want to see me about?"

"I imagine he wants to talk to you about his daughter."

It took Santana a second before he put it together. "Grace Chandler?"

"That's right," Gamboni said. "The woman who found Mai Yang's body."

Chapter 9

Santana used the phone on his office desk to call General Yang's house. He left his cell number and a voice mail asking the general to return the call. Then he went to the property room in the basement of the building and asked to see the items found on Pao Yang's body.

He pulled a brown leather wallet out of the manila envelope the property clerk brought him. The wallet contained sixty dollars in cash, Pao Yang's driver's license and a two-by-three photo of Mai Yang that looked as if it had been taken recently. On the back were written the words *Kuv hlub koj*. Santana copied the words in his notebook.

He returned to his desk and wrote out warrants for Mai Yang's and Pao Yang's phone records, knowing Kacie hadn't had a chance to do it. The cell-phone clipped to his belt buzzed just as he finished. It was Reiko Tanabe, the ME. He flipped open the phone. "Santana."

"Mai Yang died of an overdose of GHB, John."

"The date rape drug?"

"Exactly. You're familiar with its street names. EZ Lay, Liquid Ecstasy, X-rater, and Liquid Dream. It's odorless and colorless. Looks like water. GHB begins to take effect ten to fifteen minutes after ingestion. The effects last for three to six hours when taken without alcohol and thirty-six to seventy-two hours when mixed with alcohol or other drugs. Problem is, since the drug isn't standardized, it's impossible to be certain what dosage to use. In very high dosages, unconsciousness or coma can happen within five minutes. My best guess is the perp gave Mai Yang GHB and took her to Harriet Island where he duct taped her mouth to keep her quiet and raped her. He probably used a condom because I found no sperm. I did get a tissue sample from under the vic's fingernails. Maybe she scratched him. I sent it over to the BCA lab. But that can take up to two months before we get a report. You might want to see if you can speed things up."

Given Tanabe's excellent track record, Santana had no doubt that what she was telling him was accurate. "Where did the perp get the GHB?"

"The government banned pharmaceutical companies from manufacturing it in nineteen ninety, but the recipe and ingredients are readily available. Anyone with novice chemistry skills could make it. Hell, I've seen recipes for it on the Internet."

"Did you find any tracks? Any evidence of drug use?"

"No. I do three screenings in suspected homicides—one for alcohol, another for barbiturates and a third for tranquilizers, synthetic narcotics, local anesthetics, and anti-depressants. I did a gas chromatography-mass spectrometry analysis just to make sure. The GC-MS showed she had Gamma Hydroxy Butyrate in her blood."

"Anything else?"

"Isn't that enough?" she said with a laugh.

"Thanks, Reiko." He closed the phone.

"What did the ME have to say?"

Santana swiveled his chair and saw Diana Lee leaning against the cloth partition, holding a steaming cup of coffee in her hand. He figured he had to share information with her now that she was his partner. Plus, he owed her for covering his ass during the meeting with Gamboni. He knew Lee was figuring the same thing. "The toxicology report found GHB in Mai Yang's blood."

"The vic you found on Harriet Island?"

"The same."

"The Asian Crips' primary drugs are Meth and ecstasy, not GHB," Lee said.

Santana's experiences had taught him that most homicides were solved in a linear fashion. Like road signs on a highway, one clue led to the next. But he felt uneasy about Mai Yang's murder, as though the destination in this investigation already had been predetermined. He wanted to take some time to think through the evidence before going forward or heading off in the wrong direction.

"You think all the murders are connected?" Lee said.

"Maybe."

"That's encouraging."

When she smiled, he noticed that her shiny, white teeth were as straight as the creases in her khaki pants.

"I'll see if I can get a lead on Kou Yang's whereabouts," she said. "We need to find him before the Crips retaliate against the LKs."

"Before all hell breaks loose," he said.

* * *

Santana sat in an interview room at headquarters. Glen Tschida from the Officer Involved Shooting team sat across the table from him. A small tape recorder rested on the table between them. Tschida had jet-black hair, skin the color of saddle leather, and a nose like an eagle's beak. Rumors were that he was descended from Sitting Bull.

The big man sitting to Tschida's left was Joe Barton. Barton had steel-gray hair and deep-set gray eyes that seemed to have a perpetual glare.

"I think we're finished here," Tschida said, shutting off the tape recorder.

Santana had given his account of the Hawkins shooting twice and was relieved that the interview was finally over.

"You talked to the OIS team about eight months ago, as I remember," Barton said. "Just after you killed a cop."

Tschida shot Barton a look. "We're not here to discuss that, Joe."

Barton had remained silent and sullen throughout the interview. Santana figured something was bothering him. Still, Barton's words surprised him. "That cop was dirty," he said.

"He didn't have to die."

Santana didn't flinch under Barton's stare. "You want to be a little clearer?"

"You set up a cop so you could take him out. And it got your partner killed."

"Maybe you should quit reading comic books."

"And maybe you should take better care of your partners. Either that or Kacie Hawkins should draw hazard pay once she's out of the hospital. You're a loose cannon, Santana."

"It's time to go," Tschida said, standing.

Barton glared at Santana a moment longer before he stood.

Santana did the same. "Why don't you tell me what's really bothering you, Barton?"

"I just did."

"This isn't about partners getting killed or wounded," Santana said. "It goes much deeper than that."

Barton's face colored and Santana knew he had guessed right. "Why don't you spell it out for Tschida here as well. I'm sure he'd be interested in knowing what you think of minorities in the department."

"Fuck you, Santana," Barton said, and barged out of the room.

"The man isn't getting any younger," Tschida said. "He thought he deserved that transfer to Homicide more than Diana Lee."

"That's no excuse, Glen."

"No," he said. "It isn't."

* * *

David Chandler and his wife lived in North Oaks, a private, residential community of rolling, wooded hills, open fields, lakes, and wetlands, located northeast of St. Paul. In 1883, it was known as North Oaks Farm when railroad magnate James J. Hill owned the land. It was later developed as a golf course community and more recently as a conservation area. The average home sold for one million dollars.

Santana did a computer search on David Chandler before leaving the station and found a newspaper article written about him when he first became a senator. He wanted to know something about the man before meeting him.

Chandler was an only child, and, by all accounts, an excellent student. He graduated from the Georgetown School of Foreign Service with a Bachelor of Science Degree. He then joined the CIA's Directorate of Operations as a field officer. During his twenty-five-year CIA career, Chandler acknowledged field assignments in Vietnam, Laos, Lebanon, and Iraq. In the late 1980s, he was sent to Iraq to organize opposition to Saddam Hussein but was recalled for allegedly conspiring to assassinate the Iraqi leader. He left the CIA shortly afterward and became a lobbyist for a major defense contractor.

Three years later he used the connections he had established in Washington to start Tactical Systems. According to their website, the Minnesota-based company manufactured EQUIPMENT FOR THE ART OF WAR.

Chandler served as a mayor and state legislator before running for the Senate in Minnesota. He managed to win reelection twice, although by razor thin margins. His first wife, Katherine, with whom he had two children, Grace and Jared, committed suicide in Arlington, Virginia, ten years ago. David Chandler had remarried two years later.

Santana rang the chimes of the Neo-French home, and the thick, wood door swung open revealing an attractive dark-haired woman whose face was stretched unusually tight across her high cheekbones.

"You must be Detective Santana," she said in a thick, southern accent. "My husband's been expecting you. I'm Laura, David's wife."

Santana shook her hand and she ushered him into a high-ceilinged, open foyer. The temperature in the house felt as cool as her touch.

"I made some fresh coffee in anticipation of your visit. Would that be all right, Detective Santana, or would you prefer something stronger?"

"I'm fine. Thank you."

Her gracious manner suggested that she was very comfortable around men and very skilled in the art of helping men feel comfortable around her.

"David is in the study if you'll follow me."

Santana recognized a teenage Grace Chandler in one of the framed photos hanging on a wall in the living room. In the picture she stood between a beautiful, dark-haired woman Santana suspected was her mother, Katherine, and a younger blond-headed boy, Santana assumed was a brother.

Laura Chandler led him through a large cherry-wood kitchen and down a hallway to a closed door. "Please let me know if there's anything you need, Detective." Her tight skin created an odd, unnatural smile.

Santana opened the door.

David Chandler was seated on a stool at a teak bar, a half-empty cocktail glass in front of him. A younger, handsome man stood behind the bar. Santana immediately recognized him from the photo he had seen on Grace Chandler's houseboat.

David Chandler stood as Santana approached. At six-foot-one, he was the same height as Santana but he was much thinner. He squeezed Santana's hand a little too hard and held it an uncomfortable moment too long. His breath smelled of vodka and cigarettes. "This is my son, Jared."

The younger Chandler came out from behind the bar and shook Santana's hand warmly. He was an inch shorter than his father and appeared to be in excellent shape. He had an American flag tattooed on his right forearm and a gash just below his right eye.

"I believe I saw you in the ring the other night at the Myth," Santana said.

He grinned. "You go to the mixed martial-art matches?"

"I was there on business."

Jared Chandler nodded. "Well, I fight there occasionally. "You see the whole fight?"

"No, I missed it."

"Too bad. You missed my knockout. I'm undefeated."

"Congratulations," Santana said, trying to be polite. He had incorrectly assumed that Jared was Grace Chandler's boyfriend or husband instead of brother. He was surprised at how relieved and happy he felt.

"Could I get you a drink, Detective Santana?" Jared asked.

"No, thanks."

"You're sure? Not even a Coke?"

"I'm good."

He motioned toward a leather couch. Santana sat down.

A large, flat-screen television dominated one wall. The channel was turned to ESPN, but the volume was muted. Two walls were lined with bookshelves. On one shelf stood a framed photo of a young Grace Chandler and her brother dressed in camouflage. They were holding shotguns and kneeling beside a lake. A black lab sat on its haunches between them holding a dead mallard in its teeth.

Father and son took seats in leather chairs opposite Santana.

"I appreciate you taking the time to speak with me, Detective Santana. I know you're a busy man." David Chandler spoke in a deep, melodious grumble imbued with a slight southern accent.

"What is it you want to talk with me about?"

"I like a man who gets right to the point." He set his drink on the coffee table in front of him, shook a cigarette loose from a Marlboro box and lit it. He had a handsome, rugged face, evidence of hard living and experience. "I understand my daughter discovered a woman's body on Harriet Island."

"That's right," Santana said.

Smoke leaked from Chandler's mouth. "I'm sure you're aware that I have some contacts in your department and in the media."

Santana kept his gaze steady but didn't reply.

"I can assure you," Chandler said, "that Grace had nothing to do with the prostitute's death." He used the word prostitute like he would the sharp edge of a knife.

Santana heard geese honking. He looked through a window behind the Chandlers as a pair of them glided to a soft landing in a large pond nestled in the marshland near the house. The sun's rays fell through breaks in the clouds and glittered on the surface of the pond like tiny shards of broken glass. "I can't discuss details of the case with you."

Chandler gave a twisted grin. "Of course. I wouldn't expect you to. But I'd like you to be aware that my daughter had some difficulties as a child, Detective Santana."

"No point getting into that," Jared Chandler said. "It's ancient history." He stood and walked behind the bar and began mixing a fresh drink. "You sure I can't get you something, Detective Santana?"

"No, thanks."

"My son seems to feel his sister is doing just fine."

"She's managing," Jared said.

David Chandler took a deep drag on his cigarette, blew out the smoke. "My daughter has spent most of her life trying to learn socially acceptable behaviors. Unfortunately, she only knows how to speak directly. Her directness can be a problem, especially in a world filled with indirection and subtleties. You probably found my daughter somewhat rude and abrasive. Believe me when I tell you that she was not trying to insult you."

Santana recalled the interview with Grace Chandler on her houseboat. She had been direct, but he wouldn't characterize her as rude or abrasive. He said nothing.

"I'm not telling you this as an excuse for my daughter's attitude," David Chandler said, "just as a way of explanation. Grace is my only daughter. I've tried convincing her to sell that damn houseboat she's living on. Get a home in a nice neighborhood. But she won't listen to me. I'm afraid she doesn't realize how truly vulnerable she is."

"Your daughter seems to be quite capable of taking care of herself."

"Absolutely," Jared said.

David Chandler's jawbone flexed and he gave a short nod. "I wish I believed that, Detective Santana. I truly do."

"You're originally from the south," Santana said.

His brown eyes remained locked on Santana, as though he were examining a bug under a microscope. "Yes. I have a residence in Arlington, Virginia. I spend a considerable amount of my time shuttling between Virginia and Minnesota. In fact, I need to fly back tonight. There's an important vote scheduled in the Senate tomorrow on funding for the war effort."

Santana watched the two geese swimming in the pond and a small rabbit lope across the lawn toward the patio and a rectangular pool covered with a blue tarp. Then he focused his eyes on Jared. "What do you do when you're not fighting mixed martial-arts matches?"

The young man flexed powerful muscles and smiled slightly. "I run Tactical Systems. We manufacture body armor, goggles, digital compasses, laser rangefinders, and sights among other things."

"Jared spent some time in the military," David Chandler said. "I had hoped he might make it a career." He spoke with a sense of pride and regret.

"I served my country," Jared said. "Now it's time for the country to serve me." He grinned at Santana and raised his glass in a toast. "You ex-military, Detective Santana?"

"No."

He shrugged. "Well, you're serving the citizens and the country in your role as a police officer. You ought to take pride in that."

"I'm sure he does," David Chandler said. "Law enforcement is an honorable profession."

"Unlike politics," Jared said with a laugh.

"My son and daughter don't appreciate the influence politics can have. It's one way of changing the world. But there are others."

"Such as?" Santana asked.

"War."

"You've had some experience with that."

David Chandler's gaze turned inward, as if remembering something. Then his eyes refocused on Santana again. "I have. Unfortunately, 'Nam was the only war we ever lost. Now it looks like we're about to lose another."

"That doesn't sit right with you."

"It shouldn't sit right with anyone. But it's apparent this country and its leadership have lost their will, lost their way. And everything is going to hell. I'm sure you see the results every day in your job."

"What's your point?"

"My point, Detective Santana, is that it'll take more than policemen like you to save it."

A shadow floated across the room.

Santana looked out the window and saw a hawk swoop down over the patio. It caught the rabbit in its claws and rose quickly in the sky, its body a silhouette against a white cloud.

Chapter 10

Santana left the house in North Oaks feeling as though he had been looking at David Chandler through rain-soaked window glass. It wasn't quite
clear to him yet what Chandler wanted besides reassurances that he and his family wouldn't be dragged through the mud of a murder investigation.

The majority of wealthy and influential men Santana had met in his time
as a detective and police officer were control freaks, and Chandler appeared to be no
different. They expected law enforcement protection for their family as well as protection from undue media attention and unfavorable press. Santana had little doubt
that David Chandler loved his daughter and wanted her shielded from harm, but he
also believed Chandler was more concerned about his own reputation and any dirt
that would sully the family name and short-circuit important political connections.

Santana stopped by the courthouse and got a judge to sign the warrants
for Mai Yang's and Pao Yang's phone records. After he faxed them to the phone
company, he dialed General Yang's house on his cell phone and let the phone ring
four times before the general answered.

"I have some information about your daughter's death," Santana said. He
purposely avoided telling the general that he also wanted to talk about Kou Yang,
the general's son.

The general met him at the door of his Highland Park residence and led
him to the wing chairs in the study.

"The toxicology report indicates that your daughter died of an apparent overdose of gamma hydroxy butyrate," Santana said. "GHB is a date rape drug."

The general nodded slowly. "Then she was intentionally murdered."

"We don't know that for certain. She could have been given the drug accidentally or taken it herself."

General Yang sat completely motionless and silent for a time.

Santana felt as if he were viewing a corpse.

"I don't believe my daughter would willingly take drugs, Detective Santana."

Many fathers would say that, Santana knew. But the general hadn't seen his daughter for some time. It might be just wishful thinking on his part. "Mind if I take a look in your daughter's bedroom?"

"She hasn't lived here for two years."

"You never know what I might find that could help solve her murder."

Santana filled out another Consent to Search form and had the general sign it. Then he followed the general up a staircase to a large bedroom located at the far end of the second floor hallway.

The collection of framed, multicolored quilts that hung on the bedroom walls immediately caught Santana's attention. The embroidered quilts depicted scenes of mountains, rivers, livestock, stalks of grain, and peasants in conical hats.

"They are called *paj ntaub*," the general said. "The story cloths became a way of preserving our cultural identity and history. My wife stitched the ones you see in a Thai refugee camp." His voice caught in his throat, and he coughed. Then he moved around the room, explaining the story behind each cloth. "This quilt describes how we left China in the eighteen hundreds and moved south to the mountains of Laos, Thailand, Cambodia, and Vietnam. This one tells how we fought the communists and how we escaped to Thailand when the communists took over."

Santana stood in front of one framed quilt and said, "What about this one?"

"Parents are trying to calm hungry children during the long march across the border to Thailand. If a child made noise because they were hungry or afraid, we had to give them opium to keep them quiet." The general paused before gesturing toward a small, embroidered hat on the dresser that was stitched in bright red and black patterns and had a red tassel on top. "Babies wear these until the age of five. We believe it helps keep the soul of the child with the body."

Santana picked up a metal object from the dresser. It was shaped like a small turtle. Blue geometric shapes were painted along its back.

"Turtles are a symbol for long life." General Yang spoke the words with no trace of irony or regret.

"Mind if I look through the drawers and closet?"

The general made a sweeping gesture with his left hand, indicating that Santana could look wherever he wanted.

Santana walked to a nightstand next to the bed. A photo album lay on a shelf underneath a single drawer. He turned to speak to General Yang again, but the general had silently disappeared, like fog dissipating in the air on a jungle morning.

Santana picked up the album, sat on the edge of he bed and began paging through it. The photos began when Mai Yang was a little girl and were taken on birthdays and other special events like the Hmong New Year celebration. Some had been taken in school classrooms with her peers. Mai Yang appeared to be a happy child, always laughing. Then, beginning with her eighteenth birthday, her expression appeared sadder, her smiles forced.

Santana searched for another twenty minutes but turned up no clues, nothing that he thought might lead him to Mai Yang's killer.

He came downstairs and found the general sitting motionless in the study, peering out a window at black clouds darkening the sky. "Tell me what you know about Pao Yang," he said, sitting in a chair opposite the general.

General Yang stared out the window awhile before he took notice of Santana. "I know that he is dead."

"What can you tell me about his relationship with your daughter?"

"Nothing." The general's eyes were like two drops of oil.

"A photo of your daughter was found in Pao Yang's wallet. This was written on the back of the photo." Santana showed the general the inscription he had copied in his notebook. *Kuv hlub koj.* "What do these words mean in English, General?"

"It appears they were in love."

"Forgive me for asking this question," Santana said. "But I think it's relevant to the current investigation. Did you know your daughter was raped when she was eighteen?"

The general's face twitched slightly. "And how did you arrive at that conclusion?"

"I have a reliable source." Santana wanted to keep Karen Wong's name out of the conversation.

"I think you are mistaken, Detective Santana."

"Look, general. I'm sure it wasn't easy coming to a new country, raising two kids."

"Do you have children, Detective Santana?"

"I don't."

"Then you might know something about coming to a new country, but nothing about raising children."

The general stared at the standing glass case next to the desk for a time. Inside it were an old M-16 assault rifle, a .45 automatic pistol, and a .38-caliber revolver. On the wall above the case was his framed Ph.D. certificate in social sciences from the University of Paris, and a red flag with a white elephant in the middle. The elephant was standing on a pedestal under a folded umbrella. Santana guessed it was the flag of Laos before the Pathet Lao came to power in 1975.

"I'd like to talk to your son, Kou," Santana said.

"I cannot help you, Detective."

"This isn't about helping me. It's about finding out who killed your daughter and keeping your son safe."

"My son had nothing to do with Pao Yang's death."

"Then you've spoken with him."

The general sat perfectly still with no expression on his face.

"My partner was seriously wounded," Santana said.

"Detective Hawkins."

"That's right. And every officer in every department in the state is looking for your son because they think he's responsible for wounding her and killing Pao Yang's two cousins. He'll be found eventually. And some officers might not be concerned if they take him down. You've already lost your daughter. You don't want to lose your son as well."

"I didn't have anything to do with Pao Yang's murder. Or the murders of his two cousins."

Santana turned quickly in the chair and saw Kou Yang standing at the entrance to the study.

The kid's clothes were as disheveled as his hair.

"How do you know that's what I want to talk to you about?" Santana asked.

"I listen to the news."

"You agree to come with me now and I won't place you under arrest."

"What if I want a lawyer?"

"You don't need a lawyer because you can walk out of the interview any time you choose. But if you refuse to come with me now, I've got probable cause to bring you in. Then the investigation moves to another level. Maybe we can avoid that."

Kou Yang looked at his father.

The general gave one slow nod.

"Why should I trust you?" Kou Yang asked.

"Because you really have no other choice."

* * *

Santana drove Kou Yang to headquarters. He took him up to the Homicide Unit on the second floor and into one of the small interview rooms. He wanted the kid in a small, controlled environment free from distractions. He repeated what he had told Yang before and had him sign a Rights Waiver form. Then Santana gave him a pencil and a sheet of paper and asked him to write down what he did from the time he woke up the previous day until he went to bed.

Santana left Kou Yang alone in the interview room while he stood outside the closed door and spoke with Rita Gamboni.

"Did Yang lawyer up yet?" she asked.

"He hasn't asked for one."

"Did you Mirandize him?"

"He isn't under arrest."

Gamboni's face reddened. "Why the hell not?"

"I want to do a statement analysis first, so I can review what Yang writes before questioning him. It'll be easier to catch him in a lie if we have his own words on paper."

"Everyone in the department wants this kid's head on a stick."

"Look, Rita, the ME believes the perp who murdered Pao Yang was left-handed based on the direction of the knife wound across his throat. Kou Yang is right-handed."

"How do you know that?"

"When Kacie and I interviewed him, I saw a right-handed baseball glove with his initials on it. I also watched him sign the Rights Waiver form. He's right-handed."

"And you figure that's proof he didn't do Pao Yang?"

"It's not proof. But it's worth noting."

"You're ignoring something important," Gamboni said. "If Kou Yang believed Pao and his two cousins were responsible for his sister's death, that could've set him off."

"Let me do the interview first."

"I want Lee in there with you."

"Why Lee?"

"Because she knows gangs. Plus, she speaks Hmong."

"But the kid speaks perfect English."

"Get Lee in here before you start, John. We can't afford any fuck-ups on this one."

Chapter 11

Santana reached Diana Lee on her cell. While he waited for her to return to headquarters, he carefully read Kou Yang's written statement.

I got up at 10:00 because I worked until 11:00 the night before at the White Lilly restaurant. I showered and went to breakfast at the McDonald's on University Avenue in the Midway. After I ate, I drove to my parent's house to see my father. The police were there. They said my sister, Mai, had been found dead on Harriet Island. I left. Drove around. Drove to the overlook in Indian Mounds Park and sat in my car for a while. Then I drove to the house I rent with two students from St. Thomas. Two detectives came and asked me more questions about my sister. I could tell them nothing about my sister's death. I left and went to Malinas and had a few drinks. When I came out of the bar, my car was gone. I walked home and went to bed. I heard about Pao Yang's murder on television the next morning. I knew I would be a suspect, so I called my father. He picked me up and took me to his house. That's where the police found me.

Santana immediately identified inconsistencies in Yang's written statement. Truthful people generally used the pronoun "I" when giving statements.

Kou Yang had used the first person pronoun wherever it was appropriate except in two sentences. Once when he drove around and once when he drove to Indian Mounds Park. Leaving out the pronoun was an indication that he wasn't committed to the facts and might not be telling the truth.

Santana could use the inconsistencies along with Yang's non-verbal and verbal behavior to determine if the kid had murdered Pao Yang and the two gang-bangers. But first he planned to build rapport and find some common ground. If he still doubted Kou Yang's honesty at the end of the interview, or concluded that Yang had actually committed the murders, he would move immediately to interrogation, which involved a different set of skills.

During interrogations Santana never took notes. He confronted suspects with statements instead of asking questions. Confession became his primary goal rather than information gathering.

When Lee returned to the station, Santana showed her the inconsistencies in Kou Yang's written statement and explained his interview approach. "Just keep your eyes open and follow my lead," he said.

Inside the interview room, Lee stood near the closed door. Santana sat at a small table opposite Kou Yang. Santana put his legal pad, the statement Yang had composed, and a can of Coke on the table. "If you'd like something else to drink, Detective Lee can get it for you."

"I just want to tell you what I know and get out of here. You said I could leave any time."

"You can. But I want you to remember you may then be booked."

"On what charge? I didn't murder Pao Yang or his two cousins."

Santana reviewed the written statement before looking at Yang again. "After you left your parent's house, you wrote that you drove around. Where did you go when you drove around?"

"Nowhere in particular."

"Maybe you went to see Pao Yang."

"No." Kou Yang attempted to camouflage the false statement by biting his lower lip. It was a common method used to neutralize a strong emotion.

"Then you wrote that you went to Indian Mounds Park and sat in the parking lot for a while."

"That's right."

"How often do you go to the park overlook?"

"What does that have to do with anything?"

"I'm just wondering why you drove to Indian Mounds Park after you left your parent's house rather than go straight home. If the park or overlook has some special significance . . ."

"I like the view of the city skyline. I go there sometimes to think." Kou Yang set his jaw, tightened his lips and stared at Santana, freezing his facial muscles into a poker face.

"Could anyone verify you were in the parking lot?"

"I was sitting in my car. I didn't see anyone and I doubt anyone saw me."

"How long were you at the park?"

He took a little too long answering a question that shouldn't require much thought. "I don't know."

"Ten minutes? Twenty minutes? An hour. Take a guess."

Yang shrugged. "Maybe thirty minutes."

"What were you thinking about?"

"I was thinking about who might've killed Mai." He spoke rapidly and his voice was tense and pitched a little high.

"We hadn't received the autopsy report when Detective Hawkins and I spoke to you. What made you think someone had killed your sister?"

"You're homicide detectives. Homicide detectives investigate suspicious deaths. I don't believe my sister died of natural causes anymore than you do."

"Then who do you think murdered her?"

"I wish I knew." He smiled slightly, trying to mask his anger and deceit by simulating an emotion he obviously didn't feel. Suspects and liars tended to mask one emotion with another because it was easier than showing nothing.

"How long was your sister involved with Pao Yang?" Santana asked.

"Mai wasn't involved with the *neeg txhaum txim*."

"Criminal," Lee said, never taking her eyes off Yang.

He shot Lee a look, as though he had just noticed she was in the room.

"This photo was found in Pao Yang's wallet." Santana turned it over, showed him the inscription on the back. "Your sister was in love with Pao Yang."

Kou Yang's face contorted in anger. He stood up abruptly and the chair slammed against the wall. "I want out of here!"

"If you leave now," Santana said, "I'll take you down and book you."

"You said I could leave any time."

"We need to finish the interview. And you need to answer my questions. Truthfully."

"*Zaum*," Lee said, her voice echoing in the small room.

Kou Yang's muscles tensed and his fists closed.

Santana thought Yang was going to make a very big mistake and lunge at Lee. But then he exhaled a frustrated breath of air, unclenched his fists and sat down hard in the chair, as Lee had demanded.

"Stop anywhere before you went to Malinas for a drink?"

"No."

Santana wondered if Kou Yang had spotted Kacie tailing him and had driven around until he lost her. "You go to Malinas often?"

"Once in a while."

"Who did you see when you were there?"

"No one."

"You were the only customer in the bar?"

"There were other people there. But I just wanted a few drinks. I didn't feel like making conversation."

"So the bartender would remember you."

"What's the difference?"

Santana glanced at Lee.

She picked up his signal and continued. "The difference is you walking out of here free and clear, or you being locked up in a cell with a murder-one charge hanging over your head because you're not telling us the truth."

Lee's sharper tone appeared to unnerve Kou Yang. "I told you I didn't kill anyone."

"Did you report your car stolen when you came out of the bar?"

"I was afraid to tell my father. He paid for my car. I thought maybe I could get it back somehow before he found out."

"How did you expect to do that?"

"I don't know. I was really upset about my sister's death and my car being stolen. I wasn't thinking straight."

"You need an alibi," Lee said. "The more people who can verify your whereabouts, especially at the time that Pao Yang was murdered, the stronger your alibi is going to be."

"I don't have an alibi."

Santana studied Kou Yang. "How did you get home?"

"I walked."

"It's a long walk."

"Yeah. It was."

"Do you have a cell phone?"

"Who doesn't? But I use disposable phones and numbers."

Hard to trace, Santana thought.

"Why didn't you call someone for a ride?"

He spread his hands. "I needed time to think."

"Do you own a gun?"

"No."

"Ever taken any gun courses or training?"

"I've never shot a gun in my life."

"How 'bout a knife?"

"No. I don't own a knife either."

"How long have you been involved with the Asian Crips?"

Yang sat quietly without answering. His breathing sounded shallow and beads of sweat glistened on his brow.

"The numbers one and three were written on the cover of the spiral notebook you had in your house," Santana said. "One stands for the letter A and three for the letter C. ACs. Asian Crips. How long?"

"About a year."

"Sit tight," Santana said. He gestured to Lee and they stood and stepped out of the interview room. "What do you think?"

"The kid isn't being truthful," Lee said.

"I agree. I think he went to see Pao Yang after he left his father's house. And he met someone at Indian Mounds Park."

"What should we do?"

"We can let him walk and follow him."

"That didn't work the last time."

Santana wondered if Lee was being critical of Hawkins for losing the tail on Kou Yang, but he didn't want to get into it now. Before he could ask another question, Rita Gamboni came out of her office and walked over to them.

"What's your take?" she said to Santana.

"There are some inconsistencies between Kou Yang's written statement, body language, and words."

Gamboni's eyes shifted to Lee.

"Some of what Yang says is truthful," Lee said. "But not everything."

"Then I want him booked."

"I told him it was an interview and that he could walk out of here at any time," Santana said.

"Then you weren't being any more truthful than he was."

"Kou Yang claims he doesn't own a gun and has never shot one," Santana said. "Whoever shot Hawkins hit her twice, once dead center. She never got off a shot."

"Kou Yang's car was at the murder scene."

"He claims it was stolen. Someone else could've driven it. Kacie told me she didn't get a good look at the shooter's face."

"What are you suggesting?"

"Maybe we shouldn't jump to conclusions, Rita."

"Yang shot a cop and killed three gangbangers. I want you to make sure he goes down for it."

Chapter 12

Before leaving headquarters Santana called Stillwater Prison and scheduled an interview for the next morning with a Latin King gang member named Luis Garcia. Then he got in his Ford Explorer and drove across the Third Street bridge and into Dayton's Bluff, a once fashionable and wealthy residential neighborhood located on the east side of the Mississippi River. The neighborhood sat high on a plateau that sloped back from the river bluff for nearly a mile. Houses built in the late nineteenth and early twentieth century still crowned hilltop sites overlooking the river valley and the city.

The observation point that Kou Yang had described was located on Mounds Park Boulevard just south of the bridge. Eight cars were parked in the asphalt lot. Some people sat inside them talking or smoking. Others sat on wooden benches bolted to the sidewalk, enjoying the view.

Santana got out of the Explorer and walked to the railing where he could see downtown St. Paul on the banks of the Mississippi. A tugboat towed a loaded barge up river past other barges anchored along the shoreline. He could see the state capitol building to his right. Holman Field and its three runways were to his left. A train moved along the tracks in the railroad yard directly below him. Dry leaves rattled in a cool, stiff breeze and thin, red clouds scarred the horizon.

He turned away from the railing and walked south on the grass until he spotted a dirt path on his right that sloped downward at a steep angle. An orange plastic fence meant to keep people out had been trampled down. Santana nearly lost his balance as he stepped on the path and over the fence. He bent his knees and side stepped until he came to an outcropping of limestone rock that led to the precipice of a steep drop-off. He could see everything from this height, the city, the airport, the river and the train tracks.

He walked back up the hill to his SUV and looked east at the houses lining the boulevard across the road from the observation point. Kou Yang said that he had stopped here to think after being told his sister was dead. Santana believed that Yang had left out an important detail. And he wouldn't be satisfied until he knew exactly what it was.

He decided to skip his usual fast food or microwave dinner and instead eat at the Strip Club about a half-mile from the overlook. The restaurant derived its name from the steak it served rather than the entertainment it offered.

He took Mounds Boulevard north to Sixth Street and drove east past Metropolitan State University to Maria Avenue. The Strip Club was located in a nineteenth-century red stone building that offered a panoramic view of the city.

The black ceiling, electric candles, and ornate spiral staircase inside the restaurant reminded Santana of the stories he had read about the famous gangsters who once inhabited St. Paul in the1930s, a time when the city was known more for its speakeasies and its crime than its civic pride.

As a hostess led him to a table along a bank of floor-to-ceiling windows, he imagined gangsters like John Dillinger and Babyface Nelson seated around him, plotting their next heist or murder.

The hostess handed him a menu and a wine list and recited the dinner special. "Will anyone be joining you?"

"Not tonight."

She nodded and removed the dinnerware on the opposite side of the table and went away. A short time later, a waitress appeared. He saw no Sam Adams on the menu so he ordered a Corona instead.

Santana had spent much of his life alone and was comfortable in his own skin. Still, he wished sometimes that he had someone to share dinner with, someone besides his dog, Gitana, to come home to. But how much of his life could he really share?

"Hi, honey, how was your day?"

"Great. A Hmong gangbanger got his throat slit in an alley, and my partner took a bullet in her shoulder. How was yours?"

The long hours and constant danger of physical violence and death led cops to have one of the highest rates of alcoholism, suicide, and divorce in the nation. He realized it would take someone very understanding and very special to put up with him and the dangers of his chosen profession.

"Detective Santana."

He turned toward the sound of the voice. "Ms. Chandler. What brings you here?"

"Dinner."

"Of course," he said with a shrug. There was a moment of awkward silence before he said, "We have a saying in Colombia. *El que come solo muere solo.*"

"The one that eats alone dies alone," she said.

"You speak Spanish."

"*Yo podia hablar muy bien antes. Pero, no he hablado español por algún tiempo.*"

"You still sound pretty fluent even if you haven't spoken Spanish for some time."

"I need to practice."

"Well," he said. "Can I buy you dinner?"

"Actually," she said with a smile, "you could."

Grace Chandler took off her suede jacket. Underneath she wore a blue turtleneck sweater and jeans that fit her slim body like a latex glove. She hung the jacket and a matching purse on the back of the chair opposite his and sat down.

As if on cue, the waitress returned with a bottle of Corona, a second table setting and menu.

"Why don't we share a bottle of wine?" Grace Chandler said. "Or are you a Corona drinker?"

Santana saluted her with his beer. "I usually drink Sam Adams, but wine sounds good. You choose."

She scanned the list and ordered a California cabernet. Then she set down the menu, placed her elbows on the table, clasped her hands under her very lovely chin and focused her pale-blue eyes and her full attention on Santana.

"Come here often?" he asked.

"I've been here once or twice. How about you?"

"My first time."

He considered her dinner timing more than a coincidence. The detective in him wondered if she had an ulterior motive. The man in him hoped that she did.

"Do you live near here?" she asked.

"I live along the St. Croix River."

"Interesting that we both chose to live near water, don't you think?" Her smooth, unblemished cheeks were pink from the wind, and matched the shade of lipstick on her moist lips.

Santana nodded and took a long, cold drink of beer.

"How's the case going?" she asked.

"Slow."

"Is that unusual?"

"Some take longer to solve than others."

She rested her forearms on the table, kept her hands clasped and her eyes fixed on his. They seemed to glow with light, as if an electrical current were passing through them. "Do you mind if I call you John?"

"No."

She smiled. "Good. I'm Grace." She extended her right hand. "We met briefly under unfortunate circumstances. I think we should start over."

He felt restrained energy radiating like waves of heat off her skin as he shook her hand. He drank more beer.

"So what do you do in your spare time, John?"

He took some time to think about the question. What did he do? "I read. Rent some movies. Workout."

"What do you read?"

"Mostly Spanish literature."

"I don't think I've ever met a Colombian with blue eyes," she said. "They're very beautiful."

"I could say the same about your eyes."

"I got them from my mother. She was born in Barcelona." She smiled and fingered the silver butter knife on the table.

Santana wondered what David Chandler meant when he had spoken of his daughter's troubled childhood, and if Grace was aware of the meeting he'd had with her father.

"So, do you spend most of your time alone?" she asked.

"If you mean am I involved with anyone at the moment, no."

"Is that what you thought I meant?"

"Wasn't it?"

She laughed. Shook her head "Yes. Kind of clumsy, huh?"

"But effective."

She gazed at the long, jagged scar on the back of his right hand.

A *reinda* or sharp spur on a guadua tree had sliced it open as he fought for his life. The memory was still fresh even though it had happened twenty years ago.

The waitress returned with the cabernet and two wine glasses. She expertly withdrew the cork and poured a sample in Santana's glass.

He handed Grace the wine glass. "You do the honors."

She swirled the wine, inhaled and then sipped. "Wonderful."

The waitress smiled, poured them each a quarter glass. Then left the bottle.

"You can make a toast," she said. "If you'd like."

"I would if I could figure out something perfect to say."

She clinked her glass against his. "Thank you."

"For what?"

"For wanting it to be perfect."

They discussed art, movies, music, and Spanish literature during dinner. He discovered that she was smart and knowledgeable and had an infectious laugh, which, for some reason, surprised him. He consciously avoided asking about her family and her mother's suicide. She didn't ask about his family either, as if she knew their relationship would be defined by something other than their pasts.

After dinner, he walked her to her car.

"I have a confession to make," she said.

Santana waited.

"I went to the station to see you today. I wanted to ask you out for dinner. But I got there too late. I saw you driving out of the lot in your SUV." She shifted her eyes, let out a sigh. "I followed you."

"I thought our meeting was too coincidental."

She looked at him again. "I just wanted to ask you out for dinner."

"You had my number. You could've called."

"I wanted to surprise you. I hope I didn't freak you out. I'm not a weirdo or some kind of stalker, John. I almost drove away when you stopped at the overlook in Indian Mounds Park. But then when you drove here, I thought why not?" She ended the sentence with a little shrug.

"I believe you."

"So you'll call me?"

"Sure," he said.

She leaned forward and kissed him gently on the mouth. Then she stepped back and smiled.

"That's to help you remember," she said.

Chapter 13

T he next morning, Santana took Hudson Road to Stagecoach Trail and turned north toward the town of Bayport and the Stillwater, Minnesota, Correctional Facility. A few rays of sunlight broke through the morning clouds that blew across the sky like scraps of confetti. In the distance he could see a column of white smoke billowing from the tall smoke stack at the energy power plant across the road from the prison.

He turned right on Fifty-sixth Street, veered right on Pickett Street and turned right again on Sixth Street, where he parked along the curb in front of the main entrance.

He went up the steps and into the building through the two glass doors. He left his gun with the turnkey and was escorted through a metal detector and into the visitor's area, then through a door near the back of the room and into the non-contact area where he could meet privately with Luis Garcia. Santana sat on a stool facing a wall of glass and waited until a correctional officer brought Garcia through a door on the other side of the glass.

Garcia wore the standard state-issue attire: white T-shirt, denim trousers, tennis shoes. He sat quietly on a stool until the correctional officer exited and closed the door behind him. The CO could still see Garcia but couldn't hear him.

Santana and Garcia picked up the phones on their respective sides of the glass.

"Hey, Santana. It's good to see you, man."

Santana remembered how difficult it was for Garcia to sit still. Through the glass he could see that his body kept time to its own internal rhythm. "You've lost some weight, Luis."

"Yeah. I'm on a work crew. Been picking up litter along the freeways, removing graffiti, taking care of the prison grounds. They keep me real busy, you know. Maybe hope I forget the time I have to do."

Garcia appeared leaner, his Mexican Indian skin darker than Santana remembered, probably from spending so much time working in the outdoors. "I need a favor, Luis. It has to do with a case I'm working."

"Whatever you need, man. You know I don't forget you were straight with me. My mother was here last weekend. She say you stop by to check on her. I appreciate that, man."

"I promised I would."

"Words are cheap," Garcia said. "What happens after the words is what's important."

Santana had negotiated a lighter sentence for Garcia after the gang member helped him solve the murders of Julio Pérez and Rafael Mendoza, two prominent members of St. Paul's Hispanic community.

"You know much about the Asian Crips, Luis?"

"I know they are *maricas*."

"Besides the fact that they're pussies."

"They stay out of our way. We never had many dealings with them. We try recruiting some for the Kings. Didn't have much success"

"I need to talk to Eduardo Robles, Luis."

Garcia nodded his head slowly. "That is not going to be easy, Santana. The Crown don't like talking to the man, you know?"

"That's why I'm here. You need to get me in the door."

"You looking to take him down?"

"If I wanted to take him down, I wouldn't need your help or your permission."

Garcia smiled. "I always like that about you, Santana. You say exactly what's on your mind."

"I only want a conversation. But I want some trust established before I meet with him."

"I can make that happen."

"Do it. Soon."

"No problem. You still want me to drop the flag?"

"It's what you need to do, Luis. Get out of the gang."

"Only three ways out of the Kings, Santana. I could get religion. But then I have to prove I'm not faking. I could go underground. But that would mean leaving my mother."

"And the third?"

"Punch my own ticket, Santana. No return flight. Know what I mean?"

* * *

Santana was listening to a Juanes CD as he left the prison. He preferred the older Colombian music that he grew up listening to on his father's record player, but he was trying to broaden his musical tastes of late, particularly when it came to the Colombian singers becoming more popular in the States.

Ever-darkening clouds covered the sun and blades of grass bent in the wind that rolled across lawns like waves across water as Santana listened to the music flowing through the SUV's speakers, felt the rhythm and the beat deep in his soul.

Juanes was singing about the sun and how it could be turned off. But he could not turn off the light of his soul.

Santana was thinking how appropriate the song was on this cloudy day when his cell phone rang. He flipped it open. "Santana."

"It's Jenna Jones, Detective Santana. Sorry to bother you, but I think someone has been following me."

"Where are you?"

"I'm walking in Battle Creek Park."

"I'm about fifteen minutes from there."

"I know I sound a little paranoid," she said, fear evident in her voice.

The adrenaline suddenly coursing through Santana's blood was like a warning light blinking on the Explorer's dashboard. "Meet me at the picnic shell near the parking lot. And stay on the line."

It would be easy to dismiss Jenna Jones's feeling as nothing more than paranoia, but Santana had believed strongly in the power of intuition ever since he was a child growing up in Colombia. Intuition had saved his life on more than one occasion.

He took I-94 into Woodbury, then caught Interstate 494 to the Tamarack exit. He turned onto Weir Drive and then onto Upper Afton Road. The road surface was scarred with tar-covered potholes. The Explorer bounced along as Santana resisted the urge to drive more than ten miles over the posted thirty-mile limit.

"Are you still there, Ms. Jones?"

"Yes."

He heard her breathing increase as she picked up her walking pace. "Keep talking to me. And keep looking around."

"It's pretty quiet around here."

Upper Afton Road took him through a residential area and past a junior high and a large ranch that seemed out of place in a suburban community.

"I'm almost there," he said.

"I can see the pavilion. I'm heading toward it."

He turned into the entrance to Battle Creek and parked in a tar lot near a red stone building. A small sand-covered playground with green tube slides occupied a small area to the left.

Santana got out of the SUV and surveyed the park. He saw no one at the picnic tables scattered throughout the grounds. "Ms. Jones?" he said into his cell phone.

No answer. The connection had been broken.

He closed his phone and walked past a portable toilet that was chained to a light pole and entered the picnic shell attached to the building. A dozen or more empty picnic tables were fastened to a concrete floor.

He stood looking at the acres of woods, fields and woodlands, feeling the cool air blowing against his skin. Then he walked down a sloping grass hill past the playground and onto a tar walking path that snaked around the pond. He followed the path for about fifty yards until he came to a fork just beyond a hump in the tar. Ahead of him and to his right was a low, paint-peeled, wooden bench and behind it a stand of pine trees.

Santana could see no one in either direction, yet he sensed that hidden eyes were watching him.

He reached for his cell phone and hit the send button. Instinctively, he knew Jenna Jones wouldn't or couldn't answer her phone, but he might be able to hear it ring if she was close enough.

A moment later he heard a ring tone directly ahead of him. He drew his Glock and made his way cautiously toward the wooden bench. Just to the right of it he noted a short path of matted grass leading into the stand of pines. A cell phone was lying on the sidewalk in front of the bench. Santana moved slowly forward until he stood in the shadows under the canopy of pines whose lower branches were stripped bare.

Jenna Jones lay on a bed of needles ten yards to his left.

He looked for any footprints, listened for any movement around him. Then he stepped carefully across the ground, hoping that he wasn't destroying critical evidence beneath him, but knowing that he needed to get to her quickly.

As he approached, he could see that her eyes were closed and her mouth was slightly open. He saw no rips or tears in the blue jogging suit she wore, only smudges of dirt on the fabric covering her knees. He saw no petechiae or pinpoint hemorrhages produced by rupture of the small vessels on her face.

Santana checked Jenna Jones's carotid artery for a pulse. Her skin was still warm to the touch.

She hadn't been dead long.

Chapter 14

Santana and Diana Lee stood beside Rita Gamboni in the Battle Creek parking lot. Gamboni's dark blue SPPD windbreaker flapped in the cool breeze and her white-blonde hair lifted and then fell as though a comb had been drawn through it.

"My guess is, Rita, that Jenna Jones was forced to her knees and then suffocated with a plastic bag."

"If there were no marks or hemorrhages on her face and no sign of a plastic bag, it'll be just about impossible to prove that she was suffocated." The anger and frustration on Rita Gamboni's face clearly matched her stiff body language.

"Jenna Jones must've dropped the phone when the perp attacked her. It closed when it fell, breaking the connection. I copied the numbers of the recent calls she missed, dialed or received. That might give us a lead."

"Why didn't the perp take her phone with him?" Lee asked.

"He realized I was close when it rang and took off. The techs dusted it for prints, but the perp probably wore gloves. I had the feeling that he was watching me. If I'd have gotten here a couple of minutes earlier . . ."

"Deaths by homicide are full of what-ifs, John," Gamboni said. "You know that."

Santana watched as the dark body bag containing Jenna Jones's body was loaded into the back of the coroner's wagon. He remembered his interview with her two days before, remembered how he had encouraged her to leave St. Paul and return to the small town where she had grown up.

"First Mai Yang," Gamboni said. "Then Pao Yang and his two gang-banger cousins, and now Jenna Jones."

"Is Kou Yang still in jail, Rita?" Santana asked.

"He's out on bail." She looked toward the stand of pine trees where the body had been found and then at the pond where wind gusts sliced the water into small, thin waves.

Santana wanted to believe that if Jenna Jones had taken his advice and left St. Paul, she might still be alive. But he knew there were no safe harbors. Even the rich and powerful were never truly captains of their own destiny, though they certainly liked to think so. All of us were alone, bobbing in a treacherous sea. A fortunate few were lucky enough or resourceful enough and managed to survive their close encounter with a predator. Most, like Jenna Jones, never had a chance.

"You getting heat from upstairs, Rita?"

Gamboni looked at him and then at Lee without speaking. But her eyes confirmed what he already suspected. Her cell phone rang and she answered.

Santana heard her say, "Uh-huh. Okay. I'm sending detectives over right away to take a look. Thanks."

She closed the phone and said, "Kou Yang's Mazda was found in the Target lot near Battle Creek Park and towed to the impound lot."

* * *

The SPPD impound lot was located next to a metal recycling plant in a large industrial area on Barge Channel Road off Concord on St. Paul's West Side. Barge Channel Road crossed a set of railroad tracks and then dead-ended in a circular turn-around.

The impounded cars were parked in numbered rows. Signs warning of video surveillance cameras and no admission except by permission were posted on the cyclone fence surrounding the main lot. Strands of razor wire curled atop the fence.

The Mazda had been taken inside the fence to a small, secure building with a double-wide blue garage door, where it was off loaded from a flatbed truck. A SPPD patrol car had followed the truck to the lot to make certain nothing was removed from the car and that it had gone directly from the pick-up spot to the impound lot with no stops in-between.

Because Santana had probable cause to believe the car had been used in the commission of a crime, it could be impounded and legally searched for the purpose of taking an inventory of its contents. He knew the search didn't have to be conducted for the purpose of seeking evidence of a crime. Minnesota law also protected the department against claims or disputes over lost or stolen property once the car was impounded.

Santana had requested that Tony Novak and his crime-scene techs meet him at the garage. Novak had put on some pounds since his days as a middleweight Golden Glove champion, but he still moved lightly on his feet as he snapped photos of the car from different angles. His short, curly gray hair matched the color of his mustache and was gradually losing ground to the expanding bald spot on the crown of his head.

Novak was the only person from the department that Santana saw outside of work, though the socializing was limited to the boxing matches they occasionally attended together.

"We'll get prints and collect any DNA and fibers using an ALS after I finish taking the photos, John," Novak said, pushing his glasses up the bridge of his wide nose.

Santana figured it was part habit and part necessity because the black-framed glasses Novak wore looked thick and heavy.

Novak opened the driver's door and took shots of the driver's seat.

"Where's the seat at?" Santana asked.

"All the way back."

Santana recalled that Kou Yang was no taller than five-foot-seven. Whoever had driven the car recently was considerably taller than Yang. "Make sure you record the height adjustment and seat positions, Tony."

Novak nodded and made a written note. Then he handed the camera to one of the two female interns. He went to a workbench and picked up the lightweight portable alternate light source. The ALS was a small box with a cable attachment that led to an octagonal shaped lamp. It had a short handle that was attached to the base of the lamp and emitted a wide light beam.

Depending on what he was searching for, Novak used ultraviolet, blue, and green viewing filters on the ALS in combination with yellow, orange, and red wraparound goggles to view prints, fibers, blood, and serological stains that weren't visible to the naked eye.

Santana and Lee put on latex gloves and yellow goggles, while Novak snapped a UV filter on the lamp. Then he switched on the ALS and moved the lamp over the interior of the Mazda, looking for fibers and prints. Later, he and the techs would examine the exterior of the car.

Underneath the front driver seat, Novak found a paper bag from McDonald's. Santana remembered Kou Yang telling him that he had eaten at McDonald's the day Pao Yang was murdered. He opened the bag looking for a receipt with the time printed on it but found two Egg McMuffin wrappers instead.

The owner's manual, vehicle registration and a receipt for the license tabs were tucked inside the glove compartment. The car was registered to Kou Yang.

In the center console, Novak found an iPod and a set of earphones, a discount coupon for a car wash, invoices for oil changes and repairs, a cell phone recharging cord that plugged into the lighter, and a tire gauge.

Santana and Lee placed all the items in separate evidence envelopes. Dated and initialed each one. Wrote the case number and a description of every item on the envelopes. When Novak was finished with the interior of the car, he clicked off the lamp and pulled the trunk latch.

Santana and Lee removed their goggles and the two of them walked to the rear of the car with Novak.

Santana lifted the trunk lid. Immediately, he saw two small bundles wrapped with white cloth. They were resting against the left wheel well, but were in plain sight. He leaned into the trunk, lifted out the first bundle and unwrapped it.

"Looks like a .38 Special," Novak said.

Santana identified it as Taurus 85 .38 Special double-action revolver. It had fixed sights, a two-inch barrel, stainless finish and rosewood grips.

He rewrapped the gun and placed it in an evidence envelope. Then he picked up the second bundle. It was much lighter and stained with drops of blood.

When he unwrapped the cloth, he found a folding pocketknife known as a balisong or Batangas knife, but commonly called a butterfly knife. Most were made in the Philippines and had two handles counter-rotating around a tang or the metal that extended into the handle. In good knives, the metal extended all the way to the butt, giving the knife durability, weight, and balance. When the balisong was closed, the blade was concealed within grooves in the handles. For amusement, gangbangers often manipulated the blade in a technique called flipping. In the hands of a skilled user, the knife blade could be opened quickly with one hand.

"You think this is the knife used to kill Pao Yang?" Novak asked.

"I do. And I'd bet ballistics will match the gun with the bullets that killed the two gangbangers."

* * *

A strong wind gust blew yellow leaves off an oak tree in the front yard of General Yang's house. Santana rang the doorbell and glanced at Lee and then at the gray sky overhead. The low clouds made the earth seem smaller and more confined.

When he turned to ring the bell again, he saw General Yang, dressed in a black silk shirt and black pants, standing in the open doorway. The general's face was a blank slate, his hooded eyes revealing no feelings, no emotions.

Diana Lee looked down at her shoes as though she were deliberately avoiding eye contact with him.

"I'm looking for your son," Santana said. "He wasn't at his house. I figured I might find him here."

"You figured wrong, Detective Santana."

"May we come in?"

"Not this time. Not unless you have a warrant." His voice was flat but firm.

Santana wasn't surprised by General Yang's lack of cooperation, nor could he blame him. When he had taken Kou Yang in for questioning, Santana had promised the general that his son could leave headquarters at any time. But Gamboni had insisted that Kou Yang be booked and charged. Now that his son had made bail, it was apparent that the general was taking a hard line and wouldn't allow Kou to voluntarily come in again. "Has your son been with you all day?"

General Yang said nothing.

"We found his Mazda."

"The car that was stolen."

"That's what your son claims."

"So that must be what happened, Detective Santana."

"We also found a handgun and a knife in the trunk. I believe they were used to murder Pao Yang and his two cousins."

"That sounds very convenient. Did you find my son's prints on the weapons?"

"The lab is working on it."

"I suspect the prints they find will be my son's."

Santana knew that the general's statement wasn't an admission of his son's guilt. "You think someone is trying to frame him?"

"You're an intelligent man, Detective Santana. What do you think?"

"I think you should convince him not to skip bail and to talk to me. If he's innocent of the charges, I'll prove it."

General Yang seemed to consider his answer before he finally responded. "My son is neither a murderer nor a fool, Detective Santana. He trusted you once. He will not make that mistake again."

Chapter 15

Santana finished updating his daily case summary and his hour-by-hour investigator's log on his office computer.

Diana Lee was sitting at her desk, but her eyes were watching him. "You are unhappy about Gamboni's decision to detain Kou Yang on murder charges."

"General Yang wasn't real happy about it either. Did my talking with him make you feel uncomfortable?"

"The general is a very influential man."

"That shouldn't make any difference in a homicide investigation."

"No, it shouldn't."

Santana wanted to learn more about Diana Lee's background. He sensed now might be a good time to break down her wall of reticence. "Were your parents Laotian?"

"My father was Laotian, but my mother was born in Thailand."

"Did they meet in Thailand?"

"No. They met when they were studying in Paris. They returned to my father's village to marry just before the war spread into Laos. After the U.S. pulled out of Laos and Vietnam, they escaped to a Thai refugee camp. My parents were among the first refugees to the States thanks to General Yang."

"The general helped your parents?"

"He pressured the U.S government to get my parents out of the refugee camp in Thailand."

The words spilled out of her now like a confession. Santana wanted to keep the momentum going. "How did your parents feel about the U.S. leaving Laos?"

"My father never saw any of his family again." Her amber eyes glowed like a hot yellow light.

Santana felt a familiar ache in his chest as he recalled the vivid dream he'd had of his younger sister, Natalia. He wondered if he would ever see her again.

"Coming to the U.S. was difficult for my parents," Lee said. "They were educated people who spoke French and Hmong. But they didn't speak English. There were very few Hmong in the U.S. then. My father held onto his dream of returning to Laos some day. But eventually he sank into depression. Today, he hardly says a word and rarely leaves the house. My mother has been his caretaker."

"You were raised in LA?"

"In Fresno."

"How was Fresno?"

She stared at the computer screen, as though her memories were written there. "I have two brothers and a sister. My parents changed our first names so we would be more American. My given Hmong name is Gao. But changing our names didn't help. I remember my father taking the battery out of the car every night so it wouldn't get stolen. I remember the houses we rented being set on fire, the windows constantly being broken by stones. I remember landlords telling us we had to move, and how my father could never get a loan to buy a house in a safe neighborhood. I remember kids in school telling each other to watch their pets whenever I was around."

Santana wasn't sure what to make of her last statement.

Lee apparently saw his confusion because she said, "They thought we ate dogs." The look on her face was one of pain and sadness, as if she was watching her childhood home burn to the ground.

Santana remembered the racism he had encountered. How there wasn't a day that went by that he didn't wake up knowing he was Hispanic.

"I went directly from college to the LAPD," she said. "Patrolling the streets was like diving into a cesspool. Writers glamorize the city as if slitting someone's throat is more exotic in LA or London or Tokyo. But murder is ugly and violent no matter where or how often it happens."

"Why did you leave LA?"

"St. Paul has the largest Hmong community in the country. There are more opportunities here. And I thought I could help the department deal with the Hmong gangs."

"Can you put your gratitude to General Yang aside and deal objectively with this case?"

"I can," she said.

Santana decided he needed to bring Lee up to speed. "I found a photo of Mai Yang in Pao's wallet. She'd written 'I love you' on the back of it in Hmong. The photo was taken recently."

"You never told me that."

"I'm telling you now."

"Well, I'd like to know . . ." she stopped, appeared to reconsider her response. "That could be Kou Yang's motive for murdering Pao Yang."

"It certainly could be," Santana said. "If Kou Yang killed Pao and his two cousins, then he was searching for something in Pao's house."

"What?" Lee asked.

"I don't know." Santana shut down his computer, stood up and pushed in his chair.

"Going home?" she asked.

"To the range."

"Shooting helps ease the tension and frustration?"

"Sometimes."

"That sounds like a good idea."

* * *

They left the Homicide unit and walked across the skyway to the shooting range located in the LEC.

When Santana graduated from the academy, most officers shot ten months a year. But the cost of ammunition had skyrocketed due to the war. Now the whole department gathered and shot together once a year. All bullets were purchased by the city. Officers could practice more often, but only at the department's discretion. Any officers belonging to private gun clubs had to provide their own ammunition but could use their department issued Glock. SPPD officers used practice rounds for training and hollow-point, jacketed rounds for street duty. During qualifying, they shot the service ammunition rounds and obtained new rounds to carry the following year.

Santana always used the ammunition last issued to him by the department so that his ammo remained fresh. Before qualification became mandatory, he had heard stories about veteran cops whose ammo misfired in critical situations because they never practiced at the range and never requested fresh ammunition.

He and Lee picked up ear covers and targets. Santana took his time getting ready and watched Lee as she assumed a Weaver stance. Santana likened it to a boxer's stance where weight was distributed equally on the balls of both feet and a bit forward. The stance was taught at the academy and allowed officers to move and shoot accurately.

Lee bent her knees and her elbows slightly and kept her left arm perpendicular to the ground to reduce the muzzle flip caused by the recoil when the gun was fired. This made it much easier and quicker to focus on the target again for an accurate repeat shot. Santana watched her fire a few rounds before he stepped into his stall.

During the hour-long qualification training, the SPPD used moving targets and metal stands. Santana shot from behind windows and mailboxes and from both kneeling and prone positions. He was required to shoot at seven yards and then gradually move back to twenty-five yards. He knew the majority of police officers were killed at short range. He also knew there was little correlation between an officer's target scores at twenty-five yards using sights, and his ability to hit a suspect at close range during a gunfight. Sight shooting generally went out the window once the shooting started.

Santana worked on a different skill set today. He began by facing the target and assuming a Weaver stance. He got a proper grip on his Glock while it was still in the Kydex holster. As he drew and pointed the muzzle toward the target, he took a step forward with his right foot, throwing the gun out toward the target about eye level as if he were trying to punch someone. Hours of practice had taught him that unless his strong foot was moved forward toward the target, the technique felt awkward. He kept his wrist locked and the elbow of his right hand slightly bent and locked as he smoothly squeezed the trigger.

He counted his rounds until he had one round left in the chamber. Then he dropped the empty mag and reloaded. If he lost count and emptied both the mag and the chamber, the slide would lock back. It would take precious seconds to reload and then release the slide before firing again. He had been taught never to empty his gun unless he was out of ammunition. In the event of a shootout, he would count the suspects rounds if possible.

Because he might be wounded in combat and be unable to use his right hand effectively, Santana always spent some time practicing shooting with his left hand.

He consistently earned the maximum score of 300 on his required qualification tests by placing sixty rounds in the X ring inside the five-point ring. When he was in close, he practiced firing repetitions of two in the X-ring and one in the head.

After thirty minutes of firing rounds from varying distances, they turned in their targets and were issued a new box of ammunition.

Santana noted Lee's excellent accuracy. "Nice shooting."

She smiled as they walked to the parking lot. "I could say the same for you."

"I learned early in my training, Diana, that good tactical shooting requires practice and discipline. What you do in practice is what you'll do in a shoot out. Always practice as if your life depends on it."

"Good advice. I noticed you practiced one-handed shooting."

"I do."

"How come?"

"Whenever you hold the Glock with both hands in front of your face, you block the lower portion below the upper torso of the target area. It's difficult to recognize whether a possible threat is reaching for a gun or a wallet. The closer you get to the target, the greater the visual impairment. You might perceive movement but you can't see what's being moved. And I have no intention or desire to accidentally shoot an unarmed citizen."

"That makes sense. I'll work on it."

They stopped beside her car.

"Why did you cover my ass in the meeting with Gamboni?" he asked.

"I think partners should look out for each other."

"I do, too."

"What did Gamboni tell you after I left the meeting?"

"That David Chandler wanted to see me."

Lee blinked, her head jerked back and her lips retracted as if she had been startled by a gunshot. The sudden changes in her facial expression were momentary, but Santana had clearly seen them.

"You know Chandler?" he asked.

"I know of him."

"Why is that?"

She didn't respond immediately. Her reticence suggested that he had asked her to share a secret rather than answer a question.

Santana said, "You remember Grace Chandler from our meeting with Gamboni. She found Mai Yang's body on Harriet Island. Grace is David Chandler's daughter."

Lee nodded slowly. Her face was a blank slate now.

Like most cops, Lee had years of practice controlling her expressions. And, like most cops, she was good at it. But Santana had learned to read facial expressions as part of his master's in criminology degree, and knew he was better at reading Lee's facial expressions than she was at controlling them. He waited.

"When I worked for the LAPD," she said at last, "David Chandler attended a conference on terrorism. I was a member of the security detail assigned to him."

"What do you remember about him?"

"Not much. We never spoke. What did Chandler want?"

"He claimed he was concerned about his daughter. But I think he was worried more about his reputation than her welfare."

"I take it Chandler didn't impress you much."

"We have a saying in Colombia. *Es la plasta que no tapó el gato.* He's the shit that the cat didn't cover."

"But Gamboni sent you to see him."

"She didn't have a choice in that decision and neither did I."

Lee stood silently, gathering her thoughts. Finally, she said, "I felt like there was something going on in the meeting with Gamboni that didn't involve the current case."

Santana knew Lee had felt the undercurrent of tension between him and Gamboni. Still, he felt no need to debate the issue. Nor did he feel as though he wanted to acknowledge that her perceptions were correct.

When he didn't respond, she said, "Sorry. Whatever's going on is none of my business."

"No," he said. "It isn't."

* * *

Kacie Hawkins was dozing when Santana walked into her room at Regions Hospital. But she turned her head at the sound of his footsteps and gave him a warm, if brief, smile.

"How you feeling, partner?" he asked.

"Better now. I love flowers. Thanks."

Santana set the vase with the bouquet on a windowsill.

Hawkins sipped water from a straw in the glass on the bed tray in front of her. Then she said, "Can I see the card?" The water had moistened her throat, cleared the raspy sound in her voice. "Just hold it so I can see it," she said. "It hurts like hell to move my arm."

Santana held the card in front of her while she read and then opened it when she nodded. He watched as her eyes glistened and she blinked away the tears.

"Thank you, John. That's sweet."

He stood the card next to the vase, pulled up a chair and sat next to the bed.

"Turn down the television and tell me what's going on with the case," she said.

Santana used the remote to lower the volume. Then he told her what he knew, leaving out his opinions.

"You're not buying it," Hawkins said when he finished.

"Not all of it."

"You mean not any of it."

"I have my doubts."

Hawkins gave a little laugh and then winced as she coughed. "My meds are running out. The nurse'll be in soon to give me another shot. I can't believe I'm actually looking forward to being doped."

Hawkins was a light drinker. She rarely took any medication, even an aspirin. Santana knew she must be in pain.

"You've never been easy to convince of anything, John. That's what makes you a good cop. And a royal pain in the ass downtown."

"Thank you."

"You're welcome. I figure I can be honest with you because I'm lying here wounded and you're feeling guilty because you thought you could protect me. So forgive me for taking advantage of the situation."

"No need to apologize, Kacie."

She sipped more water. Then took a breath and let it out slowly. "You're the best cop I know, John Santana."

He shrugged, uncomfortable with the compliment and unsure how to respond. He decided to stick to the case. "The Mazda is problematic."

"The car could've been stolen after Kou Yang committed the murders, John. When the thief heard it was hot, he just dumped it in the Target lot. Probably never looked in the trunk."

"That's a possibility."

"But you think unlikely."

"I think the car was stolen. But by the perp who committed the murders."

"So that he could plant the evidence in the trunk."

"He or she," Santana said.

Hawkins gazed up at the ceiling and said nothing for a time.

Santana was wondering if she was about to fall asleep when she looked at him and spoke once more.

"As soon as I get out of here and back in shape, I want to be your part-ner again." Hawkins licked her dry lips and continued looking at him as though she were trying to read his mind. "How do you like working with Lee?"

Santana thought Hawkins might be feeling insecure about their partnership and wasn't surprised by her question. He liked working with Hawkins. She had the makings of an excellent homicide detective. Maybe he would feel the same way about Lee in time if they continued working together. But he would press Gamboni to let him partner with Hawkins again once she recovered. Besides, he had no idea where Lee stood on the issue. He hoped she wouldn't complicate matters by requesting that she and Santana remain partners.

"Lee is fine," he said. "But you're my partner, now and in the future. And my loyalty has nothing to do with guilt over you getting shot."

Hawkins smiled through the pain etched in her face. "Do you know much about Lee?"

"I know she worked with LAPD before she worked with our gang unit."

"She told you that?"

"Yes."

"You know, John, she wasn't Gamboni's first choice to fill Nick Baker's spot."

"I heard rumors. But I try and stay out of department politics. What did you hear?"

"Chief Ashford told Gamboni he wanted a Hmong detective in the Homicide unit. That's how she got the job."

"And you've got a problem with that?"

"I don't have a problem with Lee being Hmong. I have a problem with her not being the most qualified. Joe Barton requested the transfer and should've gotten it. Everybody in the department knows it."

"So when did you become such a Joe Barton fan?"

"When I worked with him in Vice."

Santana recalled his interview with Barton and Glen Tschida. He wondered if Kacie knew what an asshole Barton really was. He decided to keep his opinion to himself. For now.

"You know, Kacie, not every detective's request is honored no matter how good or how connected they are. The bureaucracy is always shifting depending on the political winds. New mayors appoint new chiefs. New commanders head departments. It can make your head spin trying to keep up with it all."

"That's true."

"I don't care who's in charge as long as they're competent," Santana said. He felt the same way about his partners. But he sensed there was more to Hawkins's story. "Is there something you're not telling me, Kacie?"

Hawkins inhaled and let out a slow breath. "What did Lee say to the OIS investigators?"

"I'm assuming the same thing she told Gamboni and me."

"And what was that?"

"That she ran to the front yard when she heard shots. Saw you wounded on the ground."

"What else?"

"She didn't shoot at the car because there were houses and businesses in her line of fire."

Hawkins gave a slight nod and settled her head on the pillow, her eyes staring at the ceiling. "The Mazda went right by her, John. She had a shot and didn't take it."

"You were down, Kacie. Maybe you thought . . ."

"I saw what happened before I passed out." Her brown eyes were now locked on his.

"What are you suggesting, Kacie?"

"Put the pieces together, John. Lee recognized Kou Yang and knew he was General Yang's son. The general is the most important man in the Hmong community."

Santana considered what Hawkins had said. Then he remembered General Yang had gotten Lee's parents out of the refugee camp in Thailand and into the United States.

"Your scenario only works if Kou Yang was driving the car, Kacie. You said you never got a good look at the shooter's face. I'm still not convinced it was Kou Yang."

"If that's true, John, then it's even worse. It means Diana Lee couldn't pull the trigger. It means nobody is watching your back."

Chapter 16

That evening, Santana slipped on a pair of Everlast bag gloves and worked on the speed bag and the heavy bag in the spare bedroom he had converted into a gym. As he threw lefts and rights, hooks and upper cuts into the heavy bag, he imagined he was hitting the body of the perp who had shot Kacie Hawkins and murdered Mai Yang and Jenna Jones. Each punch fed the physical aggression that was hardwired into his brain, kept the demon inside him at bay.

He wondered if the wiring got crossed in some of the predators he had known and if faulty wiring had something to do with the nature of evil. He thought about his job and his mission and how many predators he could stop before one of them stopped him.

He was dripping sweat when he switched the bag gloves for a pair of lifting gloves and settled under a bench press bar. He did one set with 175 pounds to warm up, then racked another fifteen pounds on the bar and pressed his weight ten more times. The last ten reps at 205 left his pecs and triceps feeling as though they were on fire.

He showered with hot water and finished with a burst of cold. Then he toweled off and put on a sweatshirt, jeans, and his running shoes.

He ate a dinner of black beans and rice and took a phone call from Stillwater Prison. Luis Garcia confirmed that Eduardo Robles, the current leader of the Latin Kings, had agreed to a meeting the following day. Santana wrote down the time and location.

He called Grace Chandler but got no answer. He left a message on her voice mail.

Then he sat in a lawn chair on his deck and drank a large shot of *aguardiente* Cristal. The drink was a mixture of sugar cane and anisette imported from the Caldes region of Colombia, and it flamed his throat and esophagus before settling in his stomach.

Gitana rested her head comfortably on her front paws as she lay to the right of the lawn chair, beside the tattered rubber duck she loved to carry everywhere. Though her eyes were closed, Santana knew she was aware of his every movement.

The briefcase that lay open at his feet contained his daily call sheet tracking his work hours, case files, and his Glock. Everything written about the case would eventually be contained in the murder book.

The sliding glass door leading to the master bedroom off the deck was half open. Santana could hear flamenco guitar music from a Paco de Lucia CD floating through the screen.

He had taken guitar lessons as a child in Colombia and had always wanted to play again. Recently, he had ordered a new Martin D-28 acoustic guitar and anticipated its arrival. Unconsciously, he rubbed his left thumb across the tips of his fingers, remembered how calloused they once were from pressing down on the guitar strings.

Santana liked to sit outside as much as possible now. Soon, snow and bitter cold would force him indoors for months at a time. Something he had never grown used to since leaving his home in Manizales where the temperature averaged sixty-five degrees year around.

The scent of pine lingered in the breeze. The dark-gray sheet covering the sky for most of the day had torn away, leaving strips of ragged, purple clouds staining the pink horizon.

His thoughts kept returning to Grace Chandler and the logic of starting a relationship in the middle of a murder investigation, particularly when the subject of his interest had discovered the victim's body. But then logic had little to do with most male/female relationships. Santana could no more predict when he might meet someone he was attracted to than he could predict Minnesota weather. He could easily count on one hand his significant relationships with women. There was one in high school, one in college and another when he first joined the force. And then there was Rita, his former partner. They were involved before she became the first female commander of the Homicide Unit.

Santana set the empty glass on the deck beside his briefcase. He closed his eyes and focused his thoughts once more, searching for a loose end that he might use to unravel the complexities of the current case.

The lab testing would be completed soon. Santana believed Kou Yang's prints would be found on the weapons. He believed the blood on the knife would belong to Pao Yang. Kou Yang also had motive. Pao Yang had been in love with Kou's sister, Mai. Maybe Kou thought Pao Yang had killed his sister. But that hardly explained why Pao Yang's cousins were killed or what Kou was looking for in Pao Yang's house.

Kou Yang was out on bail and conceivably could have killed Jenna Jones as well, but again what was his motivation? Was it because Kou somehow held Jones responsible for his sister becoming a prostitute?

Difficult cases were nothing new for Santana. Experience had taught him to keep an open mind despite the caged demon thrashing inside him, demanding justice. He needed to control the demon, control his growing feelings of anger and vengeance. Setting the demon free would shut down his thinking process and encourage him to make rush judgments, to cut corners, to cross the line. Santana had known cops, good cops who were now doing time with the same perps they had once put behind bars. He believed a line had to be drawn between right and wrong. He had straddled it on occasion, but in his mind, he had crossed it only once. And that was long before he carried a badge.

Gitana began whining softly, and Santana opened his eyes and peered down at her. She was sitting on her haunches now, gazing intently at the river as though she had located a downed duck in the water.

"What is it, girl?"

Quietly, she stood on all four legs, her eyes still fixed on something only she could see. She took one tentative step toward the railing along the edge of the deck. Then she gave a short whine and stopped.

As Santana leaned over to pat the soft, dense fur on her back, he felt something blow past the space just occupied by his head. The sliding door behind him exploded, sending jagged fragments of glass hurtling like shrapnel through the air.

Santana dived toward the deck floor, grabbing Gitana by the collar, and pulled her down with him. His heart was jacked up and pumping adrenaline through his system, and his senses were on high alert. He could see little in the twilight beyond the trees. But he knew from the sound that the bullet had been fired from a high-powered rifle, that he and the dog were vulnerable lying uncovered on the deck. His eyes kept searching the woods as he reached into the open briefcase and wrapped his right hand around the Glock.

Santana had two ways to go. Forward or back. Attack or run. It had been that way for more than half his life.

"It's all right," he whispered to Gitana. "Stay."

He crawled toward the deck's edge, grabbed a post with his free hand, swung his legs under the rail, and dropped over the side and into the gathering darkness.

Chapter 17

Fifteen feet below the attached deck, Santana hit the soft ground on both feet and then shoulder-rolled behind the cover of an oak trunk where he crouched on one knee. He took two deep breaths to slow his heart and steady his nerves, and waited for a second shot.

He had spent hours in crisis rehearsal training and understood the importance and principle behind mental imaging. He knew a learned trait became natural and instinctive only after thousands of repetitions. He had trained his mind and programmed his body to respond automatically to crisis situations.

Now, he used his training and imagined himself as the sniper selecting a good location for the shot. He was familiar with external ballistics. How far a bullet traveled had a lot to do with air friction, the bullets shape, weight, launch velocity and launch angle. The wind had calmed, so it was conceivable that the shot had come from the other side of the river. He remembered reading once that the longest reported range for a military sniper kill was a little over a mile and a half. The I-94 Bridge across the St. Croix was just over a half-mile long. The high ground across the river offered an unobstructed view of his deck. But if the shot had come from the Wisconsin side of the river, he had no chance of pursuing, catching or killing the sniper.

But that scenario assumed that the shooter had military training. Police snipers generally operated at shorter ranges, typically during hostage situations.

Whoever had fired the shot could have had either military or police training or both. All that really mattered was accuracy. Had Santana remained stationary in the lawn chair instead of leaning over to calm Gitana, he would presumably be dead.

He looked up at the deck. Saw the dog peering down at him. She had crawled to a point where she could watch him, but had stayed low to the ground as though she understood the gravity of the situation.

Electing to keep her rather than leaving her in a shelter had been a wise decision that had ultimately saved his life. Had the incident happened in his native Colombia, people would be saying that he had *la siete vidas del gato*, or the seven lives of a cat. Santana wasn't sure how many lives he had left or how many he had to begin with, but he hoped it was the larger number—nine—in the American version of the saying.

He knew the landscape and woods, having walked it often with Gitana. The leaves would provide cover and allow him to move quickly and undetected toward the riverbank. Like the dark, wet dirt beneath him, the leaves were soft from the recent rain. If the sniper were close, they wouldn't crunch under Santana's feet when he moved, alerting the shooter of his position.

He leaned a shoulder against the tree trunk and took another deep breath. The rich, damp smell of earth reminded him of an open grave. He had no equipment to calculate the trajectory of the bullet, which would help him determine where the shot might have come from, but he remembered that Gitana had looked out toward the river.

Santana peered around the tree trunk. The land sloped gently away from the back of his house toward the water. He mentally mapped a route that would get him to the river and possibly closer to the shooter. Then he moved quickly, staying low, zigzagging from tree to tree, varying the times he remained behind each one, never establishing a pattern.

He made his way to the riverbank where fresh footprints blemished the soft ground around him. He looked back at Gitana still crouched on all fours. No tree branches interfered with a sight line to the deck. The shot had come from this general area, but whoever had taken it was long gone.

* * *

Santana usually made Gitana sleep on the floor, though she was never happy about it. Tonight, however, when she sat on her haunches at the foot of the bed, placed her head on the sheets and gave him a look that only someone without a heart could ignore, he made an exception.

When he called her, she leapt quickly onto the bed in excited anticipation and showered him with her tongue before settling down beside him with a satisfied huff of air.

Five hours after he fell asleep, Santana found himself being dragged over the outcropping of a cliff by a dog that had a hold of his left ankle. He awoke abruptly from the nightmare, kicking at the empty air, his fingers clenching the damp bed sheets, his panicked moans echoing in the darkness.

Gitana lay stretched out beside him, her tail pointed toward the footboard, her head raised slightly off the bed spread.

"Go back to sleep," he said.

While she promptly complied, he described the dream in a journal he kept on the nightstand.

Santana had always possessed the ability to vividly recall his dreams. Now, whenever he woke up after five or six hours of sleep, he would write in his journal and then remind himself to look for dream signs when he fell asleep again and was in a dream state. Both techniques sometimes allowed him to actively participate in his dream environment while the dream was in progress and helped him understand the dark images and objects that had haunted his sleep since the age of sixteen.

He recalled that being attacked by an animal in a dream was a warning to be careful with those around him. He needed to take notice of people in his waking life that exhibited the same qualities of the dog that attacked him in his dream.

He wrote down what he remembered but couldn't recall the type of dog. He thought that the dream might have been about Gitana. Perhaps she was trying to save his life by pulling him off the deck after the shot had been fired. Maybe the dog he saw in the dream shouldn't be interpreted as a warning at all. But why hadn't he recognized or remembered Gitana?

He closed his eyes and tried picturing the dog again. He could only recall that it was black with tan markings. Then his thoughts gradually shifted to the sniper and whether the latest attempt on his life was related to the current case or to the Estrada twins he had killed twenty years ago in Colombia.

Learning to live with the inevitability of his death hadn't come easy for Santana. Whether there was another life beyond the one he currently lived was a question he no longer considered. He lived in the moment, lived for his mission and his purpose. He believed his innate instincts, his skills as an investigator, and luck had kept him alive up to this point and nothing else. He knew he would never complete his mission, but he would survive for as long as he could.

As false dawn approached, he concluded that he had no way of knowing the motive behind the shooting, at least not yet. The attempt on his life might have nothing to do with his past and everything to do with the present.

Most citizens would have immediately called 911 and reported the incident. Most police officers would have called their departments and reported an attempt had been made on their life. But Santana saw advantages in keeping quiet. It would allow him to investigate the shooting without interference. It would also send a message to the sniper that he wouldn't panic, wouldn't come unglued psychologically or emotionally. Santana saw that as an advantage as well.

He rose slowly from his bed at sunrise, feeling slow, lethargic and cold. He walked downstairs with Gitana closely at his heels. Because of his odd work hours, a contractor had installed a dog door in a wall. An electronic chip in her collar activated the door that gave her access to an enclosed dog run Santana had constructed in the backyard. He fed her and then walked upstairs again and examined the brick fireplace on the wall opposite the sliding glass door and deck.

The bullet had blown a circular hole about the size of a small fist in a single brick located halfway between the hearth and the ceiling. Small chips of shattered brick were scattered on the bedroom floor twenty feet from impact. But the brick had kept the bullet from completely penetrating the sheetrock covering the interior wall.

His decision to add a bedroom fireplace to compliment the one in the living room had proved fortuitous. Had the bullet hit sheetrock first rather than brick, it might have continued on its way and he may never have found it.

He punched out a hole with a ball peen hammer large enough to fit his latex gloved hand. The retrieved cartridge was a .308 Winchester, a common round used in sniper rifles and available nearly everywhere. He had hoped for a less common round that would be easier to trace.

He placed the bullet in an evidence envelope and walked to the center of the bedroom and studied the lawn chair still sitting open on the deck. Then he shifted his eyes to the bullet hole in the brick. He looked at both objects a second time and then a third. It was clear the bullet had been rising as it blew past his head. That would make sense if the shot had been fired from ground level near the river.

He swept fragments of broken glass into a dustpan, dumped the glass in the trash with the rest of the shattered door, and carefully examined the decking one more time. He didn't want Gitana cutting a paw. After showering, he ate a breakfast of arepas, hot chocolate, and eggs.

His knees were sore from the fifteen-foot drop off the balcony, so before throwing the eggshells in the garbage, he rubbed the oil from inside the shell on his kneecaps. It was something his mother had taught him when he was young. He was never certain the egg juice had any medicinal value, but psychologically, it made his knees feel better.

He called a glass repair company and set up an appointment to replace the glass in the sliding door. Then he called Tony Novak at home.

Chapter 18

The sky the next morning was slate gray, the wind brisk and cool. Santana stood on the sand beach in front of his house, wearing a leather jacket. He could smell dead fish in the wind, hear water lapping against the shore and cars crossing the I-94 bridge over the St. Croix River. The chill in the air signaled that fall would be short lived, and what lay ahead would be bleaker and colder and darker, like death itself.

Santana watched Tony Novak attach a 35-mm camera to a tripod above a clear foot impression in the sand. Novak placed a scale next to the long axis of the impression and a second scale perpendicular to the heel. He used a hypodermic syringe to drain a small amount of water from the impression, but left two grass clippings and a small piece of leaf that had been trampled into it. Removing the material might destroy the print. Novak then snapped black-and-white and color photographs of the foot impression before casting the impression with dental stone he had pre-mixed in a zip-lock bag.

"You don't have to tell me what the hell's going on, John. But it looks to me like someone walked along the beach from the north and then knelt right here." Novak squinted at the impressions in the sand and then at Santana's deck. "If I were a betting man, I'd say someone fired a shot from a kneeling position in the direction of that deck up there. The shooter knelt on his right knee with his left foot forward and the left elbow on the bent knee."

"That would make him right-handed," Santana said.

"Yes, it would. His target was someone sitting or standing on the deck. I'm guessing you got real lucky or whoever fired the rifle was a poor marksman."

Santana wondered now if the perp who slit Pao Yang's throat and the perp who fired the sniper bullet were the same person. "This is between you and me, Tony. No one else can know."

Novak nodded as though what he was being asked to do was common practice. "I've worked with you long enough, John. I trust your judgment. Give me some time to study the impression. I'll let you know what I find."

* * *

Santana had attended Hmong funerals before and understood how important rituals were to the family of the deceased and their clan. Families often had long waits before they could bury their dead because only three Hmong funeral chapels existed in the city. But General Yang was an influential man in the Hmong community. The services for his daughter, Mai, were held quickly.

Santana parked in a large, paved and striped lot overflowing with cars off Eaton Street on St. Paul's West Side. As he exited the car, he could see the dome of the St. Paul Cathedral to the north. Cars zoomed along Highway 52 to his right and further east a plane landed at the Holman Field airport.

There were two entrances to the one-story brick mortuary. A blue awning hung over the entrance to the chapel on his left and a red awning marked the entrance to the chapel on his right. Posted signs on the glass doors indicated Mai Yang's funeral was in the east chapel, Pao Yang's in the west.

Santana entered through the east doors and was immediately struck by the heavy smell of incense and the sight of dozens of fresh flowers arranged in sympathy baskets and on stands in large floral sprays. An elderly man swayed back and forth in front of the crowd seated around the edges of the room on metal folding chairs. The old man was playing a bamboo mouth organ called a *qeej*. Santana had heard it pronounced "geng." Gold and silver folded papers were attached to the walls. The paper represented the spirit of money that would later be burned and sent on to the next life with Mai Yang.

Hmong funerals normally lasted three days except for extreme cases where a family may not have enough financial resources. They believed it took that long to give a soul instruction for its journey to the world of her ancestors.

Mai Yang's body was dressed in traditional Hmong funeral attire and placed in an open Hinoki wood casket with a mahogany red finish. One end of a string had been tied to the little finger of her right hand and the other end to the horn of a bull. The horn represented the bull that would be sacrificed to provide food for the funeral visitors and for her journey to the afterlife. City codes now prohibited the Hmong from killing a bull directly outside a funeral home. Instead, a bull would be slaughtered later at the stockyards in South St. Paul.

Santana spotted Diana Lee sitting in a folding chair on the far side of the room near General Yang and his son, Kou. Lee's black hair hung straight and loose over the shoulders of a navy-blue pantsuit. She acknowledged Santana with a nod.

He watched as a group of women walked to Mai's casket and knelt down beside it. With their heads bowed and one hand covering their faces, they began wailing. The women were close relatives of Mai Yang. They would cry several times during the funeral and stay awake for three days to show their support for the general and their clan. Ten minutes after they began crying, the women abruptly stopped and walked away from the casket, their tears drying quickly. They reminded Santana of the *Plañideras* in Cartagena who were hired to cry at funerals.

Santana got Lee's attention and motioned for her to follow him outside.

The sun had broken through the thinning cloud cover, and the angle of its rays created long shadows in the parking lot.

He wondered if Hawkins's concerns about Diana Lee had triggered last night's dream, wondered if the person he should be cautious about was his new partner. But witnesses often made mistakes when describing crimes and suspects, especially when under duress. Hawkins could be wrong about Lee, wrong about what she thought she saw. Santana needed to satisfy his curiosity, assuage his doubts, learn exactly what she had told the OIS investigators.

Lee came out the door wearing a long wool coat. "What's up?"

"What exactly did you tell the OIS investigators?"

Worry lines wrinkled her brow. "Why? Have they talked to you again?"

"No. They haven't."

"Then what's the problem?"

"I don't know that there is one. But I'd like you to run through what you recall for me one more time. I'm still not convinced Kou Yang was the shooter."

Santana felt he was being honest with Lee about Kou Yang, even if he was being less so regarding his motivation for asking about the shooting. But if Hawkins's perceptions were inaccurate, he didn't want Lee believing that he thought she had done something wrong, or, worse yet, had lied to the OIS investigators.

"I was coming out of the garage behind the house when I heard two shots," Lee said. She closed her eyes. Stood perfectly still. "The shots were close together, one after the other. I drew my Glock and ran toward the front of the house. It was raining hard and difficult to see." She spoke calmly, with no inflection, as though she were hypnotized and watching a movie of the shooting playing on the back of her eyelids. "I saw Hawkins down and someone running toward the Mazda. I yelled for him to freeze."

"How did you know it was a him?"

She held her eyes shut. "I'm just using him for the sake of description. But I believe it was a man by the way he moved, the way he ran. I couldn't see his face because he wore a hooded windbreaker."

"How tall was he?"

"I'm not sure. He was moving away from me."

"Did he have a gun?"

"Yes."

"Do you remember in what hand he carried it?"

She held out her left hand, as if testing her impression. "Left hand."

"You're sure."

"I'm sure because I didn't see anything in his right hand, which was facing me. When I yelled and he turned and pointed the gun at me, it was in his left hand."

"Then what happened?"

"I remember moving behind a tree trunk, figuring he was going to fire. He didn't. But it gave him time to get to the car and start it."

"Which direction did he go?"

"The car was parked along the curb facing west. That's the way he went."

"So he drove right by you."

"Not right by me. I was approximately fifteen yards from the road."

"You didn't fire."

She opened her eyes. Looked at Santana for a long moment before replying. "Like I said. It was raining hard. If I shot and missed, a bullet could have hit a house or a business."

She had recounted the shooting quickly, without hesitation. Santana wished she had kept her eyes open, but he hadn't detected any tells indicating that she was lying or distorting the truth.

"Did I help?" she asked.

In truth, he thought, no. But he wanted to keep the focus on Kou Yang and not on his reasons for asking her to describe the shooting. "You can't ID Kou Yang as the shooter."

"That's what I told the OIS investigators."

Santana decided he would drive by Pao Yang's house later and take another look at the scene. Just to satisfy his curiosity.

"I'm going back in now," she said

"How long are you staying?"

"Until this afternoon."

"I'll come with you."

As they entered the building again, Santana saw a man give General Yang some dollar bills. The general appeared to thank him. Then he got up from his chair and headed for a door that connected the two chapels. He gave no indication that he had seen Santana. But Santana was certain the general knew he was there.

Seeing the general taking the dollar bills reminded Santana of something he needed to check out. "I need to speak to General Yang," he said to Lee.

The detectives followed the general into the next chapel.

A shaman dressed in black pants and jacket, and a conical red hood, sat in a chair at the head of Pao Yang's closed casket. An older man and woman were seated on each side of the casket. They were beating drums with sticks that had a piece of red cloth attached to one end.

"What's the shaman doing?" Santana asked.

"Making certain evil spirits don't leave Pao Yang's body and come near the family again in the next life. The two people seated in chairs on each side of the casket are Pao Yang's oldest aunt on his mother's side and his oldest uncle on his father's side."

A younger man standing at the head of a short line near the casket was speaking in Hmong to the body.

"He's settling financial, emotional and spiritual accounts," Lee said. "No one wants Pao Yang's spirit to return to haunt him."

Santana saw General Yang go down a set of steps. "I'll see you later," he told Lee. Then he followed the general down the stairs and into a lounge that smelled of cooked rice and chicken.

Men were sitting at round tables playing cards, eating and drinking pop and beer, chatting as they passed the time, trying to keep awake, waiting to be called once again to their duties upstairs. A few men gave Santana a reflexive glance, then quickly returned to their conversations and card games.

Already General Yang was seated at one of the tables with three other men, eating from a plate of chicken and rice. The general raised a forkful of rice to his lips. He paused, held the fork steady as his eyes locked on Santana's.

It was at that instant Santana confirmed that General Yang was eating with his left-hand.

Chapter 19

Santana sat behind the wheel of the Crown Vic and stared out the windshield at the Hmong funeral home and the bone-colored sky.

According to the ME, the perp who killed Pao Yang was left-handed due to the angle and direction of the knife wound in Yang's throat. Based on cases Santana had investigated, he knew that ten percent of the population was left-handed. Left-handedness was more common in males than in females. One of a pair of twins was likely to be left-handed. And people who were left-handed had a slightly higher risk of psychotic mental disorders.

As far as Santana knew, the general had no identical twin and no history of mental illness. But he had fought in Laos and certainly would be familiar with guns and knives.

The general could have killed Pao Yang because he knew Pao was dating his daughter and presumed him responsible for her murder. If that were true, then the general wasn't likely responsible for his daughter's murder. But if he thought Pao Yang was somehow responsible for his daughter becoming a prostitute, he might have killed them both. But would he set up his son, Kou, to take the fall? And, Santana thought, if the sniper was right-handed, maybe General Yang hadn't been the one who attempted to kill him, but could it be his son, Kou?

Santana needed more connections, more evidence to make a case that General Yang was responsible for all the murders. He needed to know if General Yang or his son, Kou, had called Jenna Jones or vice versa.

* * *

Malinas was a small sports bar that served American and Hmong food. Located in a two-story brick building on Dale and Van Buren, it had three full-size pool tables, a dance floor, and a poker table.

Three Hmong teenagers were shooting pool and listening to "Hotel California" by the Eagles when Santana entered. They all looked at him, and then quickly shifted their gaze back to their game.

He sat on a stool at the bar and ordered two eggs rolls and a Coke. He had eaten a variety of good egg rolls in his time, but the Hmong made the best. While he waited for his food, he showed the Hmong bartender his badge and Kou Yang's booking photo. "Recognize him?"

The bartender wiped his hands on the apron tied around his waist and took the photo from Santana. He held the frame of his glasses with his right hand as he studied the photo and then shook his head.

"His name is Kou Yang," Santana said. "He was in here a couple of days ago. Were you working then?"

"Yes," the bartender said, handing the photo back to Santana. "I work that day."

Santana waited for more information and quickly realized he wasn't going to get any.

The conversation between the three young Hmong men playing pool had suddenly become quieter and less animated. Santana knew they had made him for a cop. "Kou Yang came in here late afternoon or early evening."

"I don't know everyone who comes in."

"Anyone you see in here that might recognize this kid?"

The bartender gestured toward the pool table. "You have to ask."

Santana figured he would be wasting his time. But he got up from the stool and showed the photo to each of the young men around the pool table. None of them could identify Kou Yang.

Santana sat down on the bar stool again and ate the delicious egg rolls when they were served. At least lunch wasn't a waste of time.

Before he left, he gave the bartender a business card. "If your memory improves, give me a call."

Santana's cell phone rang as he was leaving the bar. He unclipped the phone from his belt, recognized the watch commander's number at the station. He flipped open his phone. "Santana."

"We had a code three on the West Side, John. Shots fired. Sounds like a drive-by involving the ACs and the LKs. We got Eduardo Robles here. Says he wants to talk to you."

* * *

"Robles tells me he had a meeting set up with you today," Diana Lee said. "Was there a reason you kept me out of the loop?"

Santana could tell she was making a concerted effort to disguise the frustration in her voice.

They were standing outside the door of an interview room at headquarters. He was relieved the Homicide Unit was deserted and Gamboni was behind a closed door in her office. He didn't like airing disagreements in public.

"I thought we were working this case together," Lee said.

"We are."

"I'm not sure I understand your method of collaborating."

Santana knew Lee would be upset with him for setting up the meeting without telling her. He felt he owed her an explanation for keeping her in the dark. "A former LK gangbanger owed me a favor. I thought I could use the contact to get Robles to talk."

"Like Robles wouldn't talk to me?"

"Has he?"

Her gaze shifted to the floor.

He took it as a signal that Robles had refused to speak to her. "Look, Diana. Both of us want to know if the LKs know anything about Pao Yang's murder. Why don't you tell me what happened this afternoon."

Her eyes found his again. "Apparently, a carload of ACs drove over to the West Side and fired some shots at Robles and his LK gangbangers."

"Looking for payback," Santana said.

"As predictable as the rising sun. Fortunately, no one was hit. We're still looking for the shooters. But we've got some angry citizens."

131

Santana could see that her lips were pressed together and her lower eyelids were tensed in anger.

"Anything else I need to know?" she asked in a voice that masked her feelings.

He quickly recapped what Tony Novak had told him earlier about the prints, blood, and ballistics.

Lee's mouth parted in disbelief, but she held her tongue.

"Let me do the talking when we interview Robles," Santana said.

"But if we've got the murder weapons, a motive, and a prime suspect in Kou Yang, why waste our time with Robles?"

"As long as he's here, let's see what he has to say."

Eduardo Robles settled back in his chair as Santana and Lee entered the interview room. Cool. Confident.

He wore a gold bandana around his closely shaved head and a black sleeveless T-shirt and baggy, faded jeans. The thumbnail on his right hand was quite long, indicating that he used it as a scoop to snort cocaine. A five-point crown with two pitchforks crossed and the tines pointing down was inked on his left bicep. The letters L and K flanked the crown. ADR was tattooed on his right forearm. He wore a teardrop tattoo near the corner his left eye.

Tattoos provided Santana with information about who Robles was, what he had done and where he had been.

A pitchfork with the tines pointing down was a devil symbol used by the Latin Kings and Bloods. The Crips used a six-point crown and a pitchfork with the tines pointing up. ADR stood for *amor de rey*, which meant love to the king. The teardrop represented a family member or friend of Robles who had died in prison.

"You Santana?" Robles said.

Santana sat down across the table from him. "That's right."

Robles glanced at Lee who stood with her arms crossed and her back against the door. Then he focused his eyes on Santana. They were as dark and dead as those of an animal mounted on a wall.

"Detective Lee had you sign a Rights Waiver form, Eduardo, so you know you're not under arrest. Yet."

132

"Hey, man. Who's the victim here?" he said with feigned outrage. "You need to find a carload of *Chino cabróns.*"

Chinos or *Rolos* were labels Santana and his boyhood friends called anyone born in Bogotá, Colombia. But he knew Robles was using the word as a derogatory term for Chinese or anyone with Asian ancestry. "Let's forget about the Asian assholes for a minute. You spoke with Luis Garcia about our meeting."

"Yeah. Garcia said you were a straight shooter, Santana. He said you look out for his mother while he does his nickel in Stillwater."

"I stop by when I can."

"Luis said I could trust you."

"It's a two-way street, Eduardo."

Robles nodded slowly and leaned forward with a smile that had no feeling. "*Hablaré con usted, pero no con la mujer.*" His voice was soft but clearly loud enough for Lee to hear.

"So, don't talk to me, shitbag," she said.

Santana was surprised that Lee understood some Spanish and by her outrage. Robles seemed equally surprised. He glowered at her as he might a shoe if he stepped in something unpleasant. The spark of anger that long ago had fried the emotional wiring in his brain was palpable. But he bit his lip, sat back in the chair and locked his fingers behind his head.

Robles was older and smarter than most gangbangers running the streets of St. Paul. Less inclined to be intimidated or to supply information to the police unless he determined it was in his or his gang's best interests.

"Lee and Santana," he said, waggling an index finger between them. "What are you anyway? Half the minorities on the SPPD?" Robles had a Mexican accent and spoke as though he had been educated in a classroom as well as the street.

"We're not here to discuss the department's hiring practices," Santana said.

"Hey, Latinos need more role models."

"Like you?"

"I do what I can, man."

"Cut the bullshit, Eduardo."

Robles spread his hands.

"The LKs have a problem with the Asian Crips?" Santana said.

"No problem we can't handle."

"Pao Yang's throat was slit three days ago."

"You know, Santana, I was real disappointed to hear that. I didn't sleep all night I was laughin' so hard."

"Why don't you tell us what you know?"

Robles rested his elbows on the table. "You think I took out that *pinché pendejo*?"

"Maybe not you personally. But maybe you green-lighted the killing."

"The Kings had nothing to do with it."

"The ACs apparently believe you're responsible."

"They going to wish they didn't."

"You're not thinking of retaliating, are you?"

Robles sat back in his chair and said nothing.

Santana had seen more than his share of teens and young men like Eduardo Robles. He was always disappointed but never surprised that someone this young could be as empty as a shell casing.

Two years ago the feds had arrested twenty-six LKs on drug and firearms charges. It was one of the largest drug busts in Minnesota history. Called operation Wild Kingdom, the yearlong investigation was led by the SPPD and agents from the DEA. The indictments contained thirty-one counts, including one count charging all twenty-six defendants with conspiring to distribute and possess with intent to distribute methamphetamine, cocaine, crack cocaine, and marijuana. The LKs had controlled much of the methamphetamine, cocaine, and marijuana that flowed into the state from Mexico and from Chicago, the city where the LKs began and the city where they were now the dominant gang.

The arrests of some of its most violent members in St. Paul had reduced the gang's ability to be suspects as well as victims, and the violent crime rates involving LKs had declined on both sides of the river over the last two years. But Santana knew that taking out a few gang members was like the game Whack-a-Mole. As soon as the department concentrated on cleaning up one area of the city, gangs appeared in another part of town. Robles had arrived from Chicago and taken control of the LKs soon after the core leadership had been arrested.

"I heard Pao Yang was organizing the Asian Crips," Santana said. "Maybe trying to cut into your drug market now that you're vulnerable."

"We just a group of *pochos* watching each other's backs. Like a club. *Que no?*"

"Pochos" was a common slang term for an Americanized Mexican.

"And you," Robles said, looking at Diana Lee, "are a *chica caliente.*"

"Wow. A lowlife gangbanger thinks I'm hot. Thanks for making my day."

"*No problema.*"

Robles looked at Santana again. He either had missed Lee's sarcasm or chose to ignore it. "Why should I help you out, man?"

"Because you don't want to take any heat for Pao Yang's murder."

Robles thought about it. "You know, Santana, I think I might give you some information, 'cause you help out Luis."

"And help yourself in the process."

"The way the world works, man."

"Maybe in your limited universe, Eduardo. But you're in my world now. And you're going to help me out or you're gonna wish you had."

There was a long silence before Robles spoke again. "I hear things."

"Like what?"

"Like maybe the *Chinos* selling something."

"Am I supposed to guess what?"

"*Caballo*, man. You know, horse. Mexican mud."

Lee uncrossed her arms and stepped away from the door. "Heroin?" she said.

Robles nodded.

"You sure?" she asked.

"I'm not lyin', man."

"Where's the heroin?" Santana asked.

"Pao Yang had it."

"Maybe that's why you took him out?" Lee said. "You wanted the smack."

"The *Chinos* are the channel swimmers. I don't use that shit. You loco."

"Easy, Eduardo," Santana said. "We need to know the source of your information."

"We caught a *Chino* from the Crips bangin' one of my *vato's* sisters. My homeboy was stompin' the shit out of him when the *Chino* said he'd help us score some dust if we let him go."

"You know where we can find this Crip?"

"You got him."

"We do?"

"Sure," Robles said. "Over at the morgue. Benny Vue. He's one of the two *cabróns* ate a bullet at Pao Yang's house."

Chapter 20

Santana parked the Crown Vic along the curb in front of Pao Yang's house, and he and Lee stepped out.

Small puffs of cumulus clouds smoked the clear sky overhead. A thin veil of white cirrostratus clouds covered the sky to the west. Jagged black thunderheads rose from the horizon and merged with the white clouds creating what appeared to be a range of snow-capped mountains. The scene reminded Santana of the Andes and of his boyhood home in Manizales.

As they walked up the sidewalk to the house, Santana could hear a dog barking and a baby crying somewhere in the neighborhood. His mind was focused on the unpleasant memory of Kacie Hawkins lying wounded in the grass. He remembered thinking for one terrifying moment that he was responsible for Hawkins losing her life. Then he remembered the wave of relief and joy he had felt when he realized she was still alive.

Now he needed to figure out why Pao Yang and his two cousins had been murdered and if their murders were somehow connected with Mai Yang's death and Kacie Hawkins's wound.

Santana and Lee gloved up; she removed the crime scene tape across the front door, and they entered the house.

Rays of sunlight shooting through the windows cast an amber glow throughout the living room, as though a fire lighted it. The forensic techs had completed their work. But familiar scents still hung in the air. Vapors from the superglue. Aluminum from the dusting powder. Ammonia from the urine. And copper from the blood. Santana thought that blood smelled like warm pennies.

The furniture had been dusted with a combination of black and silver-gray latent print powder. On light-colored surfaces, the latent prints appeared dark, making them easy to photograph. On dark-colored surfaces, the prints appeared light. When lifted with tape and placed on a white backing card, a latent print appeared dark. Nowadays, the lab techs carried just one powder, one brush and one color of backing cards. They only had to compare the dark ridges of the latent print to the dark ridges of the inked print.

Santana's thoughts shifted from the powder to the gruesome scene of blood-spattered walls and dead gangbangers slumped in chairs around the kitchen table. Learning to live with the bloody images associated with homicide was something he accepted as part of his profession, but he had never gotten used to it. Once he became desensitized to the violence, it would be time for him to find another job.

He and Lee stood in the living room studying the details. Then he took out a small tape recorder from a pocket of his leather jacket and turned it on. He spoke into it, setting the date, time, and location before narrating what he saw.

Faded hardwood floors that creaked like hinges on a rusty door as they stepped on the boards. Beige walls potholed with dents. Mismatched furniture sprinkled with fingerprint powder. No paintings or bookshelves. No framed photos of family and friends. An old TV with rabbit ears and a fourteen-inch screen. Three copies of *SAM* magazine on the coffee table featuring scantily clad Asian women on their covers. No phones, no answering machine. Santana wondered if Pao Yang only used a cell phone or a throwaway phone as gangbangers preferred to do.

According to Diana Lee, Pao Yang had come to Minnesota from California. Santana recalled that the gang's last reputed leader was in prison serving an eleven-year sentence for raping young Hmong women as part of a gang initiation ritual.

He and Lee worked together as they began searching each room in the house. Two detectives testifying in court as to what they found was always better than one. A lone detective could be accused of planting evidence, and Santana had no intention of letting that happen.

The two bedrooms, like the house itself, seemingly belonged to no one. Santana felt as if he had entered a cheap hotel room that offered a place to sleep and nothing more.

They pulled out drawers and looked inside and underneath each one of them. They searched behind mirrors and under and inside mattresses and box springs.

A closet with a foldout door in the larger bedroom had an odor like old gym shoes and contained the standard AC gang attire. Blue T-shirts, baggy jeans, and athletic shoes. Santana inspected the mail, which consisted of overdue utility bills and junk advertisements. He found no bank or mortgage statements or title indicating that Pao Yang owned the house.

They went to the kitchen. Blood spatter had dried on the walls. Ceramic plates crusted with food and water glasses powdered with fingerprint dust were still on the table. Dirty dishes floated in filmy water in the sink. Santana again noted the open drawers and cabinets.

They emptied a set of salt and pepper shakers, two boxes of Wheaties cereal and a jar of Folger's Instant Coffee and a sack of sugar. After an hour of searching, the house looked as though a tornado had blown through. But they still had found no heroin.

"Maybe the smack's not here," Lee said, leaning against the kitchen counter.

Her smooth, copper skin sparkled with beads of sweat, and her dark hair was pulled back and held in place with a tortoiseshell clip. Santana remembered that women in Colombia called it a *cocodrilo* or crocodile clip because of its long, pointed teeth.

"It's here," Santana said.

"What makes you so sure?"

"Whoever shot the two gangbangers and Hawkins was after it. And he was willing to risk coming here in broad daylight to get it."

"Maybe he found it. Maybe he was on his way out when the three of us arrived."

"I don't think so. Someone doing a thorough search would've left the house looking like it is now."

"Not if he found the smack right away."

Santana recalled the initial crime scene in the kitchen.

"Not all of the drawers or cabinets were open that day, Diana. I don't think the perp was that lucky or Pao Yang that careless. I think the perp had just started looking when we showed up."

"Then where are the drugs?"

"We've been looking for powdered heroin."

"So?"

"So there's liquid heroin as well."

"Not as common," she said.

"But not unusual." Santana opened the refrigerator door.

Inside he found an unopened pound of ground beef, a stick of butter, three eggs, five cans of Budweiser, and a carton of whole milk. The freezer contained a half-gallon of chocolate ice cream and four empty ice cube trays.

"Take a look," Santana said, handing her the half-gallon of ice cream.

She pulled off the cover and dipped an index finger in the carton. Then she tasted the tip of her finger. "Chocolate ice cream."

She tossed the carton in the sink.

Santana pulled out the milk carton. It was nearly empty. He poured the contents in a glass on the counter.

"Your turn," she said.

Santana picked up the glass and smelled the sour milk. "Why don't you try it?" he said, offering the glass to her.

"You are kidding, right?"

"Yes. I'm kidding."

The five beer cans were sealed and he cracked opened each one.

"It's a little early for me," she said as he held a can out to her.

"We're not having a party, Diana."

She shrugged and took it.

They poured the cans in separate glasses. All five cans contained beer.

"Now what?" she asked.

Santana opened the last cupboard in the kitchen. Four one-liter bottles of Baileys Irish Cream liqueur sat on a shelf.

"Did Pao Yang strike you as Baileys Irish Cream drinker?"

"I don't know. What do you think gangbangers drink?"

"Not Baileys." Santana pulled one of the bottles off the shelf. Offered it to her.

"I'm not much of a drinker."

"Well, here's your chance." He unscrewed the cap and immediately smelled a glue-like odor.

Lee smelled it, too. She held his gaze, and then she grabbed an empty glass out of an adjoining cupboard and banged it on the counter.

Santana could see that her eyes were jittering with excitement and light, like fireflies in a dark sky. He poured a small amount of thick liquid from the open bottle of Irish Cream into the glass.

"It's liquid heroin," she said, looking at Santana. "And it was here all along."

✢ ✢ ✢

Heavy raindrops hammered the window in Rita Gamboni's office. A low, dark sky had brought an abrupt end to the day and an early start to the night.

Rita Gamboni leaned forward in the chair behind her desk and looked at Santana, then at Lee, then at Pete Canfield, the Ramsey County Attorney, sitting in the three chairs in front of her desk. In his pin-stripped suit and razor cut hair, Canfield could have just stepped out of the pages of *GQ Magazine.*

"How much heroin do you think we have?" Gamboni asked. The lipstick and makeup she always applied so carefully in the morning had faded, leaving her mouth and complexion looking nearly as white as her blonde hair.

Santana thought she looked more tired than usual, and he wondered if it was from the increasing job pressure or from something else.

Before he could respond to Gamboni's question, Lee said, "One pound of opium is refined down to less than two ounces of heroin. A kilo is two point two pounds of opium and nets the grower sixty to one-hundred-thirty dollars. A kilo goes for four to six thousand dollars. Wholesale price on the street is between ninety and two hundred thousand dollars. Dilute it for street sale and you can make one and a half to two and a half million dollars. I'd say the heroin in the Irish Cream bottles is worth one million dollars."

"Impressive," Gamboni said.

Lee lowered her head in embarrassment. "I've always been good with numbers."

"I've notified the DEA, John," Gamboni said.

"What about Kou Yang?"

"He's lawyered up."

"How many murders we charging him with?"

"Three so far," Canfield said. "Plus, the aggravated assault charge for shooting Hawkins."

"We need to make sure everything is airtight," Gamboni said.

Between the open metal slats in the blinds, Santana could see streaks of lightning webbing the dark sky and hear long cracks of thunder that sounded like wood ripping apart in a log splitter. "Tell me why Kou Yang would kill Pao Yang and then Benny Vue and Kevin Xiong," he said to Gamboni. "They all belonged to the same gang."

"Maybe he wanted the smack. He wanted revenge on Pao Yang for humping his sister. He goes to Yang's house and Vue and Xiong are there. Kou Yang didn't intend to cap them, but he's got no choice."

Canfield nodded in agreement. "I like Gamboni's scenario, John. Kou Yang has means, motive, and opportunity. And he's got no alibi for the time of the killing. You said he was lying to you and Lee during the interview. What more do you need?"

"What about his sister and Jenna Jones? Why would he kill them?"

"What's your take on that, Detective Lee?" Gamboni asked.

Lee glanced at Santana. "I'm not sure what to think."

"Really?" Gamboni said. She kept the two detectives waiting before she spoke again. Maybe hoping Lee would change her mind. "I'm sure you'd like to tell me what you think, Detective Santana."

"I think it's highly unlikely that Kou Yang murdered Jenna Jones and his sister, Mai."

"But you agree that he killed Pao Yang and his two cousins, Kevin Xiong and Ben Vue," Canfield said.

Santana had noticed that Canfield had developed a bad habit of rubbing his gold cufflinks between his thumb and forefinger whenever he posed a question to which he didn't know the answer beforehand. He wondered if he should tell Canfield before an observant defense attorney used it against him. "All the evidence says so."

"That's not what I asked, John."

Santana knew Canfield to be trustworthy and more than competent, one of the few high-ranking attorneys in the city who placed integrity above political ambition. "We're giving the kid far too much credit, Pete. We're supposed to believe that Kou surprised Pao Yang while he was alone behind a restaurant in Frogtown and cut his throat. The next morning he shoots two of Pao Yang's gangbanger cousins while they're eating breakfast and then wounds Kacie Hawkins while he makes his getaway. And this is a kid who never had so much as a parking ticket."

"Maybe Pao Yang got careless," Gamboni said. "Or maybe he wasn't worried because he knew Kou Yang and had no idea what was about to happen."

"Reiko Tanabe is convinced that the perp who killed Pao Yang was left handed. Kou Yang is right handed."

"So he used his strong hand to keep him quiet and to hold him steady while he cut his throat."

"Even if we have evidence tying Kou Yang to three murders, we've got nothing tying him to the murders of Mai Yang and Jenna Jones."

"Then I suggest that you and Detective Lee find some evidence," Gamboni said.

Chapter 21

Santana took an old freight elevator with a manually operated wooden door up three floors to Grace Chandler's artist's loft in a warehouse in downtown St. Paul. He was tired from the long day. But when Grace called and asked to see him, he couldn't turn her down.

Easels, canvases, and frames were scattered throughout the large room, which smelled of paint and was broken up by wooden pillars. Concrete covered the floor and metal pipes split the open spaces between the exposed beams in the eleven-foot ceiling. A brown foldout couch and two, worn overstuffed chairs circled a throw rug and a square glass-topped coffee table in the middle of the room.

Grace gave him a hug and kiss, but both seemed obligatory. "Would you like a glass of red wine or a beer? I'm baking a pepperoni pizza."

"I'll take a beer."

Santana sat down in an overstuffed chair.

She brought him a cold bottle of Sam Adams.

"How did you know?" he asked.

"The night we had dinner at the Strip Club. You mentioned you usually drank Sam Adams."

"I'm impressed."

She sat on the couch opposite him and gave him a tight smile. He didn't need to be a detective to see something was bothering her. "What's wrong, Grace?"

"Nothing."

She averted her eyes, looked down at her paint-splattered denim blue shirt and jeans. Then she lifted her chin, inhaled deeply and released a frustrated breath. "Okay. I can't hide anything from you. I'm upset because you spoke with my father the other day and didn't tell me."

"You talked with him?"

"He called."

"I didn't tell you, Grace, because I figured you might react this way. I didn't want to spoil the evening."

Her shoulders and facial muscles relaxed slightly. She started to smile and then held back. "Keeping secrets is no way to start a relationship." Her voice was softer now, less accusatory.

"If it helps, I came here to tell you I'd met with him."

She nodded slowly and looked into his eyes, as if the truth would be revealed there. "What did my father tell you when you spoke to him?"

Santana had no desire to hurt her. But he had no desire to be dishonest either. Then he wondered if she already knew what her father told him and if this was some sort of test. "Your father told me you had some difficulties. He didn't elaborate."

She shook her head in resignation. "My father never wants me to have an opinion contrary to his."

"And you resent that?"

"Wouldn't you?"

Santana had no way of answering the question since both his parents had been dead by the time he was sixteen. "Your father has done well."

"He inherited a substantial fortune from my grandparents. That helped."

"Do you see him often?"

"We don't have much in common."

"Different political leanings?"

"My father wasn't around much when I was young. I don't think he's ever forgiven the country for pulling out of Vietnam and losing the war. When he was elected senator, he asked the press not to interview me. He convinced them I had," she paused and made quotation mark gestures, "emotional issues. He said I'd never recovered from my mother's death, which wasn't true. But I gave one interview anyway to an alternative publication. It didn't go well. I never gave an interview again."

Santana wondered what had happened during the interview. He made a mental note to find out. "You don't believe your father is serving the public interest."

"Like most politicians, the only interests he's serving are his own." Her face was more reflective than angry. "I remember he used to take me flying when I was young. It was about the only thing we enjoyed doing together." She smiled at the memory. "I think he's trying to act like a father again. It's just too little, too late."

"Does your father still fly?"

"He has his own plane."

"What about hunting? I saw a photo of you and your brother duck hunting."

"We used to hunt together with my father. Not anymore."

"Do you keep a gun around the houseboat?"

"Yes," she said. "A rifle. Not a handgun."

Santana wondered what type of rifle it was and had an urge to ask her if it was a Winchester. Then he grew angry with himself for even thinking that Grace could have attempted to kill him.

The oven timer rang.

She left her wine glass on the coffee table and got the pizza out of the oven.

While she cut it into slices, Santana studied a finished canvas leaning against a brick wall. Red streaks of paint ran like drops of blood over a black background as though they had been spilled on the canvas rather than painted. Her other paintings scattered around the room were all very dark and brooding. Her style seemed to have its roots in surrealism and reminded Santana of some of the early abstract expressionistic paintings popularized by Jackson Pollock and Willem de Kooning.

Grace put the pizza slices on a large plate and set the plate on the coffee table. "I'm actually a good cook. One of these days I'll prove it to you."

"I like pizza."

"Maybe you could show me how to cook some Colombian dishes."

"I could do that."

"Are you going to work the whole weekend?"

"What did you have in mind?"

"Would you like to come to Lake City with me on the boat tomorrow?"

"It's pouring."

"It's supposed to clear up."

Santana knew by accepting her invitation he was committing to more than just a boat ride. Still, he couldn't deny his growing attraction and feelings for her. "Can I bring my golden retriever, Gitana?"

She smiled. "Of course. Gitana means Gypsy in Spanish, doesn't it?"

"Yes," Santana said.

Her face became thoughtful as her eyes gazed into space. "I haven't had a pet since I found my cat . . ." She stopped abruptly.

"What happened to your cat?"

She shook her head and refocused. "She . . . died."

Santana rolled the dice and asked about her mother. "How old were you when your mother died?"

She wiped her mouth with a napkin. Drank more wine. "I was twenty-four when Katherine died. My brother was eighteen."

Santana thought it strange that she called her mother by her first name. "You weren't real close to her?"

"No."

"Was your brother?"

"No one was close to Katherine. Even her friends called her the ice princess."

"How did your brother react to your mother's death?"

"He didn't."

"Didn't react?"

"Never has."

Santana thought of his own mother, Elena. He and Grace Chandler had both lost their mothers. One by murder, one by suicide. He still carried a photo of his mother in his wallet. He doubted Grace carried a photo of Katherine in hers. "Are you and your brother close?"

"When we were younger," she said. "Not so much anymore."

"What changed?"

"Jared joined the Army after high school. My father wanted him to make the service his career. But Jared wanted to run the business. Equipment for the art of war is how my father advertises it." She drank some wine and looked at him now with hard interest. "You know Katherine's death was ruled a suicide, don't you, John?"

"I know."

"Always the detective," she said with a trace of sarcasm.

"When your father asked to meet with me, I did some checking."

"I thought we could forget our pasts, John, and maybe start fresh."

Santana had never forgotten his past and never would. Still, he had been reluctant to ask about her past for fear she would ask about his. "I'm not judging you, Grace."

"Please don't."

He moved from the cushioned chair to the couch and embraced her. She reciprocated. He took it as a positive sign.

"I know we just met," she said. "I know your job comes before our relationship. I can live with that."

"I'm just curious by nature, Grace."

She slipped out of his arms, took his right hand in hers, and ran an index finger over his scar. "How did you get this?"

"I cut it on the spur of a guadua tree. Guadua is like bamboo, only much heavier."

"Did you cut it by accident?"

"I did." *While I was fighting for my life.*

Her pale-blue eyes were luminous. She held them steady on his. "You don't like talking about your past anymore than I do."

"I prefer other subjects."

"Can we really understand and know each other today if we never talk about who we were yesterday?"

He let the question hang for a time in the dead space between conversations before replying. "I don't know."

"Maybe that's why we're both alone now, John."

He cupped her face in his hands. "Let's give it chance."

"I want to. You just have to promise me that you'll be careful."

"I will," he said, wishing it were a promise he could keep.

Chapter 22

The sky did clear early Saturday morning as Grace had predicted. The day was sunny and mild, and the breeze sweeping through the trees smelled of the river and of dry autumn leaves.

Grace launched the boat like a seasoned captain. She schooled Santana on the charts, the river currents, and instruments. Then she asked him to take the helm while she played with Gitana. The dog spent most of her time moving from starboard to port and back again, watching ducks and geese and any other animal that moved along the shoreline or in the riffles of water.

They docked in Lake City, located on one of the most photogenic spots on Lake Pepin, and ate dinner at the Harbor Café overlooking the river. Then they strolled hand in hand on the river walk between joggers and roller bladers. Lake Pepin was one of the finest sailing lakes in Minnesota, and though it was late in the season, many sailors were taking advantage of the beautiful fall weather. Grace took scenic photos with her Nikon SLR camera. Once, she asked a passerby to take a photo of the two of them.

As Santana watched the sailboats tacking into the wind, he recalled a line from a Pablo Neruda poem, a line from the book that had mysteriously fallen off a shelf and onto his bedroom floor, a line that had convinced him his sister was still alive. "Little boats that sail toward those isles of yours that wait for me."

Later, small clouds of water vapor misted in the cool air as they walked along the dock toward her houseboat. White light from a full moon spilled across the smooth surface of the water like milk poured out of a glass.

Grace shivered and he slipped his arm around her shoulder, felt her lean against him.

She flicked on a light, lit the logs in the wood-burning stove in the living room of the houseboat. He could smell the kindling burning, hear the crackle of the birch bark as the logs caught fire. The flames cast a soft glow throughout the room.

She went behind the galley counter and poured Baileys Irish Cream into two cocktail glasses. "Ice?"

"No, thanks."

She slipped a disc into the CD player. "You like smooth jazz?"

"Sure. Especially sax. Who's the artist?"

"Kirk Whalum. The song is called "Anytime." She flicked off the light, sat beside him on the couch and handed him a cocktail glass. Her perfume smelled like a mix of oranges, jasmine, sandalwood, and musk.

The night was very quiet, the water beneath the boat still. The mellow sound of Whalum's saxophone drifted like smoke into the room. Santana watched the logs burning and drank the Baileys, which reminded him of the heroin found in Pao Yang's house. He pushed the thought aside, felt stress ebbing like a slow tide from his muscles. He took comfort in the stillness, felt no need to make small talk. He liked that Grace seemed comfortable with the stillness as well. He settled back on the couch.

"Comfortable?" she asked.

"Very. And a little tired."

"I know what you mean. I don't have the energy level I once had. I think I'm getting old."

He looked at her beautiful face glowing like an ember in the firelight. Then he reached out and gently touched her cheek with his hand. "In Colombian we say, *Tu eres tan joven como la piel que tocas.* You are as young as the skin that you touch."

She smiled and averted her eyes for a second in embarrassment. "I like you, John Santana."

"You don't know me."

"I'm a quick study."

He said nothing. Just looked at her for a time.

"Do I need to ask or are you going to tell me?" she said.

"Yes," he said. "I like you, too."

"That wasn't so difficult, was it?"

"No." He set his drink on the coffee table, took the glass from her hand and set it next to his. Then he leaned over and kissed her soft, full lips.

Her mouth opened and she gave a little moan and wrapped her arms around him and pulled him tight against her. He felt her tongue, felt her heart pounding in her chest or maybe it was his own heart or maybe both.

She broke off the long, deep kiss and took his scarred hand in one of hers and led him to the bedroom.

They undressed each other quickly in the moonlight and then threw back the covers and plunged into bed like swimmers seeking cool water on a hot summer day.

She lay on her back with her arms over her head, her body luminescent in the pale moonlight as he kissed her neck, her full breasts, and her belly. He moved between her legs, but she laced his hair with her fingers and pulled him gently up to her face.

"I want us to come together," she said in a whisper. Her breathing was rapid and heavy, as though she had run fast and for a long distance. She guided him with her hand and inhaled sharply as he slid inside her.

He held back at first. But he could feel her body tensing underneath him. Feel her warm breath soft as a feather against his neck and the heat between her legs. Feel her arms tightly wrapped low around his back as she moved in perfect rhythm with him now like a slow, sensual dance.

He kissed her mouth and her neck. Then he rose up on his hands and moved faster inside her. As she arched her back and let out a cry, he felt pressure building inside him and then suddenly release.

And for a time there was no past, no future, only the two of them, only this moment.

* * *

While Grace slept peacefully, Santana lay awake, listening to her soft breathing and to the echo of distant voices. He knew he could fall in love with her, and this both excited and troubled him. He had never spent much time thinking about marriage and children because he was a marked man. The shooting incident on his deck was proof of that. Knowing that he could be killed at any time was a destiny he had come to accept. He had focused all his energies on his job and his mission. He wished at times that his life could be different. But he had made a decision years ago to kill the Estrada twins. He knew full well the consequences of his actions. Now, as he thought of a possible future with Grace, he worried that his past decision would put her life in jeopardy. Even Gitana was at risk. The assassins who hunted him would never hesitate to kill the dog, his wife, or his child, nor would they hesitate to use his family to get to him. Fear for his sister's life was the main reason he had been reluctant to look for her. If Natalia was alive and safe in a convent as he hoped, he might lead the assassins directly to her.

Santana believed he had survived for years in the shadow of death in part because he was alone. He had no one but himself to worry about. But he also had no one to care about. The death of his wife, his child, or sister would undoubtedly unleash the demon that had driven him to kill the two brothers. He had fed the demon and kept it at bay through his mission and his job. He feared that if he lost another loved one like he had lost his mother, Elena, he would never again be able to contain the demon. He would become like the assassins who hunted him.

* * *

Santana slept soundly for the first time in ages and awoke before dawn with no memories of dreams or nightmares that usually disturbed his sleep. He rolled over on the queen-sized bed, peered out the sliding glass door that opened onto the stern, and saw Grace, dressed in jeans and a white, cable-knit sweater, standing with her fingers curled around the railing, gazing at the harbor still lit by pinpoints of light in the gray dawn.

Santana dressed. Then he opened the slider and stepped out onto the stern.

Grace turned when she heard the door open and smiled. As he closed the door behind him, she came to him and wrapped her arms around his back and laid her head against his chest. "Good morning, sleepyhead."

He folded his arms around her. "How come you're up so early?"

"No reason," she said, unconvincingly.

He waited a beat. Then he said, "Remember, I'm a cop."

"Twenty-four hours a day?"

"Three-hundred sixty-five days a year."

She let out a little sigh. "I'm going to have to get used to that."

There was implied commitment in the words she spoke. Surprisingly, he felt comfort rather than panic. "What is it?"

She lifted her head, looked up at his face. The cold had colored her cheeks and a slight breeze had mussed her hair. "I haven't been with anyone for a long time, John."

"I haven't either."

"Really?"

"Really."

She laid a cheek against his chest again. Stood quietly with her arms around him for a while before she spoke once more. "It's okay if it was only for one night."

"Is that what you want?"

"No," she said. "But I can come on a little strong. I'm worried you'll feel . . . obligated. God, that's such an ugly word."

"I wouldn't use obligated to describe what I'm feeling, Grace."

"I like the way you call me Grace."

He could feel her shivering in his arms. "Let's go back inside where it's warm."

She laughed as he picked her up and carried her back to bed where they made love again. She was still a passionate lover, but more playful this time, teasing him about his whiskers and how they rubbed her complexion red. But that didn't prevent her from kissing him.

Santana attributed her playfulness to the conversation they'd had and to the tenuous level of trust they shared after one night of intimacy.

Grace prepared a large breakfast of scrambled eggs, turkey sausage, bread, and hot chocolate before they headed up river again toward St. Paul. The cool air and intimacy left Santana feeling more relaxed than he had been in months. It was a welcome change. But as they neared the St. Paul Yacht Club on Sunday evening, his thoughts once again shifted to the current case.

As he left Grace and drove from the yacht club to his house, the weather seemed to reflect the shift in his thoughts and the conflict raging inside him. Bolts of lightning split the hard black sky and thunder rattled the window glass in his house throughout the night. The storm finally moved off to the east on Monday morning, leaving roads slick and shiny with moisture. Road spray misted the SUV's windshield as Santana drove along Interstate 94 toward St. Paul. Wiper blades squealed as they swept across fogged glass.

A cool front had rolled in behind the storm, dropping the morning temperature ten degrees. Santana flicked on the defrost switch and cracked opened the front windows.

In a dream the previous night, he had fallen through thin ice and into a cold river. He knew intuitively that he was standing on shaky ground when it came to the current case. That he was taking risks and needed to remain cautious. All the evidence pointed to Kou Yang as the murderer. Yet, he still had more questions than answers.

The SPPD crime lab on the third floor of the Griffin Building had a red phone and buzzer attached to the wall outside the door. No one could enter without an escort, not even the chief.

Tony Novak let Santana in. They walked by the front desk and down a hallway. Then past a red grocery cart donated by Target. The cart was filled with rifles and handguns seized at crime scenes. The guns needed to be taken back to the property room in the basement.

Novak wore tennis shoes, loose-fitting jeans, and a black T-shirt with yellow C.S.I. lettering across the chest. CAN'T STAND IDIOTS was written underneath the lettering.

The new lab was considerably larger than the old one. Besides a small lab that contained super glue and gravity chambers, and a larger lab that resembled a chemistry classroom, the lab personnel had their own cubicles, a conference room, a kitchen with a break room, a large closet where cold case files were stored, a dark room, and a computer room that was connected to the AFIS data base and the National Integrated Ballistic Information Network.

Novak's desk was located near a large cabinet with glass doors. The cabinet held a collection of old guns stored in the event the forensic techs needed to know how a particular gun worked.

Novak sat down at his cluttered desk and opened a file folder. "We got latent prints on both the knife and the .38 Special found in the Mazda's trunk. Quite a bit of oil in the prints, which suggests the perp was young or excited or both. In any case, he sweated more than usual, which produced more oil. Kou Yang was inked when he was booked. The whorl pattern on the knife and gun match the pattern on his fingerprint card. I found twenty-two matching minutia points as well. It doesn't prove he used the knife or the gun to commit murder. But I'd swear in court that his prints are on the weapons."

"What about the blood, Tony?"

"Pao Yang had A-positive blood. Same as on the knife."

"And the ballistics?"

"The bullets that killed the two gangbangers at Pao Yang's house were fired from the .38 found in the Mazda's trunk."

Evidence implicating Kou Yang in at least three murders kept mounting. Anger over his sister's death appeared to be his motive. It seemed likely that he shot Kacie Hawkins as well. But at least two questions remained. Why kill his sister? And why kill Jenna Jones?

"See if the BCA can match the DNA found on Mai Yang's body with her brother's DNA," Santana said.

"I've already sent samples to the BCA lab."

"Anything on the duct tape found on Mai Yang's body?"

"No prints. I'm still working on the brand. Even if I figure that out, it may be sold through numerous outlets. If you could find the roll the piece came from, I could match the torn edges."

"What about the foot impression?"

Novak opened the bottom drawer of his desk and removed a cast of the foot impression he had made from a footprint on the beach near Santana's house. "I considered the design features first. It's the weakest comparison and identification feature, but it narrows the field since the variations in outsole mold design are distinguishable. And they'll be repeated during the manufacturing process."

He held up the mold with one hand, pointed with the index finger on the other hand. "The heel area in the outsole had a distinctive groove and identifying logo. I'd say the shooter wore a size-eleven Nike Air athletic shoe. I didn't find any random cuts, gouges, abrasions, or flaws in the sole made during the manufacturing process. But the photos revealed shadow points, which are indicative of foreign debris attached to the outsole. That makes this impression unique from all other shoes. Plus, there's a significant wear pattern on the outside of the heel. The perp who wore these Nikes is going to wear down all his shoes in the same way. You bring me another old pair of his shoes, John, and I'll be able to identify the same wear pattern."

Chapter 23

Santana took the elevator down one floor to the Homicide Unit and went to his desk. Diana Lee wasn't in yet. Neither was Rita Gamboni or the other detectives in the unit.

He poured himself a cup of hot chocolate from the thermos he had brought from home and opened his briefcase. He took out the list of numbers he had copied from Jenna Jones's cell phone and Mai Yang's and Pao Yang's call out sheets he had obtained from the phone company. For thirty minutes, he searched for matching numbers on the three lists but came up empty. Then he used the reverse directory, which allowed him to match phone numbers with a name and address.

He had checked nearly all the phone numbers and their corresponding addresses before he got a hit he recognized. One of the callers was listed as Rashid Hassan. And the call to Jenna Jones had been made the day after Santana met him in her apartment.

* * *

3M's corporate headquarters was located four miles east of downtown St. Paul just off Interstate 94. Santana veered right on the McKnight Road exit, which curved under the freeway, and followed it east for a half-mile until he arrived at an entrance near the main building, a fifteen-story tower of glass, aluminum and stone just north of the Interstate.

The low brick lab buildings scattered throughout the huge campus all appeared to be the same. He drove around and backtracked a couple of times before he found the correct building number, parked and headed for the lobby. A sign at the entrance reminded employees that they were required to present their badge to the door readers when entering and exiting a building.

The woman behind the waist-high counter was a heavy-set African-American woman with a name tag that identified her as Yolanda.

Santana showed her his badge and asked to speak to Rashid Hassan.

"Do you have an appointment, Detective Santana?"

"I don't. I called ahead, but all I got was voice mail. The operator directed me to this building."

"Let me see if Mr. Stratton, Mr. Hassan's immediate supervisor, has returned from his meeting."

"I'd like to speak to Rashid Hassan."

"I'll just be a minute," she said. "If you'd like to take a seat." She gestured toward a small lounge to Santana's left that contained a round, glass-topped table and a couch and chair with matching red cushions.

Santana figured the strict procedures were for security reasons and for the employees' protection. And Yolanda wasn't about to bend or break the rules for a detective or for anyone else.

He sat in the cushioned chair studying a map of the grounds hanging on the wall above the couch. According to the map, the campus had four hundred thirty acres and twenty-eight buildings. Santana counted each one just to make sure.

Minutes later, a serious looking, balding man wearing wire-rimmed glasses, brown trousers, a white shirt, and brown tie held in place with a silver clip, walked out of a corridor and toward Santana. "I'm Donald Stratton."

Santana stood and shook Stratton's outstretched hand. "John Santana. St. Paul P.D."

"Please follow me," Stratton said, nodding at Yolanda as they passed.

Santana followed him down a concrete-block corridor painted soft beige to an office. Stratton sat behind a metal desk, Santana in a swivel chair in front of it.

According to the framed glass certificates on the walls, Donald Stratton was a member in good standing of the Environmental and Engineering Geophysical Society, and had undergraduate and graduate degrees in environmental engineering from Michigan State University. A single framed photo of a studious looking woman resting on top of the three-drawer file cabinet in the corner of the room told Santana that Stratton was married but probably had no children.

"How can I help you?" Stratton asked. He smiled a polite but tight smile, like a man unaccustomed to talking to people, especially cops.

Santana took out his notebook and pen. "I don't know that you can. I wanted to speak with Rashid Hassan."

"You're a detective?"

"Homicide."

Stratton's body stiffened. He sat forward in his chair. Placed his forearms on the desk and clasped his hands together as though he were about to say a prayer. "Has something happened to Rashid and his family?"

"Hassan isn't here?"

Stratton shook his head. "He took some vacation time."

"How long ago was that?"

"So Rashid and his family are fine?" Stratton said, ignoring Santana's question.

"As far as I know."

Tension leaked out of Stratton's body like air escaping from a balloon. "Rashid took a vacation three weeks ago."

"Do you know if he stayed in town?"

"His mother had taken ill. I believe he went to Pakistan to see her."

Santana wondered why Rashid Hassan would be in Jenna Jones's apartment five days ago if he had gone to Pakistan. Then again, if he had left three weeks ago, he could have returned. Maybe Hassan was taking a few more days of vacation. Maybe he and his family went somewhere else. "What kind of work does Hassan do for 3M?"

"He's a an environmental engineer."

"You have quite a few environmental engineers working here?"

"Some. Others are chemical engineers and material scientists. Most of our employees are local nationals. We have fewer than three hundred employees not residing in their home countries."

"I take it Rashid Hassan is one of them."

"That's correct."

"What else does the company do besides environmental engineering?"

"We also work with fiber optics, electronics and manufacturing." Stratton leaned back slightly, appeared relieved to be discussing business rather than Rashid Hassan. "Our worldwide sales total about twenty-four billion dollars. We have companies in more than sixty countries, and our products are sold in nearly two hundred countries. We employ in the neighborhood of seventy-five thousand employees."

"What is Hassan's field of expertise?"

"He works with soil contamination and groundwater cleanup. You may have heard that some chemicals we once used in a few of our products have shown up in wells in the area and in the Mississippi."

"I read about it in the paper."

"Rashid has been working on a general cleanup plan and detailed feasibility study we plan to submit to the state later this year."

"What can you tell me about him?"

"I can tell you that he's been with us for two years now. He's very good at his job."

"What else?"

"If you'd like more information, I'd have to check with HR and our legal counsel. That might take some time."

"Mind if I take a look at Hassan's office?"

"I'd have to speak with the director of the lab."

"Could you do that now?"

"He's away at the moment."

"Vacation?"

"No. Meetings. He should return later this afternoon."

Santana made a note. Then he removed a business card from his wallet. They both stood.

"Is there something important you're not telling me, Detective Santana?"

"I'd ask you the same question," Santana said, "if I thought I'd get an answer." He handed his business card to Stratton and left.

Chapter 24

The route from victim to perpetrator in a homicide investigation was rarely a straight line. Santana often faced detours and dead ends and clues that led nowhere. Though his visit with Donald Stratton had been less than productive, he had learned that Rashid Hassan had taken a sudden and unexpected vacation. Whether that information would lead somewhere remained to be seen.

Santana had written down the address he had found in the reverse directories. He had also copied the information from Rashid Hassan's driver's license into his notebook the day they had met in Jenna Jones's Battle Creek apartment. The same day Mai Yang's body had been discovered on Harriet Island. He saw nothing strange in Hassan's behavior that day. A married man with a family and a good job would appear nervous and upset if a police officer caught him soliciting sex from a prostitute. But now Santana began rethinking his initial conclusions. Perhaps Hassan had had much more to hide.

He took Interstate 94 to 694 and then caught Highway 5 east through Oakdale and past the Imation headquarters near the western edge of Lake Elmo, a small suburb about ten miles from 3M.

The four-lane highway soon narrowed to a two-lane tarred road posted with yellow and black signs warning of deer crossings. Most of the area was farmland now, and Santana found it surprising that large open spaces and farmland still existed this close to the city.

The speedometer needle dropped from fifty-five to forty miles per hour as he entered the city limits. He turned right on Lake Elmo Avenue and drove through the town, which consisted of a gas station, barbershop, beauty shop, library, a few small businesses, and the Lake Elmo Inn, a well-known restaurant where Santana had taken a date on occasion. With its clapboard and brick buildings and old homes featuring porches with spindles, the town had a very rural feel to it.

The road through town crossed a set of railroad tracks and curved around a lake on his right. Two miles outside of town, Santana saw Hassan's address on an aluminum mailbox along the side of the road. He eased the Crown Vic to the left shoulder and pulled even with the driveway.

The two-story, prairie-style house was set well back from the road. It had a hipped roof, a gabled dormer, and a one-story front porch supported by heavy, squared piers. A small barn that had been converted into a garage stood at the end of a long driveway to the right of the house.

Santana lowered the driver's side window, stuck out his left hand, and opened the mailbox.

Empty.

He closed the mailbox lid and turned into a dirt and gravel driveway that cut through the grass in the front yard. Then he parked next to a tall, white oak tree whose leaves were turning yellow and stepped out of the Crown Vic.

The temperature had flatlined at a crisp sixty-five degrees, and the wind was dry and cool. A thin coat of clouds that looked as though they were burned white-hot by the sun covered the sky. The wind chimes hanging on a branch above Santana rang in a slight wind that smelled of charcoal and grilled beef and gasoline.

He followed a concrete sidewalk past shrubs in the dirt bed along the front of the house, strode up the four steps onto the porch and rang the doorbell. He waited a few seconds and rang the bell again.

Nothing.

No mail in the mailbox. No newspapers on the front stoop. If Hassan and his family had gone on vacation, he would have stopped the mail and newspaper delivery.

Santana located Hassan's phone number in his notebook, dialed, and heard a phone inside the house ring five times before he broke off the connection. Then he peered in each of the two casement windows flanking the front door but saw nothing through the thin curtains besides a living room and a small bedroom.

The rectangular alarm company sign that stood like a sentinel in the dirt bed indicated the house was wired for security. Hassan had made the common mistake of posting a sign identifying the alarm company, thinking it would frighten burglars, instead of unintentionally giving them information they could use to disable the alarm. Better to buy a generic sign from a hardware store, Santana thought.

He went down the steps and stood on the sidewalk. He had no warrant and no probable cause to enter the premises. Still, he had entered homes before without warrants and probably would in the future. The nearest neighbor appeared to be at least a half-mile away. He decided to check the backyard first.

He crossed the sidewalk and headed down the side of the house and into a back yard that gave out onto an empty field. He could see a swing set with two seats swaying gently in the breeze.

Santana walked to the garage and cupped his hands around his eyes and peered into a small, dusty window in a padlocked side door. A red compact took up one of the two spaces. He couldn't see the make or model.

Behind the garage he found an eight-by-ten-foot rectangular fire pit that had been dug in the ground. White stones circled its outer edge. Two, five-foot-tall steel tripod supports at each end of the pit held up a six-foot rotisserie steel spit. He remembered that when he was a child his father used to roast pigs over a similar pit. The smell of charcoal, beef, and gasoline were stronger here. But Santana also detected a sulfurous odor and a coppery, metallic smell.

He found a rake beside a cord of dry birch and oak stacked against the back of the garage and pushed it through the surface of pasty white coals and ash that had the texture of coarse sand.

Then he moved around the edge of the pit, raking the ashes, until the tongs caught on something and he dragged it to the surface.

Chapter 25

The fire pit behind Rashid Hassan's garage had been cordoned off with yellow crime scene tape and uniformed officers were maintaining the perimeter. Log entry limited movement into and out of the restricted area.

The temperature had remained steady, the wind gentle, and the smell of gasoline, beef, sulfur, and copper strong.

Tony Novak and his forensic techs were videotaping, taking distant and close-up photos, and drawing scaled diagrams.

"The techs dug up two bodies," Reiko Tanabe said, looking at Santana, then at Diana Lee. "One female adult. One female child. I'll have to extract DNA from bone marrow. Match it with dental records to determine the identities."

The charred corpses reminded Santana of the black, mummified bodies pulled from the lava after the Nevado del Ruíz volcano erupted in Manizales when he was thirteen, killing hundreds, including many of his friends.

Santana looked at Lee, saw that her face was the same color as the ash. "You all right, Diana?"

She shook her head and then darted toward the field on the other side of the pit.

Santana and Tanabe exchanged glances. Neither spoke. They waited.

Three minutes later, Lee rejoined them.

Santana pulled a Kleenex out of the travel package Lee held in her hand and wiped the corner of her mouth. "Missed a little."

"Thank you."

Tanabe pointed to the largest burned body lying in the pit. "Notice the way the arms are raised up in a defensive position and the right fist tightened like a boxer."

Having seen severely burned bodies before, Santana knew the pugilistic pose could be mistaken for a defensive posture of a victim being attacked or an indication that the victim was alive prior to the fire. "It had to take awhile to burn the body this badly, Reiko."

"And high temperatures," she said. "A wood fire burns at a temperature of about sixteen hundred degrees Fahrenheit. In a crematorium where a body is supposed to be fully reduced to ash, the temperature can reach twenty-seven hundred degrees. Even then, the bones aren't fully decomposed and the large fragments are ground up in the final preparation. But this body was roasted like a pig for quite a while."

Lee shook her head slowly, as if she had no answer for why one human would choose to inflict such pain on another.

Tanabe squatted beside the charred body. Studied it for a time. "The scalp has burned away exposing the cranial vault. The skin of the chest, arms and legs has burned away exposing the charred muscles underneath. The left hand indicates there was blunt force trauma prior to burning. At least one of the three bones in the arm was likely fractured."

Santana could see that the fingers of the left hand were extended and not closed as in a fist.

"A burned body is brittle," Tanabe said. "I'll make sure the techs wrap it in a clean white sheet in the position it was found." She stood, looked at the two detectives.

"I'm guessing the victims are Rashid Hassan's wife and daughter," Santana said. "But we'll need to make a positive ID. Let's see what we can find in the house, Diana."

As they walked toward the front door, Lee said, "How did you know Hassan had a wife and daughter? And what were you doing here?" Her tone of voice indicated the question was asked more out of curiosity than recrimination.

"I met Rashid Hassan a week ago in Jenna Jones's apartment. Caught him soliciting sex. He had a photo of his wife and daughter in his wallet. I warned him and let him go. But when I crosschecked Jenna Jones's phone calls with the reverse directory, Hassan's number came up. He called Jones again the day after I let him go."

Bolt cutters had removed the front door lock. Santana examined the doorjamb and frame but saw no sign of forced entry. The security alarm had not been activated and did not go off when the door was opened. He and Lee gloved up and walked into the house, getting a feel for the place, looking for something that appeared out of order and created cognitive dissonance. Wondering if they would find Rashid Hassan's body inside the house.

The furniture was made from polished natural wood. Embroidered patchwork tapestries hung from the walls. Persian rugs covered the hardwood floors and multi-colored throw pillows accented the couch and matching chairs. The rooms were accented with incense holders, porcelain ceramics, and an expensive looking porcelain tea set.

The faces in the framed photos on the marble side tables matched the faces of the woman and child Santana had seen in the photograph in Hassan's wallet. Magnets on the stainless steel refrigerator in the kitchen held up crayon drawings of animals.

A driver's license Diana Lee found in a purse in the master bedroom suggested the female adult's body in the pit was thirty-three year old Farah Hassan.

A young female tech was dusting the home office for prints. "Not much here," she said. "Very odd for a family home."

"No dishes in the sink or dishwasher," Lee said. "No dirty clothes in the hamper or laundry room. No trash in the wastebaskets. The beds are made, the clothes in the closets neatly hung. The house looks like no one has lived in it for a while."

"Maybe no one has," Santana said. "Check the garage, Diana. I'll check the young girl's bedroom. Try to put a name with the face."

The daughter's bedroom had light-blue walls and a wallpaper border with seashells. A yellow patterned comforter covered the bed and art prints with fish and dolphin designs hung on the walls. There was a vanity with a large mirror behind it, a student desk with a corkboard back for posting notes, a CD case storage area and a desk lamp. Dolls and stuffed animals and soft pillows were placed neatly on the bed and bookshelves. A large art table stood in a corner of the room. Atop it were crude clay models of bowls and animals.

Santana remembered how he liked working with clay when he was a kid. Liked the feel and smell of it.

He estimated the dead young girl was about the same age his younger sister, Natalia, had been when he fled Colombia. He remembered the recent dream he'd had about his sister, how she had been right there in his bedroom with him, close enough to touch. Then his thoughts shifted to the dead girl in the fire pit.

Her name was Safia.

She had printed her name on a series of animal drawings Santana found in a desk drawer. The drawings were addressed to mommy and daddy.

Santana sat on the bed and viewed each drawing as he used to do with Natalia. She had always wanted his praise and approval. He was her big brother. He would always look out for her. Always protect her from harm.

You didn't even say good-bye.

He told himself that he would return to Colombia and find her one day. But time had passed quickly. He hadn't returned. Hadn't found her. Hadn't kept the promise he had made to himself.

He surveyed the room. Looked at the clay models on the art table, at the framed photo of Safia on a bookshelf. She had been a beautiful little girl with dark hair and large dark eyes. Santana had heard all kinds of explanations for why a man might murder his wife and daughter, but none of them had ever made any sense to him.

Talk to me, Safia. Help me.

He stood up, set the drawings on the bed, and went downstairs to the basement. On a long, rectangular table, Santana found a home chemistry lab with glass beakers, Erlenmeyer flasks, a wickless alcohol lamp and stand, graduated cylinders, test tubes, thermometers, plastic funnels, tubing and clamps, rubber stoppers, glass eye droppers, and stirring rods. He saw no chemicals, but on the floor underneath the table he found a small piece of clay about the size of his thumb.

He picked it up and rolled it around in his hand and then sniffed it. It had an oily smell, different than he remembered. He returned to the young girl's bedroom and picked up a piece of clay from the art table. It had a more familiar smell. For no particular reason other than its smell, he put the first piece of clay in an evidence envelope and listed it on the evidence recovery log.

"John?"

Santana looked up. Saw Diana Lee framed in the bedroom doorway.

"What do you have there?" she said, pointing to the evidence envelope in his hand.

"I don't know for sure. It looks and feels like clay but doesn't smell like it."

"I found some trash in the garbage bin in the garage," she said. "Usual junk. Kleenex, tin cans, banana peels, crumpled paper."

"Bills?"

"No bills. A drawing."

"Of an animal?"

She shook her head. "No. Why?"

Santana thought about it. Remembered the drawings he had placed on the bed. "Where's the drawing you found?"

"In the garage."

"Show me," he said.

A red Honda Civic was parked in the left stall of the double garage. Tools, shovels, rakes, and hoses hung on silver hooks screwed into the walls. A snow blower stood in a corner.

"I ran the plate through the DMV," Lee said. "The Honda is registered to Farah Hassan."

Santana studied the garage floor opposite the Honda. Bent over and ran a finger through an oil slick. Then he took out a small flashlight from his coat pocket, flicked it on, squatted, and shined the light on the cement floor underneath the Honda. "The Honda isn't leaking oil," he said. "Hassan is probably driving his own car. Get out an APB. We need to find him. If he's responsible for the murders, he may have already left the country. And see what you can find out about Farah Hassan." He stood, turned off the flashlight and put it in his pocket. "Where's the drawing?"

Lee led him to a workbench beside a large plastic garbage bin on two wheels. She pointed to a drawing that was unfolded on top of the workbench. "It looks like a maze."

It was drawn in pencil rather than crayon, but on the same eight-and-one-half-by-eleven-inch manila cardstock as the animals drawn by Safia Hassan. Someone had drawn a tall building over the maze.

"This was done by someone other than a child with limited art skills," Santana said.

"Maybe the father or mother drew it."

"Maybe."

"Why is it important?"

"I don't know that it is. But I'm sure it wasn't something the daughter drew."

"Why not?"

"Her drawings are hung on the refrigerator door, in her father's office, her bedroom. Parents don't throw out drawings their daughter made especially for them."

Brothers don't throw out drawings their little sister made either.

"Most fathers don't murder their wife and child, John."

"True enough. But log the drawing on the evidence inventory and bag it."

Chapter 26

Santana and Diana Lee sat at a table in Alary's, a downtown sports bar not far from headquarters. Recently renovated, it was decorated with police, fire and sports memorabilia and now featured twenty-two flat-screen plasma TVs, a sidewalk patio with chairs and umbrellas, and a bevy of young, pretty waitresses in tight T-shirts and short skirts. It was a meeting place for sports junkies, off-duty police officers and firefighters, attorneys, and city and state workers.

"You feeling any better?" Santana asked. He was working on his second Sam Adams, Lee on another Coke.

She stared at her half-full glass, shook her head. "A mother and child burned like that. It's not something you can easily forget."

Santana thought about Safia Hassan and about her father, Rashid Hassan, and about roasting him like a pig. "It's better not to forget."

Lee looked up from her drink. "Then how do you get past it?"

"I never get past it, Diana. I use it for motivation."

She drank more Coke, Santana more beer.

"Does the violence and cruelty one human inflicts on another ever surprise you anymore, John?"

Santana had learned firsthand about violence and cruelty long before he became a homicide detective. What he saw on a daily basis now only reinforced his opinion. "Unfortunately, no."

She gave a nod and then sat quietly for a time. "I guess it's one of the downsides of homicide."

"Maybe staying in the gang unit might've been a better career choice?"

"No. I can deal with this. It's important for me and for my clan that I'm successful at this, John. Do you understand?"

"Yes."

"It's difficult for me to be assertive. I struggle with it every day. Even though I was born and raised in the States, I'm still a product of my culture. We were always taught to respect authority and defer to the elders."

"Meaning men," Santana said.

"Yes. I don't like to make waves."

She had taken off her suit jacket. Santana saw the small tattoo on her right forearm.

Lee noticed he was looking at it. "It's the symbol for a Chinese dragon. It represents good luck."

"Why not just a dragon?"

"Having a dragon tattooed on your body can bring you bad luck. In ancient China it was forbidden to have the likeness of living creatures on the body. Some people today have the word dragon tattooed under the symbol. But that's like writing the word dragon under a tattoo of a dragon. It's silly."

Santana believed his luck was a result of intuition, skill, and preparation. "So what kind of luck do you expect, Diana?"

"Love, health, success, protection from evil spirits, even good parking spaces."

"Cops always get good parking spaces," he said. "At least when we're on duty."

She smiled. "I don't mean to get personal, but does your faith help you cope?"

"I'm pretty much on my own."

Lee nodded, as though she expected his answer. "I think tragedies can either strengthen faith or weaken it."

"I respect your beliefs, Diana. But there's no rational or spiritual explanation for the cruelty we saw today."

She thought about Santana's statement. Drank some Coke. "So you believe in evil."

"I believe there are evil people."

"What do you think happens when you die?"

Santana had considered the possibility of his own death since the age of sixteen. He never dwelled on it and never let it depress him. But he had come to terms with it, come to know it as he would a friend who moved in and never left. "There's a Robert Browning poem entitled "Prospice" in which he wrote about the black minute at the moment of death."

"You think that blackness is all there is?"

"Browning thought there was more."

"But you don't."

"No. I don't."

Lee nodded her head slowly as she contemplated his reply. "Do you fear death, John?"

"I don't fear it. I'm just not in any hurry to test my hypothesis about the afterlife."

She smiled. "We believe in reincarnation of the soul. People can come back as new members of Hmong families, animals, rocks, trees, and flowers."

Santana thought he would like to come back as a detective. Maybe take a few more of the scumbags off the board.

"Our soul is called *Plig*." Lee pronounced it "Plee." "It is in your body when you're awake and out of the body when you're dreaming."

"Really?" Santana said, thinking about his own dreams.

"Yes. If your soul meets a good spirit then you'll have good dreams. We believe there is a soul for all parts of the body—the eyes, the hands, the heart—thirty-two in all. The *winjan* is the strongest soul and all that exists after death. The *winjan* either goes to heaven or is reborn depending on how you lived your life. The *winjan* becomes a wandering spirit if a proper death ceremony is not performed." She paused a moment and then continued. "We're taught that we have a finite number of days on Earth. The number of days we have is determined at birth."

"Do you know how many days you have left?"

"Yes," she said. And left it at that.

* * *

Santana returned to headquarters after leaving Alary's and went downstairs to the property room in the basement where he asked the property officer to bring him the evidence collected at Rashid Hassan's house. A few minutes later, he signed a release for the evidence envelope containing the clay he had found in Safia Hassan's bedroom.

Santana located Jeff Jenkins of the Ordinance Disposal Unit in the huge garage underneath the Griffin Building, organizing the truck the unit used to dispose of explosive devices.

"Hey, Santana. How you doin'?" With his fine, boyish features, wire-rimmed glasses, and thin frame, Jenkins looked more like a college professor than a bomb squad expert or a man in his mid-fifties.

"I'd like you to take a look at something, Jeff."

"Sure."

He jumped down from the back of the truck and took the piece of clay from Santana. "Where'd you get this?"

"Found it in a house of a homicide victim. Looks like clay, but I'm not sure."

Jenkins shook his head. "It isn't clay. It's C-4."

"Isn't that military issue?"

"Yeah. The U.S. military is the primary manufacturer of it. This all you found?"

Santana nodded. "Is there any other place you could get it, Jeff?"

"The military has reported occasional small thefts. Someone could've pulled the formula off the Internet. And Vietnam War veterans have been known to keep small amounts as souvenirs." He smiled. "I wasn't one of 'em."

"Is it hard to make?"

"Well, it isn't something you're going to put together after taking high school chemistry. And cooking up the explosive at home is tricky and dangerous. You'd have to know what you're doing. Basically, you take RDX in powder form and mix it with water. Then add the binder material, dissolved in a solvent, and mix the materials with an agitator. You remove the solvent through distillation and remove the water through drying and filtering. The biggest problem is acquiring the RDX. But there's a lot of it overseas. One hundred forty metric tons went missing from an unsecured depot near Baghdad at the start of the war. You could also take RDX out of bombs, artillery shells, and land mines. And it would be fairly easy to smuggle and safe to carry."

"The C-4 felt like clay but smelled oily."

"That's because it contains a little motor oil. The additive material is made up of polyisobutylene, which is used in the manufacture of synthetic rubber. The polyisobutylene makes it relatively safe to handle and highly malleable. You can mold it into different shapes to change the direction of the explosion. What you get is a relatively stable, solid explosive with a consistency similar to modeling clay."

"How do you set it off?"

"You'd need a detonator or blasting cap to apply some energy to start the chemical reaction. Even shooting it with a rifle won't trigger the reaction. Lighting C-4 with a match just makes it burn slowly, like a piece of wood. That's why the military uses it. We used it in 'Nam to heat water or C-rations. It burned hot and gave off a chemical smell, but it heated the food quickly. You just had to remember to let the stuff burn out completely. But a small amount of C-4 packs a wallop. Less than a pound of it could potentially kill several people."

Jenkins inspected the C-4, rolled it in his hands. "The explosion actually has two phases. The initial explosion creates a very low-pressure area around its origin. After the outward blast, gases rush back in to the partial vacuum, creating a second, less-destructive inward energy wave. The initial expansion inflicts the most damage. Gases are expanding at over twenty-six thousand feet per second. At that expansion rate, John, it's impossible to outrun the explosion like they do in action movies. You find anymore of this, you let me know."

* * *

Dusk was settling over the landscape as Santana parked the Crown Vic along the curb beside Pao Yang's house. He wanted to take another look at the scene where Kacie Hawkins had been wounded. Wanted to know if Diana Lee really had time to pull the trigger as Hawkins had suggested.

He got out of the car and walked under the gnarled oak and across the lawn to the elm tree where Diana Lee said she took aim at the Mazda. The tree was roughly fifteen yards from the street.

He fixed his gaze on the house where yellow crime scene tape still hung at an angle across the broken screen door like a bandage on a wound. Then he looked at the small, rectangular, cinder-block office across the street and the cyclone fence encircling the metal warehouses. He stood still in the quiet air, focused his eyes on the baseball diamond behind a row of houses to his right and pictured the scene in his mind as the car sped west along the street. Imagined Lee raising her gun, drawing a bead on the driver.

It was raining hard that day, making it difficult to see clearly. Santana factored the rain into the scenario he was creating in his mind because he wanted to give Lee the benefit of the doubt. She had expressed concerns about her bullet missing the car and hitting one of the houses, so he factored that into the scenario as well. But as he visualized the Mazda speeding past the baseball diamond and then the row of houses, he concluded that she had at least two seconds to pull the trigger before her field of fire would have endangered anyone in a house.

It was a short amount of time but enough to take the shot.

* * *

That evening, Santana logged into his home computer and accessed the web page for Google. He typed Grace Chandler in the search box. Shortly, he had a list of articles referencing her name. He scrolled down the page until he found the link to an interview she had given to the *Twin City Weekly*, an alternative paper. The interview had been conducted prior to an art exhibit at the Women's Club in Minneapolis, which featured her paintings.

In the interview, Grace had spoken mostly about her art. How she saw her work as pure emotion transferred directly onto the canvas. How it was meant to be apolitical. But near the end of the article, the interviewer had begun asking personal questions about the family.

Q. Did you support your father's run for senator?

A. No.

Q. Did you vote for him?

A. I don't agree with his politics, so why would I be expected to vote for him?

Q. You didn't get along with your mother.

A. That's putting it mildly.

Q. How did her death influence your art?

A. It didn't.

Q. There were rumors that her death wasn't accidental.

A. My mother was a very troubled woman.

Q. Did she commit suicide?

A. That's the cause of death listed on the death certificate.

Q. What about news reports suggesting she might have been murdered?

Santana wondered what reports the interviewer was referencing. He sat forward in his chair and continued reading.

A. I don't know what you're talking about.

Q. Do you believe your mother was murdered?

A. No comment.

Q. Did you or your father or anyone in your family have anything to do with her death?

A. This interview is over.

Santana cautioned himself not to jump to conclusions. There could be logical explanations. But the interview had raised serious questions in his mind.

Chapter 27

When Santana arrived at headquarters the next morning, he made a long distance call to the Arlington, Virginia, PD. He was passed along the line to three different people before he got a homicide detective named Matt Colburn on the line. Santana explained for the third time who he was and why he was calling.

"Yeah. I was the lead detective," Colburn said. "I remember the Chandler case generated lots of publicity and even more heat. The high-profile cases always do."

"What were the findings?"

"As I recall, Katherine Chandler took two .22 caliber bullets in the chest. That's uncommon in suicides, as you know, but not rare. Maybe she flinched when she pulled the trigger. Or maybe the first bullet missed a vital organ or both."

"What did the ME conclude?"

"The first bullet wasn't fatal. The second one pierced the heart and killed her instantly. But two shots eliminated the accidental death scenario."

"Who found the body?"

"The daughter. She was visiting for the weekend and was sleeping in the bedroom across the hall. Claimed she heard two shots, ran into the bedroom and found her mother lying on the floor. She picked up the gun and put it on the desk. Then she called nine-one-one."

"You find any backspatter or gunshot residue on the daughter's hands?"

"Just her prints. The mother had GSR on her hands but no backspatter. There was no backspatter on the weapon or inside the barrel that would indicate a contact shot. The gun was registered to Katherine Chandler. The husband said she kept it in her nightstand."

"Anyone else home?"

"The senator was out of town. The son was out with a friend."

"Any evidence of an intruder?"

"The bedroom had French doors that opened into a patio and garden. David Chandler maintained that his wife always locked the patio doors when he was away. They were closed but unlocked. Someone could've come in that way, but we found no footprints, no evidence of an intruder."

"What's your take?"

Colburn let out breath and was quiet for a time. "David Chandler was convinced his wife committed suicide. She had a history of mental-health issues. She might've taken her life."

"But you're not sure."

"According to statements we collected from her friends, Katherine Chandler was a strict Catholic and wouldn't kill herself. And her relationship with her daughter was strained at best. They had quite a few arguments, some in front of friends, including one the night Mrs. Chandler died. The daughter had opportunity and motive. I always thought she might be good for it, but couldn't prove it. In the end, Katherine Chandler's death was ruled a suicide."

"Anything else you remember?"

"Well, it might not seem like a big deal, but it always troubled me."

"What's that?"

"Katherine Chandler's watch was missing."

Santana's pulse quickened. "A watch?"

"Yeah. It was a gold Rolex with her name inscribed on the back. A gift from her husband. We searched the house and grounds but were never able to find it. I figured the perp took it."

Grace had insisted that she had found Mai Yang's watch near the parking lot on Harriet Island after her morning walk and before she discovered Mai

Yang's body. Her explanation had seemed plausible though Santana had wondered why she had waited so long before admitting she found it. And now he had been told that her mother's watch was missing as well.

Coincidence or pattern?

"Leave me your number," Colburn said.

Santana gave Colburn his cell number and his fax and phone number at headquarters.

"I'll fax you the report. If I think of anything else, I'll call you," Colburn said.

Santana thanked him and hung up.

His gut instinct told him Grace wouldn't kill her mother, that she didn't have it in her. But he knew that line of thought was influenced by his personal feelings for her rather than fact. Everyone, he believed, had it in them given the right set of circumstances. Still, a case for suicide could be made given Katherine Chandler's history of mental illness.

Santana sat back in his chair and imagined how it could have gone down. Grace knows her mother keeps a loaded gun in the nightstand. She either gets the gun beforehand or when she enters the room. She wears gloves and shoots Katherine Chandler once. Then she puts the gun in her mother's hand and shoots her again in the heart, killing her instantly. That would account for the gunshot residue on her mother's hands. Before Grace disposes of the gloves, she unlocks the patio door. Then she waits for the ambulance and police to arrive. Cold. Calculating.

Santana wondered what kind of mind could even imagine Grace doing something like that. But, of course, he knew. It was the kind of mind that made him a good detective and a lousy boyfriend.

* * *

Thick gray clouds blanketed the sky and branches bent in a gusty north wind as Santana approached the wood-slatted bench on the riverbank where General Yang sat.

"I've been expecting you, Detective Santana." The general wore a long, black wool coat and leather driving gloves.

Santana sat down beside him.

"You came to my daughter's funeral last Friday for a reason."

"I wanted to pay my respects."

The general nodded. "But that is not the only reason you came to the funeral or why you are here." He kept his eyes focused on the Mississippi River.

"I needed to know if you were right or left-handed."

"I could ask why you desire that information, Detective Santana, but I suspect it has something to do with Pao Yang's murder."

"The perp who killed him was left-handed."

"The fact that the murderer and I are both left-handed could merely be a coincidence."

"Yes, it could. Then again, you had motive."

"And what would that be?"

"Pao Yang was a known gangbanger who was in love with your daughter. He may have killed her accidentally or intentionally with GHB. Maybe you wanted revenge. And unless you can provide me with a solid alibi, you had opportunity as well. Where were you the night Pao Yang was killed?"

"I was home."

"Any witnesses?"

"I'm afraid not."

Santana wasn't convinced the general was telling the truth, but he moved on. "How's your son holding up?"

"I wish he were stronger."

"Like you?"

"No, Detective Santana. Not like me." He regarded Santana now with eyes that were as void of light as a black hole in space. "I have done my share of killing during war, Detective Santana. And I cannot deny I would kill again if I thought it necessary. But I would never let my son be charged with a crime I had committed. I can assure you of that."

"Do you have any idea who might want to murder your daughter and frame your son?"

"No."

"I'd like to talk to your son again, general."

The general considered his request. "You believe my son is innocent."

"Let's say I'm not convinced of his guilt."

"I will discuss your request with his lawyer. See what can be arranged."

The wind blew dead leaves in swirls across the brown grass and ripped paper from a kite caught between the branches of a tree.

Santana wondered if the Mississippi reminded the general of the Mekong and all the death and horror associated with it. "Do you think the war in Vietnam and Laos was a mistake?"

The general faced the river again. "In hindsight, of course. We lost our homes, our families, and our country. But we thought the greatest military in world could never be defeated by a bunch of peasants. And we would benefit. We thought wrong." The general drew a breath and let it out slowly. "I was always proud of my men. They fought bravely and honorably. We constantly disrupted the southern flow of North Vietnamese troops through Laos along the Ho Chi Minh Trail and rescued American pilots who were shot down. But by end of the war, we were using thirteen- and fourteen-year-old children to replace the casualties. Thousands of us gathered at the mountain air base in Long Tieng, the C.I.A.'s last outpost, waiting for planes to take us to safety. But there was no evacuation plan. Fifty thousand were left behind. Most fled into the jungle and wound up as refugees in Thailand or became boat people. The rest were killed by the Pathet Lao."

He spoke in a controlled voice, but Santana clearly heard the undercurrent of anger in his tone. "Did you work closely with the military?"

"Mostly the C.I.A."

Santana remembered that David Chandler had been a C.I.A. operative in Laos and he felt his heart quicken. "Did you meet David Chandler during the war?"

General Yang looked at Santana once more and gave a nod. "David Chandler has always been a supporter of the Hmong in this state and nationally. He supported our repatriation to Minnesota."

Santana wasn't sure why the new information had set off an alarm in his head. Then it came to him. "Did David Chandler know your daughter and your son?"

"He knew them as children, but over the years, we have drifted apart."

Santana thought it strange that neither man had mentioned his relationship with the other, though it proved nothing. Grace had never mentioned it either. He needed to find out why.

* * *

"There was a three-point-five centimeter entrance wound over the back of the neck at the level of sixth cervical spine in the child," Reiko Tanabe said, reading from the autopsy notes she had compiled in two separate red file folders.

Santana and Lee were sitting at a square table with Tanabe in the cafeteria at Regions Hospital. Along with the autopsy reports, the files contained photographs and diagrams of both sides of the two bodies found in the pit, including close-ups of burns and injuries.

"The sixth and seventh cervical vertebrae were fractured," Tanabe said. "I recovered a twenty-two-caliber bullet. Ecchymosis caused by blood escaping into the tissues from ruptured blood vessels in the area indicated that it was an ante mortem injury." She closed the cover and opened a second file folder. "The woman's body is a little trickier. Fire causes skin to shrink and shrinking skin often splits. That can be mistaken for blunt trauma injuries. Severe flexion of joints from thermal effects can also fracture bones. Skulls often crack along suture lines as a result of the swelling of brain tissue or expansion of gases inside the skull as the body heats. So I have to be careful with my conclusions. But there was blunt force trauma to the left hand prior to burning. The ulna was fractured. There was a similar-sized entrance wound over the left side of neck in the adult female, about two centimeters away from midline and four centimeters below the angle of mandible. The second thoracic vertebrae was fractured. I recovered another twenty-two-caliber bullet. Ecchymosis was present in the surrounding area. Oozing of blood from the wound kept the area wet." She looked up from her notes, drank from a coffee cup.

"So they were dead before they were burned," Santana said.

Tanabe glanced at her notes. "The epidurals in the frontal, parietal and temporal areas were over a centimeter thick, chocolate brown in color and had a honeycomb appearance. That suggests postmortem burns. I found no carbon particles in the respiratory passages of both victims and the blood was not cherry red in color. It's my conclusion that death could not have occurred due to antemortem burns. I believe both victims were first shot. Soil samples indicated they were then doused with gasoline and set on fire."

Lee let out a long breath.

"Anything else you can tell me, Reiko?" Santana asked.

"I can tell you that I won't get much sleep if you keep sending me bodies."

"I wish it were different."

"I know you do. But Hmong autopsies take more time. I have to make sure there's no metal left in the bodies."

"I didn't know that."

"It's part of our culture," Lee said. "We can't have any metal in caskets and none left in or on a body before burial. Not even zippers in clothes or lead from the war."

"No plastic bag inside for organs or outside on the body either," Tanabe said. "I can't keep specimens. All body parts have to be returned."

"How come?"

"Someone could use any organs left out of the body or metal buried with the body to put a curse on surviving family members," Lee said.

"Speaking of metal," Tanabe said, peering at her notes once more. "I received the Hassan family's current dental and medical records. I can use them for identification purposes while I'm waiting for the DNA results. Rashid Hassan's medical records were included. The upper end of his right femur was replaced with a metal ball and the hip socket in the pelvic bone with a metal shell and plastic liner."

"What's that mean?" Lee asked.

"Hassan had right hip replacement surgery. His right leg was slightly shorter than the left due to the surgery, so he probably walks with a slight limp."

Santana leaned forward. "Are you sure Hassan walked with a limp, Reiko?"

"Unless he used a shoe insert. You could check his closet. See if any of his shoes had inserts."

"Why the concern?" Lee said.

"Because the Rashid Hassan I met in Jenna Jones's apartment didn't walk with a limp."

Chapter 28

Diana Lee was seated on the couch in the living room of Rashid Hassan's house, Santana on a cushioned chair facing her. The thermostat in the house had been turned down to sixty degrees, so Lee was still wearing her long wool coat.

They had searched Hassan's closet and found no inserts in any of his shoes.

Lee said, "If Rashid Hassan walked with a limp, John, and the man you saw didn't, then it could mean someone is impersonating him."

"It could."

"But why?"

"I don't know. What did you find out about Farah Hassan?"

"She was a stay-at-home mom. I couldn't locate any close friends or relatives. I checked with the daughter's school. Farah Hassan called them a week ago and claimed that the family would be out of the country for a few weeks. Maybe whoever was impersonating Rashid Hassan made her make the phone call so that the school wouldn't become suspicious?"

Santana nodded and studied the framed photos on the fireplace mantel and the photos on the end table next to the couch. He noted the clear rectangular mark in the thin layer of dust coating the tabletop beside him. "Look at the framed photos around the room, Diana. You notice anything unusual?"

She stood up, walked to the fireplace mantel and peered at the photos. Then she gazed at the photos on the end table next to the couch. "No," she said at last.

"Take a walk around the house. Tell me what you see or don't see."

Santana waited.

Lee returned to the living room five minutes later. "There are no photos of Rashid Hassan. Only photos of his wife and daughter."

"Very good."

"It could be Hassan didn't like his picture taken."

"Not even with his daughter?"

"Not likely."

Santana pointed to the rectangular mark in the dust on the table beside him. "I think there was a picture frame here that the perp removed."

"But Hassan surely had friends who would recognize an impersonator," Lee said. "And anyone at work would know."

"Maybe the impersonator was only interested in assuming Hassan's identity for the short term. That could explain Jenna Jones's murder. She could identify him."

"But you saw him, too."

Santana considered the possibility that the attempt on his life was connected to the current case rather than his Colombian past. The more he thought about it, the more sense it made. He and Jenna Jones may have been the only two people who knew the man calling himself Thomas Carlson was impersonating Rashid Hassan.

"Maybe the actual Rashid Hassan didn't kill his wife and child," Lee said. "Maybe he's dead."

"That seems likely."

"But where's the body? Why wasn't it in the pit with his wife and child?"

"I don't know. But I think whoever assumed Rashid Hassan's identity is buying himself time."

"Why?"

Santana shook his head. "Let's drive over to 3M. See if they have a current photo of Rashid Hassan."

* * *

186

Yolanda, the stern gatekeeper in the lobby of the building where Rashid Hassan worked, recognized Santana from his previous visit. She was more personable and less suspicious than before, but no more accommodating regarding the company's visiting rules. Santana and Lee could not enter the corridors of the building without Donald Stratton. The detectives waited ten minutes until Stratton appeared and escorted them to his office.

Santana introduced Lee. Stratton retrieved an extra chair from an adjacent office and they all sat down.

"I heard on the news that two bodies were recovered at Hassan's house," Stratton said. "It's just unbelievable to think something like this could happen."

Lee glanced in Santana's direction, waiting for him to take the lead.

"Was Hassan working on anything unusual?" Santana asked.

Stratton shook his head.

"Was Hassan acting differently recently?"

"No. Rashid always seemed happy. He enjoyed his work."

"Do you have a current photo of Hassan? Perhaps an ID card."

Stratton opened a desk drawer and took out a stack of ID cards. He shuffled through them as though he were sorting a deck of cards. Halfway through the stack he stopped and dropped a card on the desk. "This photo was taken recently."

Santana picked up the card. He saw immediately that the man he had met in Jenna Jones's apartment was not the man pictured on the photo ID card. "Did Hassan walk with a slight limp?"

"As a matter of fact he did. I believe it was a result of hip surgery he had a few years before he came to the U.S."

"We'd like to take a look in his office."

Stratton hesitated. "I'll have to okay it with human resources and our legal department."

"We could get a warrant."

"I don't think that will be necessary, Detective Santana. Can I get back to you later?"

"Sooner is better," Santana said.

* * *

187

Grace Chandler had prepared a dinner of chicken fettuccine, salad, and warm French bread. A long, thin candle lit a small table on the houseboat and logs burned in the fireplace.

Santana enjoyed the contact, the intimacy he shared with her. Allowing the current investigation to come between them seemed as careless as sailing into a storm. Still, distrust was as much a part of his Colombian culture and upbringing as was the Catholic religion. Colombians called it *malicia india*. The term came from the Indians who had quickly learned how untrustworthy their Spanish conquerors could be. Through intermixing, *malicia india* was in Santana's genes and in his blood. It had served him well as a homicide detective. But he was angry with himself and worried now that his distrustful nature could undermine Grace's feelings for him and his feelings for her.

"How do you like the wine?" she asked.

"Fine," he said, refilling their wine glasses from a chilled bottle of Pinot Gris.

Her smile was as thin as the lemon slice in the water glass. Her melancholy expression indicated that she saw a disaster in the making and no way to prevent it. "Is there something on your mind, John?"

"You didn't tell me your father knew General Yang."

Grace's jaw dropped slightly in surprise. Then she reached for her glass and drank some wine before answering. "I guess I didn't think it was important." Her weak voice didn't match her words.

"Did you know Mai Yang?" Santana kept his voice neutral and without accusation.

"No, John. I did not."

"Had you met her before?"

"Yes. Years ago, when she was very young."

He assumed Grace wouldn't recognize Mai Yang if she hadn't seen her for years. Even if she had seen Mai recently, it would be difficult to look at her face when it was crawling with maggots. "How about the general?"

"I remember meeting him once or twice when I was a child, but I haven't seen him in years either. I'm sure he wouldn't recognize me if we passed on the street."

Santana watched for tells that she was lying and felt guilty for doing it. A battle was raging in his head between the need for answers and his desire for her. Try as he might he could no more ignore the questions in his mind than he could deny who he was. If their relationship was going to last beyond a few nights of intimacy, he had to know the truth. He had to be able to trust her. And he couldn't trust her until she provided concrete answers to his questions.

"Did your brother know the general?"

"I'm sure he met him when he was younger. I doubt it ever went beyond that."

Santana watched the flames turning logs into white ash. The fire reminded him of Rashid Hassan's wife and daughter. No matter what his feelings or desires were for Grace, he needed to know who murdered them, and who murdered Mai Yang and Jenna Jones, and Pao Yang and his two cousins. Santana couldn't allow himself to believe that one life was worth less than another. Not if he expected to be an effective homicide investigator. Everyone deserved the best that he had.

"Tell me about your mother's death," he said.

"We already talked about it, John. Nothing has changed."

Except he had learned Katherine Chandler's watch had disappeared after her apparent suicide. And Grace had found or taken Mai Yang's watch after finding her body. Or, Santana hated to think it, after Grace killed her. "You never mentioned that your mother might've been murdered."

Her complexion darkened. "Where did you get that idea?"

Santana felt as if he were about to dive off a high board without knowing if there was water beneath him. "I spoke to the lead detective who investigated her death."

Sparks suddenly lit Grace's eyes. "And why would you do that?"

Santana hesitated, unsure how he should respond.

"Because you think I had something to do with it, don't you?" she said, her voice rising in anger.

He felt as if he had just thrown something valuable overboard and had no way to get it back.

Grace pushed her chair away from the table and stood. "I think you should leave now."

Santana had knowingly taken a risk by telling Grace that he had spoken with the lead detective investigating her mother's death, and it had backfired as he suspected it would. He got up and retrieved his leather jacket from the couch.

"How could you think I had something to do with my mother's death?" She was looking at him with a mixture of anger and regret. Her pale-blue eyes were filling with tears

He wanted to remind her that she had told him she hadn't gotten along with her mother. But he knew that would cut any remaining lines tethering their relationship. "I never said I did."

"But you implied it, John."

"No. The detective who investigated the case implied it. I don't know if he's any good at his job."

Grace crossed her arms as if she had felt a sudden chill. Seconds later her body began shaking, and Santana could see tears raining down her face, though she made no sound.

He went to her and held her in his arms and waited. Wind gusted and wood snapped in the fireplace like broken branches. Tears of wax slid down the candle.

Grace wrapped her arms around his waist, laid a cheek against his chest.

It felt good holding her, comforting her, protecting her. He wanted to believe that she was innocent. But doubts still lingered like embers in ash.

Finally, she stepped back and looked up at him. "I didn't kill my mother, John. You have to believe me." Her eyes were wet and red, her nose stuffy.

"Do you think someone did?"

"I don't know," she said, and laid her cheek against his chest again. "I don't know."

* * *

City light flowing through the angled blinds of the bedroom washed the darkness with a harsh, white light.

Santana could hear the wail of a distant siren and the soft rhythm of Grace's breathing as she lay beside him. Their lovemaking had been very tentative at first and then more aggressive, as though intimacy was a growing hunger that needed to be fed. He felt relieved the sudden storm between them had passed. Yet, a flood of questions still remained unanswered.

He reached up and closed the blinds. Then he drifted into a dream in which he was a sailor on a ship lost at sea, looking for a beacon that would show him the way. Cannon balls suddenly rained down on the ship as explosions lit the night sky. He felt the ship sinking underneath him, felt the breath squeezed from his lungs. He couldn't move his arms, couldn't breathe.

A voice called to him. "John! Wake up!"

He awoke and sat up with a start.

Grace leaned on an elbow. Reached out and touched his arm. "John?"

He said nothing at first. Waited until his heartbeat slowed.

"Are you okay?"

"I was drowning."

She sat up and put an arm around his shoulders. "It was just a nightmare."

"No," he said, staring into the darkness. "It was a warning."

Chapter 29

Grace asked Santana if he wanted to stay for breakfast the next morning, but he begged off, promising he would phone her later. He left the houseboat before sunrise and returned to his home on the St. Croix.

Gitana lathered him with wet kisses when he opened the door and bent down to pet her. Then she waited impatiently as he put on a running suit and athletic shoes. He slid his compact G-27 Glock into an inside-the-waistband holster he wore over his right kidney. Santana refused to hide behind the walls of his house, but he was no fool. He figured whomever shot at him was still out there. He needed to be armed and ready for any confrontation, for the next attempt on his life.

As he jogged with Gitana along a tar road that paralleled the river, questions about his dream lingered like the water vapor fogging the air. He knew from previous experiences that his dreams and nightmares became more vivid when he was close to solving a case. He was still unclear as to what the metaphors represented, but he trusted that his intuition and memory would soon connect symbolism with reality.

His thoughts shifted from last night's dream to David Chandler's relationship with General Yang. The connection between the two former military men, their families, and Mai Yang's murder appeared to be nothing more than coincidence. But Santana believed there were few coincidences in life and even fewer in homicide investigations.

When he and the dog returned to the house, Santana prepared a large bowl of food for her. Then he showered, put on a fresh mock turtleneck, wool trousers, and shoes with thick soles. For breakfast he ate scrambled eggs, chorizos, an arepa, and hot chocolate.

He had two messages on his cell phone. The first message was from Rita Gamboni. She had scheduled a nine-o'clock meeting in her office with a DEA agent named Roy Blanchard. The second message was from Donald Stratton informing Santana that he could search Rashid Hassan's office at 3M.

The sun broke in and out of the thin layer of gray clouds that dusted the sky as Santana drove toward St. Paul. Daily morning temperatures hovered in the forties now, and he turned the heater on high until the SUV's interior warmed to a comfortable level.

He thought he had budgeted enough time to make it to headquarters by nine, but he was ten minutes late getting to Gamboni's office due to traffic. Gamboni, Lee, and a man in a charcoal suit Santana assumed was Roy Blanchard were waiting for him.

Gamboni let out an impatient sigh as Santana sat down in one of the three chairs facing her desk. She had verbally criticized his tardiness on previous occasions, but this morning she let her exaggerated sigh serve as the sole reminder of her frustration.

She introduced Santana to Blanchard. He was medium height and with broad-shoulders, thinning blond hair, and a ruddy complexion. He had a soft handshake and wore a cheap suit.

Santana noted the gun bulge under his suit coat.

"Now that we're all here," Gamboni said, giving Santana a cool stare, "I'd like agent Blanchard to brief us on an undercover operation the DEA has been conducting. Their investigation might help us identify the source of the heroin found in Pao Yang's house."

Blanchard leaned forward in his chair and fixed his light-brown eyes on Santana and Lee.

"We recently infiltrated a drug ring that's been smuggling black-tar heroin grown and refined on Mexico's west coast across the U.S. border to a distribution center in Los Angeles. The heroin is usually smuggled across the border in the dashboards or gas tanks of vehicles. From LA, it's transported across the country by female juvies or senior citizen males to avoid suspicion. The ring also sends the smack through overnight delivery services or the U.S. mail, often hidden in lamps and other small appliances. We figure they're distributing more than eighty pounds of heroin each month, worth more than seven million dollars. Diluted to street purity, a little over two pounds of heroin produces more than a thousand doses."

Blanchard let them process the information and then continued.

"Couriers bringing money back to Mexico buy an old car and stash cash throughout its body. Then they drive across the border and dump the car at a predetermined location. The drug ring is well organized, disciplined and professional. As soon as we intercept drugs in one city, the members of the drug cell are rotated to another city where heroin remains to be sold. They're moving into territory usually controlled by Colombian or Dominican rings. We're trying to bust them before a drug war breaks out and our city streets start looking like Juarez or Nuevo Laredo."

"You think the heroin we found came from Mexico?" Santana asked.

"Most of the black tar recovered so far from the Mexican drug ring has been about thirty to forty percent pure. Well below the purity of Colombian white heroin, which is why we believe the ring is independent and has no ties to Colombian cartels or to the major Mexican cocaine trafficking cartels. The heroin you recovered was eighty-five percent pure, much purer than the stuff coming out of Mexico. I don't know how familiar you all are with the drug, but that high of a purity level is dangerous to users because it allows them to smoke or inhale it rather than injecting it. And users think if it's not injected it's not as dangerous, which is, of course, a crock of shit."

Gamboni asked, "So, do you think the heroin that detectives Santana and Lee recovered came from Colombia?"

"It could have. But there are two other possibilities. One is the Golden Triangle of Myanmar, Laos, Vietnam, and Thailand. But heroin production in Southeast Asia has declined dramatically in the last decade. So it's more likely your heroin was trafficked out of the Golden Crescent in Iran, Pakistan, or Afghanistan, an area that produces ninety percent of the world's opium. The thing is, relatively little heroin produced in Afghanistan is distributed in the United States because of high demand for the drug in Asia and Europe."

"So where does that leave us?" Gamboni asked.

"I have an idea where our heroin might've come from," Santana said.

Everyone in the room stared at him.

"Let me explain." Santana began with the discovery of Mai Yang's body on Harriet Island. Then he recounted his interview with Yang's roommate, Jenna Jones, in their Battle Creek Apartment, and his subsequent meeting with Thomas Carlson, the man carrying Rashid Hassan's identification. "The man I met in Jenna Jones's apartment ten days ago is not the Rashid Hassan who works for 3M."

No one spoke for a time.

Then Gamboni said, "Are you absolutely sure, John?"

"Positive. I saw his ID photo. We need to go back and check his office at 3M. I got clearance this morning. But we know the real Rashid Hassan had hip replacement surgery and walked with a slight limp. The man I met had no limp. But he had an accent. Whether he's actually from Pakistan, I don't know for sure."

"You're suggesting this impersonator brought heroin into the country from Pakistan."

"I'm saying he might have, Rita. We haven't been able to locate him. I think when Rashid Hassan went to Pakistan to visit his ailing mother somebody took his place and reentered the country using his name. He could have shipped the liquid heroin into the country in the Baileys' bottles."

"That's possible," Blanchard said. "South American heroin availability is decreasing because of the Colombian government's crackdown on drug traffickers. The Colombians and Dominicans still control most of the U.S. distribution. They get white heroin from their sources in Asia or Europe. But street gangs are gaining more control of the retail heroin market in large cities."

"Like the Asian Crips and Latin Kings," Lee said.

Gamboni rested her elbows on the desktop. "This guy who's impersonating Hassan certainly could've murdered Hassan's wife and child and then destroyed evidence by burning their bodies. Killing her would stop her from making any phone calls to Pakistan or to the State Department looking for her husband."

"Most South American heroin is transported into the country by couriers on commercial flights," Blanchard said. "The major points of entry are New York and Miami. If this guy came from Pakistan, he probably came through New York. I can look at recent passenger arrivals from that POE. Then crosscheck those with recent passenger arrivals in the Twin Cities. In the meantime, Commander Gamboni, I suggest you and your detectives let the DEA handle the case."

She looked at Blanchard as though he were a stain on her new dress. "You're telling me you don't want our help?" Gamboni spoke with an edge in her voice.

"No, Commander," Blanchard said with a placating smile. "I don't think we need it. Your detectives have done a good job of locating the heroin. I appreciate their efforts. Now it's up to the DEA to locate this Hassan if he truly is the source."

"I see."

"I wouldn't want them getting in the way of our investigation."

"No," Santana said. "We sure as hell wouldn't want that."

"I'll handle this, detective," Gamboni said.

Blanchard gave Santana his best hard-assed glare. "This is exactly what I'm talking about, Commander. Your detective has a reputation as an adrenaline junkie. That's not what we need going forward in this investigation."

"Why don't you let me handle my detectives," Gamboni said.

Blanchard raised his hands in a gesture of surrender. "No problem. I'm just offering some advice."

"Save it."

Blanchard stood. "I'll keep you up to date on our progress."

"Do that," Santana said. "We'll be waiting with our heads up our ass."

Blanchard's eyes flared with anger. Then he regained control, gave a tight smile and left Gamboni's office.

"Asshole," Gamboni said when the door closed. "I'll be damned if I'm going to let the DEA criticize my detectives and tell me how to run my department." She picked up a pen from her desk and tapped it lightly against the desktop as though she were beating a snare drum. After a time, she stopped and said, "Let me hear your thoughts, John."

"Diana should search Hassan's office."

"And you?"

"I'm working on another angle."

"Would you care to share it with us?"

"Not yet."

"I see." Gamboni began tapping her desktop with the pen again, only harder. "Detective Lee, why don't you head for 3M and see what you can find in Hassan's office."

Lee stood without looking at Santana and left the office.

"Let's hear it, John," Gamboni said, tossing the pen aside.

Santana knew that what he was about to say would displease her. But he saw no way around it. "I'm working on a connection between General Yang and David Chandler."

"Chandler?" she said, incredulously.

"Yang and Chandler met in Laos during the Vietnam War."

"What the hell does that have to do with the current case?"

"I'm not sure. But there's a connection."

"Maybe the connection is between you and Grace Chandler."

Santana felt heat in his face. "How did you find out?"

"Does it matter?"

"Apparently it matters to someone."

"One of David Chandler's friends saw you having dinner with Grace Chandler. He mentioned it to the senator."

"Is there a problem with my seeing his daughter?"

"Why don't you tell me, John? Is there a problem?"

Santana wanted to avoid discussion about Katherine Chandler's death and Grace's possible involvement. But he wasn't sure how much Rita knew and what Chandler had told her. He decided to remain vague. "No problem I can see."

"Well, I guarantee there will be a problem for the department if you continue to hassle David Chandler," Gamboni said. "He's a senator for God's sake."

"So he gets a pass?"

"He doesn't need a pass, John. He's concerned about his daughter, who apparently has had some issues."

197

"Is that how Chandler phrased it? Issues?"

"That's how I'm phrasing it."

"He wants me to stay away from his daughter?"

"You're both adults. I can't order you to do that regardless of what David Chandler wants. But you're putting the department in a difficult situation."

Santana wondered if Rita would order him to quit dating Grace if she could. But maybe he was only imagining that she still had feelings for him, or maybe he was actually hoping she did? And what would that mean? That he still had feelings for her?

"But I can order you to stay away from David Chandler," Gamboni continued, "unless you've got evidence implicating him in any of the homicides you're investigating. Do you have any evidence of his involvement?"

"No."

"Then it's settled," she said, arranging a stack of papers on her desk. "Jesus, eight murders in less than a week." She glanced at her watch and stood. "I have to meet with the Secret Service. The president will be here tonight for the fundraiser at the Landmark Center. And tomorrow he's scheduled a visit to the Federal Courthouse. Put your energies into finding the man impersonating Rashid Hassan, Detective Santana. I don't need anymore headaches."

Chapter 30

A ten-foot electrified fence secured the Tactical Systems building. Santana showed his badge to the security guard monitoring the front gate and kiosk. Then he parked his SUV in the visitors lot and entered the building.

Jared Chandler's secretary was a man named Mark Stiles according to the nameplate on his desk. He wore a white, buttoned-down shirt with no tie and sat straight as a rifle barrel in his chair. He appeared to be about the same age as Chandler. Judging by his posture, closely shaved head, and polite but clipped manner, Santana guessed he was ex-military.

"I'm Detective John Santana from the St. Paul P.D." He flashed his badge. "I called earlier and arranged a meeting with Chandler."

Stiles stood. "Follow me, Detective Santana."

As he was shown into a small but expensively furnished office, Santana noticed that Stiles right hand was twisted and missing three fingers.

Jared Chandler came around his rosewood desk and shook Santana's hand. "Good to see you again, Detective," he said with too much enthusiasm. "Please have a seat. Hold my calls, Mark."

Stiles gave one nod, went out the door and closed it quietly behind him.

"What can I do for you, Detective?"

Santana sat in a cushioned chair and took out his notebook and pen. Thin rays of light sliced between vertical blinds covering the wall of windows on his left.

"You recall we met briefly at your father's house."

"Yes."

"You mentioned at the time that you'd served in Afghanistan."

"Two tours."

Santana watched Chandler carefully. "Your father seemed somewhat disappointed that you left the Army."

Chandler started to reply and then hesitated as though he needed to rethink his answer. "I believe I explained that running this business was more important than another tour in Afghanistan."

Hanging on the wall behind Jared Chandler's desk were framed photos of him in his Army uniform and one photo of him in a pin-striped suit shaking hands with former Vice-president Dick Cheney.

"Your company has weapon contracts with the government?"

"Of course."

"Your weapon's business ever take you back to Afghanistan?"

"Occasionally."

"Been there recently?"

"About three months ago."

"How about Vietnam? Ever been there?"

Jared shook his head. "No, I haven't. But it would be an interesting trip to make."

"I'm curious to know why you or your father never mentioned you knew General Yang."

Jared blinked. "Because I don't know General Yang or his family."

"But your father did."

"I assumed you already knew that, Detective Santana. But really, what difference does it make?" Chandler leaned back in his chair and squeezed a rubber stress ball in his right hand.

"Have you ever met General Yang?" Santana asked.

"Yes, I have."

"Did your father ever talk with you about the general?"

"Not that I recall."

"Did he ever talk to you about his experiences in Vietnam or Laos?"

"My father was in the CIA," Chandler said, as if that answered the question.

"Have you ever met General Yang's children?"

"I might've met them when we were very young. I can't recall."

"What about your sister, Grace? Do you know if she ever met them?"

"Perhaps," he said. "You'd have to ask her."

"How close are you to your sister?"

He leaned forward and placed the stress ball on the desk. "I wish we were closer. I really do. But, unfortunately, I haven't spoken to Grace for quite some time."

"Did you have a falling out?"

"I wouldn't characterize it that way."

"How would you characterize it?"

"Grace doesn't agree with my career choices. Nor I with hers."

"She seems like a talented artist."

"Have you seen her paintings?"

"I have."

"Well, they're awfully dark. Disturbing actually, don't you think?"

"Why do think she paints such dark subjects?"

"I don't like to speculate on my sister's motives or her psyche. But I think her art may have something to do with our mother's death."

"You mean your mother's suicide?"

"However she died."

"Do you have doubts about her suicide?"

Jared Chandler mouth turned upward in a bemused smile. "My mother died ten years ago. Her death can't possibly have anything to do with your current investigation."

"Why don't you tell me what you really think?"

Chandler said nothing for a time. Just held his hazel eyes steady on Santana.

Santana waited.

"Look, Detective Santana, if you're asking me if I think my mother was murdered, the answer is no."

* * *

When Santana returned to his desk at headquarters, he found a message from Tony Novak taped to his phone, requesting that he come to the lab. Santana rode the elevator up to the third floor where one of the techs let him in.

Novak was seated on a stool. On the lab table beside him were an infrared spectrophotometer, a polarized light microscope to examine and identify the fibers and for cross-section work, and seven rolls of tape aligned in a horizontal row. "I've been working on the piece of duct tape the ME found beneath Mai Yang's body."

"So what did you find, Tony?"

"I examined the polyethylene, the fabric and the adhesive. Any or all can be used for identification purposes. Duct tape can be laminated by adhesive or it could be extruded. The extruded polyethylene won't wash off with solvent, and it will most likely have little dimples in the film at the interstices of the fabric on the other side. You can see this with a low power magnifying glass." Novak handed Santana a magnifying glass and gestured toward a piece of duct tape on the tabletop.

Santana could clearly see the dimples in the tape as he peered through the glass.

"You also have film thickness, color, and the metals used in the pigments, which is determined by Energy Dispersive X-ray. It's also possible for the polyethylene to be multi-layered. I can tell this by using a cross section."

"Interesting, Tony," Santana said, not knowing what else to say. He gave Novak the magnifying glass.

"The fabric is usually cotton, polyester or a blend," Novak said. "You have the yarn weight, both in the machine and the cross direction and the yarn twist, which is known as S or Z twist depending on the direction. The type of weave, which could be a plain weave, or inserted weft threads, which are essentially monofilaments with no twist to the filament bundle. You could also have both inserted machine and weft threads, or knitted fabric, the knit being in the machine direction. I can also look at the cloth count, both in the machine and the cross direction."

Novak's brown eyes gleamed with excitement as he smiled at Santana. "Finally, you have to look at the adhesive's color and infrared spectrum. Each duct tape manufacturer has its own formula. This is as good as a fingerprint to identifying the manufacture."

"Really?" Santana said, interested now.

"Absolutely. But I had to identify the type of duct tape first."

"I didn't know there were so many different kinds, Tony."

Novak grinned. "Well, I only had a small piece of tape to work with, John. First, I examined the edges to see if I could detect the method of slitting used. I believe it was cut with a sharp knife, but anything beyond that would be mere speculation. Next, I examined the fillers in the adhesive that weren't detectable by infrared and took measurements of the width and total thickness of the tape. I compared that information with the different types of duct tape currently manufactured."

Novak pointed toward the first roll of tape to his left. "You're probably most familiar with the cheap general purpose tape and the black tape, John. The general-purpose tape is made from low count cloth, a thin film and a low adhesive coating weight. If you hold this tape up to the light, you can see the fabric very well. A low-magnification glass can tell me a lot about the fabric."

"Next, you have your black duct tape with extruded polyethylene. It's used to seal outdoor enclosures such as air conditioner hoods. The black color resists the ultra violet of the sun." Novak said it with the enthusiasm of a child solving a puzzle. "The third type is gaffer's tape. It's used in photo, movie and TV studios and to hold down cables, fasten lights, that sort of thing." He held up the tape so Santana could clearly see it. "Gaffer's tape has a matte, low reflective backing with a clean removal adhesive."

He set the roll on the table and pointed to a fourth. "This is nuclear grade tape used in nuclear power stations and nuclear powered ships. The bleached fabric has been washed in distilled water to remove halogens. The adhesive has only a few parts per million halogens, sulfur and certain reactive metals, so it's basically corrosion free."

"Then you have duct tape with a flame retardant adhesive and a high-adhesion, high-hold, high-shear-resistance adhesive. Its identity is printed along the tape." He pointed at the UL 181 number for emphasis.

"This one here," he said, pointing to the sixth roll, "is mission duct tape, which is carried on every mission into space. If you saw the movie about the

Apollo 13 mission, this type of tape was used to jury rig the carbon dioxide filter. It has a vinyl coated backing."

Novak picked up the last roll on the table. "Cargo bay tape is used in aircraft cargo holds. It also has a flame retardant adhesive and usually a white polyethylene."

Novak positioned himself on the stool so that he was directly facing Santana. "Based on the results of my tests, I can safely say the piece of tape you found on Mai Yang's body came from a roll of cargo bay tape."

"The tape used in aircraft."

"Exactly. If I could match the evidence tape found under Mai Yang's body to a roll in the possession of the suspect, we'd have him."

Chapter 31

Santana knew he was taking a risk as he parked his car in a lot off University Avenue and rode an elevator up to David Chandler's senate office on the top floor of a six-story brick building. He had made the appointment knowing that it might upset Gamboni, Chandler, and Carl Ashford, the chief. But he was willing to take the risk if it helped bring the perp or perps responsible for the murders to justice.

Still, he worried as his Nextel phone buzzed that Chandler had alerted Gamboni or Ashford, and if the call was from one of them. But it was from Diana Lee.

Santana let it go to his voice mail. If the Chandler and Yang connection proved to be a dead end, he saw no point in taking Lee along for the bumpy departmental ride that would inevitably follow.

A heavyset woman ushered Santana into a spacious office, where he shook hands with the senator and then sat down in a comfortable padded chair in front of a light oak desk.

A large, framed-glass, campaign poster from the last election hung on one wall. A photo of the Twin Towers with smoke billowing out the windows hung on the opposite wall, surrounded by plaques acknowledging Chandler for his various accomplishments and charitable work. Built-in shelves were filled with books and photos of Chandler with the president, national and local celebrities, and his family.

Chandler sat in a high-backed leather chair, placed his elbows on the arm rests and tented his hands. "I could say I was surprised to see you again, Detective Santana. But that would be a lie."

"And you don't believe in lying."

"I take pride in always telling the truth. Whether it's good news or bad, I can best serve my constituency, my friends and family, and my country by being honest with them."

Chandler spoke with such rehearsed conviction, Santana almost believed it. "Speaking of serving your country, you never mentioned that you knew General Yang when I first spoke with you about his daughter's death."

"It had no bearing on the case."

I should be the judge of that, Santana thought, but moved on to the next question. "What's your impression of General Yang?"

"He's a fine man and a dedicated soldier. It's unfortunate that his daughter is dead and his son is apparently responsible for the murder of three men."

"Tell me about your relationship with the general."

"We don't have a relationship."

"But you knew him during the Vietnam War."

"That was then."

"Still keep in contact?"

"I see him occasionally at functions."

"When did you see him last?"

"I believe at his wife's funeral a few months ago. I'd have to check my calendar to be sure."

"So you haven't spoken to him about his daughter's death."

"I suspect the general was greatly embarrassed by his daughter's lifestyle, as I would be if my daughter had made such a poor choice."

"You're aware that I'm seeing Grace."

"Acutely."

"Does my seeing her bother you?"

He gave a slight smile. "My daughter has her own mind and her own opinions, as I'm sure you've discovered. My opinions are of no concern to her."

"They might be to me."

"I doubt that very much, Detective Santana. You strike me as a man who makes his own decisions. That's why I'm not surprised by your visit."

"Even though you pressured my commander to make me back off."

He had a relaxed grin on his face. "I would not use the term pressure. It was more of a request."

"Is it my profession you object to, Senator, or my winning personality?"

"This isn't about you," he said. "It's about Grace and her emotional well-being. My daughter was very traumatized after her mother's death. Now, she finds another body. That should be the extent of her involvement. But separating her everyday life from the murder is difficult when she's dating the detective investigating the crime."

Santana understood Chandler's argument but disagreed with his reasoning. He sensed the senator was worried about something other than his daughter's emotional well-being, but he had no idea what he was looking for and, thus, no idea how to get at it. "Tell me about your first wife's death."

Chandler's face colored momentarily. He gripped the armrests on his chair and straightened his back as though preparing to salute. "And why should I talk with you about Katherine's death?"

"You're a man who always speaks the truth. The detective who investigated your wife's death thought she had been murdered. But you insisted your wife committed suicide."

"You've been investigating my first wife's death?"

"Not investigating."

"But you've spoken with Detective Colburn."

"You remember his name."

"Of course." Chandler set his elbows on the arm rests, tented his hands once more and sat back in his chair, thinking.

Outside the windows behind Chandler, Santana could see the sun's rays stripping away the cloud cover.

"Detective Colburn had his theory and wouldn't let go of it," Chandler said. "Fortunately, the medical examiner ruled Katherine's death a suicide."

"But medical examiners can make mistakes."

"You would know more about that than I would, Detective Santana."

"I understand your wife was a strict Catholic."

Chandler nodded. "Given your background, I suspect you might know something about the faith."

"You've looked into my background?"

"Senators can be just as curious as detectives when it involves their daughter."

Santana wasn't exactly surprised by Chandler's admission. If Grace were his daughter, he would probably be investigating her boyfriend's background, too. "According to the Catholic Church, suicide is a mortal sin."

"My wife had mental health issues. I think that trumped her faith."

"Grace didn't get along well with her mother."

"She and Katherine had their disagreements. But I wouldn't characterize them as anything more. Like Grace, Katherine was strong willed and opinionated."

"Any different than you?"

He chuckled. "I've been known to have an unpopular opinion or two."

"How did your son get along with his mother?"

"Katherine was rather distant when Jared was very young. As I recall, she really began experiencing some emotional problems shortly after his birth. My wife did her best. But quite honestly, she wasn't very successful. Unfortunately, I was out of the country most of the time and couldn't offer much support when it came to raising the children. Still, I'm proud of them."

Santana knew that asking Chandler about Grace's possible involvement in her mother's death was like walking through a minefield. But he wanted to get Chandler's take, watch his reaction to the questions. "Do you think Grace had anything to do with your wife's death?"

Chandler appeared to have no emotional or physical reaction. Maybe he suspected Santana would ask the question and was prepared for it. Still, Santana expected to see at least feigned outrage. Maybe no reaction was as telling as an overreaction.

"You've met my daughter, Detective Santana. What do you think?"

"I think that most everyone is capable of killing given the right set of circumstances."

"I would agree with you. Good men and women who never thought of harming anyone or anything can be taught to kill. I've seen it with my own eyes. It's just a matter of training. But circumstances are important."

"Like war?"

"War is definitely a circumstance. But war is not the only circumstance that justifies killing. There are causes."

"Such as?"

"Freedom."

"From what?"

"Oppression. Dictatorship."

"Doesn't that usually lead to war?"

"Not always. But I believe it should."

"Are there good wars and bad wars?" Santana asked.

"I would say there are good reasons to go to war and not so good reasons. But once a country has made a commitment, then winning should be the only acceptable outcome. If our current leaders had followed that creed, we might not be in the mess we're in today."

"What if winning isn't possible?"

He shook his head as though Santana had made a ridiculous comment. "There is no war that we're incapable of winning. It's all a matter of will. We need a president and a country capable of understanding that. We believed it once, but we've lost our pride, our dignity. Someone has to have the courage to lead the way. Someone needs to give our citizens a reason to be proud of their country and their leaders again."

It sounded like more than a stump speech. It sounded to Santana as if Chandler saw himself as a leader who could do it. "Your company, Tactical Systems, certainly benefits from war."

"It's the country that benefits, Detective Santana."

"And how is that?"

"Wars keep us safe."

"All wars?"

"The right wars, yes."

"You ever return to Vietnam or Laos?"

"I've been back on a number of occasions working on behalf of the M.I.A.s."

"There are still bodies that haven't been found or returned?"

"Unfortunately, yes."

"I understand you fly your own plane."

"That's right."

Santana opened his briefcase and took out the roll of cargo tape Tony Novak had given him and set it on the desktop. "Know what that is?"

"Of course. It's cargo bay tape."

"You ever use any on your plane?"

"I might have. Why do you ask?"

Santana didn't want Chandler to know that a piece of cargo bay tape was found underneath Mai Yang's body, so he ignored the question. "Would you have any cargo tape here or at your house or hangar that I might take a look at, Senator?"

The senator's eyes shifted to the roll of tape on the desk and then back to Santana. "There are thousands of rolls of tape like that sold every day, Detective Santana."

"True enough. Are you right-handed or left-handed, Senator?"

Chandler stood. "If you'll excuse me, Detective Santana. I need to attend a benefit at the Landmark Center tonight."

"For the president?"

"That's right." Chandler gestured toward the door. "I hope your investigation ends successfully."

I hope so too, Santana thought. But as he walked out to his car, the odds seemed as long as the late afternoon shadows.

Chapter 32

When Santana returned to the Homicide Unit, he saw Diana Lee at her desk. "You find anything in Rashid Hassan's office?"

"Nothing out of the ordinary," she said.

Santana hung his leather jacket on a coat rack and sat down in front of his desk computer.

"I tried calling your cell, John, but you didn't answer."

"After you left Gamboni's office, she told me to leave Chandler out of the investigation. I went to see him anyway. There's going to be blowback."

"Partners are supposed to stick together. I can take the heat."

Santana wasn't sure that she could, but he didn't want to press the point.

"What's your angle, John? What is it you're looking for?"

"I don't know. But Chandler's got something going. And it may involve General Yang."

Lee's eyes grew wide. "Do you think the general had something to do with the murders?"

"He's left-handed. He knows how to kill."

"But would he frame his son?"

"I don't think so." Santana clicked on his computer and waited for it to boot up.

"What are you doing?"

"Looking for more information on David Chandler and General Yang. I'm missing something."

Lee rolled her chair next to Santana's while he Googled Senator David Chandler. The senator's website contained contact and background information, constituent services, recent press releases, a few videos of Chandler being interviewed on national and local talk shows, and thumbnail photos.

"It seems Chandler speaks Vietnamese," Santana said after reading the background information. He clicked on a link entitled P.O.W./M.I.A. and continued reading.

> Thousands of live sightings of American soldiers in Vietnam have been reported since the war ended. In 1980, a reliable CIA contact reported seeing about thirty Americans working on a prison road crew in Laos. The U.S. Joint Special Operations Command prepared a rescue force, but press leaks and a badly bungled CIA reconnaissance mission stopped the rescue before it started.

"Do you think Chandler was involved with the reconnaissance mission?" Lee asked.

"He was working for the C.I.A. at the time, Diana. He'd spent time in Vietnam and Laos during the war. I suspect he was involved."

Santana saw numerous photos of Chandler meeting with various Vietnam veteran groups and families of missing serviceman.

"Look at that photo," Lee said, pointing with an index finger to a photo of Chandler standing with a large group of Americans.

Santana clicked on the thumbnail photo to enlarge it. According to the caption underneath it, the picture was taken in Thailand in 1992 at the Ban Vinai Refugee Camp near the Laotian border. The Americans were from the St. Paul city council and from the school district.

"My family was in that camp when it first opened," Lee said. "I'll never forget how dusty and dirty it was. It closed shortly after this picture was taken."

Santana watched the videos on the website and then pored over more photos. After an hour, he began to think he was wasting his time. Then he clicked on a final thumbnail photo that was taken in 2004, just after Chandler had been elected to his second term as the junior senator from Minnesota. There were a dozen men in the photo including David Chandler and General Yang. A few of the men were Americans, most were Hmong. They were all dressed in short sleeve embroidered shirts and were posing for the photo in front of a temple in Chiang Mai, a city in northern Thailand. "Look at the guy second from the left in the second row, Diana. The caption says his name is Cha Yang."

"He could be one of the general's sons."

"I thought Kou was his son."

"He is. But the general had over twenty children with four different wives. Polygamy was commonly practiced in Laos, John. Kou and Mai Yang were the only children the general had with his fourth wife. She died young."

As Santana peered more closely at the photo, his heartbeat quickened. "This guy on the far right in the first row doesn't look Hmong or American."

Lee leaned forward in her chair and stared intently at the computer screen. "The caption says his name is Karim Aziz."

Santana examined the photo one more time just to make sure. "He's the guy I met in Jenna Jones's apartment, Diana. The guy impersonating Rashid Hassan."

* * *

Santana and Lee got out of the Crown Vic and walked toward General Yang.

He caught sight of the two detectives as they approached, adjusted the black scarf that was draped around the collar of his long coat.

The general was standing alone beside his daughter's headstone in the Oakland Cemetery near downtown St. Paul. The headstone was located in a grove of maple trees whose red leaves looked like flames bursting from the branches in the waning sunlight.

The name inscribed on the headstone nearest to Mai Yang's headstone was Song Yang. Santana wondered if she was the General's fourth wife. "Kou told us we'd find you here," he said.

The general held his dark eyes on the two detectives but said nothing.

Santana pulled the colored photo he had run off the Internet from his jacket pocket and showed it to the general. "The man on the far right in the first row. Karim Aziz. We need to talk to him."

The general glanced at the photo. "Then you need to go to Thailand."

"No, general," Santana said. "I saw him in your daughter's apartment ten days ago."

"You are mistaken."

Santana felt a rush of heat in his chest. He gazed at the rows of headstones that appeared to stretch endlessly toward the horizon. He had attended far too many funerals in his thirty-six years. Seen too many people die pointless deaths. "Karim Aziz entered the country illegally using Rashid Hassan's name on a phony Pakistani passport. I believe he killed Rashid's wife and child and burned their bodies in a fire pit behind the family's residence in Lake Elmo. You have any idea why he would want to do that?" He made no attempt to hide the anger in his voice.

"You are sure of this, Detective Santana?"

Trying to read the general's expression was like trying to read the face of the dead. Still, Santana thought that General Yang seemed troubled by what he had just heard. "Positive."

The general looked at his daughter's headstone and then at Diana Lee. She held his eyes briefly and then lowered her head. "I suggest you speak to David Chandler," he said.

"Why Chandler?"

"I believe he knows why Karim Aziz is in the country."

"And you don't?"

"The war has ended for me, Detective Santana. But perhaps it has not ended for others."

Santana thought about what the general had implied. Then he held up the photo. "The names of the men with you and Chandler are written here. But who are they, really?"

"Some might call them patriots, some guerilla fighters, some mercenaries."

"What would you call them, general?"

"Misguided."

"What are Karim Aziz and David Chandler planning to do?"

"I can tell you what I know. But I am not responsible for their actions."

Chapter 33

The Landmark Center was a towering Romanesque Revival structure built like a castle. It had red-tile roofs, multiple turrets and gables, a six-story indoor courtyard, stained-glass skylights, and a marble-tile foyer. The original Landmark building was constructed in 1902 and served as the Federal Court House and the site of many trials of 1930s-era gangsters like Machine Gun Kelly, Ma Barker, and John Dillinger. Renovated in the 1970s after a group of concerned citizens saved it from the wrecking ball, the building faced the north end of Rice Park in downtown St. Paul, near the St. Paul Hotel, the Ordway Center for Performing Arts, and the St. Paul Central Public Library.

In Santana's first few years with the SPPD, he had worked security details at political fund-raisers and high-end parties at the Landmark Center thrown by the rich and well connected in Twin Cities' society.

Santana angle parked the Crown Vic on Fifth Street. He and Lee badged their way through the tight presidential security and into the building.

The dinner and fundraiser were being held on the third floor in a large ballroom with a twenty-foot ceiling, marble fireplaces, carved mahogany, and linen-covered tables with place settings for eight.

Santana stopped just inside a doorway that led into the ballroom. "Diana, would you recognize David Chandler?"

"Maybe from his photos."

Santana surveyed the room.

Waiters and waitresses in black pants, white shirts, and bow ties, were serving champagne and hors d'oeuvres from shiny silver platters. Women in expensive floor-length dresses and sparkling jewelry that glittered in the chandeliered light kissed the air beside each other's cheeks and talked in excited tones about upcoming travel plans and the private high schools and Ivy League colleges their very bright sons and daughters attended. Important men in tuxes and dinner jackets huddled around even more important and influential men. They spoke in ominous tones about the economy and shook their heads in frustration over their declining stock portfolios.

"There he is," Lee said, pointing toward Chandler.

Because of his money and power, David Chandler was a man others sought out. A group of six distinguished men had congregated around him.

Santana had started toward Chandler when Rita Gamboni suddenly appeared in front of him as if she had materialized out of thin air.

Her whiteblonde hair was expertly coiffed, her red lipstick and soft makeup perfectly applied. Her long black dress accentuated her slim figure. In her one-inch heels, she was nearly as tall as Santana.

"What are you doing here, John?" Her tone was accusatory rather than questioning.

"We're here to see David Chandler."

"What?" she said, her cheeks flaming red.

Four women standing in a small group behind Gamboni stared in her direction.

Gamboni placed one hand on her left hip in a confrontational pose, and tapped the small black purse she held in her other hand against her right thigh. "I asked you to stay away from David Chandler. But you disobeyed my direct orders and went to his office this afternoon. And now you're hassling him again." Her eyes were as hard as the small diamond hanging from her necklace. They shifted from Santana to Diana Lee and then back to Santana again.

"So Chandler called you this afternoon."

"Why wouldn't he? You won't listen to me, John, and you won't leave him alone. Maybe I should talk to Chief Ashford?"

"Look, Rita, David Chandler knows the man who's impersonating Rashid Hassan. He may be involved in the murders of Hassan's wife and child."

Her jaw dropped and she stared silently at Santana. "Have you gone completely insane, John?"

"No. But I think Chandler has."

Gamboni shook her head slowly as though she couldn't believe what Santana was telling her. "I want you and Detective Lee to leave right now. First thing tomorrow morning, you both report to my office."

Lee looked down at the floor, refusing to meet Gamboni's stare.

Santana brought out the photo and showed it to Gamboni. "The man on the far right in the first row is Karim Aziz. He's the man I saw in Jenna Jones's apartment, and he's killed at least two people."

The women behind Gamboni jerked their heads in Santana's direction.

Santana took Gamboni by the arm and gently led her out into the hallway. Lee followed.

"Listen to me, Rita. We need to talk to Chandler now."

"He's a senator for God's sake. You just can't cuff him and haul him off like some gangbanger."

"Leave it to me."

Gamboni started to protest and stopped.

"You've got to trust me, Rita."

"And what if you're wrong, John?"

"Then you can have my badge."

"Is that what you want?"

"I have no choice."

She thought about it for a time. "Fine," she said, stepping aside.

"Let's go," Santana said to Lee.

They crossed the wide hallway and entered the ballroom again, weaving between small clumps of people toward David Chandler.

He was involved in an animated conversation with the men around him, but he looked in Santana's direction as the two detectives approached.

"Detective Santana," Chandler said with a tight smile. "I'm surprised to see you here." He appraised the two detectives dressed in their work clothes, as though he was a tux and they were a pair of brown shoes. "Not staying long?"

217

"We need to talk, Senator," Santana said. "Privately."

"Perhaps this conversation could wait. As you can see," he said, making a sweeping gesture with one arm, "I'm currently occupied."

"It can't wait, Senator. I think you know that."

Santana followed Chandler's gaze, saw Rita Gamboni striding toward them.

"Commander Gamboni," Chandler said. "Perhaps you can convince your detectives that we can have this conversation another time."

Santana could tell by Gamboni's conflicted expression that she wasn't sure what to do. He said, "If you'd prefer to talk in front of these gentlemen, Senator, we can do that."

The six men standing in a tight semi-circle gazed at Chandler and waited for his response.

In the background, Santana could hear the tinkle of glasses, the low hum of conversation, a ripple of laughter.

"All right," Chandler said. "But let's make this quick. If you'll excuse me gentlemen." He followed Santana, Lee, and Gamboni into the hallway, crossed his arms and leaned against the railing. "What's this all about?" His voice lacked the authority he had projected only moments ago.

Santana held out the photo so Chandler could get a good look at it. "This man standing to the far right in front. His name's Karim Aziz. Tell me about him."

"What's to tell? I met him once in Thailand."

"Why don't you cut the bullshit, Senator?"

Anger flashed in Chandler's eyes. He glared at Gamboni, waiting for her to reprimand her detective. But when he realized that she wouldn't rise to his defense, his anger quickly dissipated.

"You need to tell us everything, Senator."

"I have no idea what you're talking about."

"I know about the plans to invade Laos and retake the country."

Chandler shifted his eyes to Rita. "Commander Gamboni. Are you going to just stand there and let your detective talk to me like this?"

"I've spoken with General Yang," Santana said. "I know about the weapons. The men."

Chandler nodded slowly. "I'm impressed, Detective Santana. You would've made an excellent intelligence officer. I can see why your commander trusts you."

"What were you hoping to accomplish?"

"The Hmong supported this country during the war. The Laotian government is still hunting those who stayed behind. Now Thailand wants to repatriate the Hmong who fled Laos. They will be killed. The Hmong deserve to have their country back."

"And you propose to do that by starting another war?"

"You don't understand, Detective Santana. There are others at the highest levels of government who support the idea of military intervention."

"Are you aware that Karim Aziz murdered Rashid Hassan's wife and daughter?"

"Murder was never part of the operation, Detective Santana. Neither was kidnapping my daughter."

Santana felt a stab of pain in his heart. "Why would Aziz kidnap Grace?"

"I'm afraid he's going to kill the president and wanted assurances that I wouldn't reveal the plan."

"Jesus," Gamboni said.

Santana took some time to put it together. Then he looked at Lee and Gamboni. "Aziz is from Pakistan. He's al-Qaeda."

"No one was aware of that," Chandler said. "An unfortunate error in judgment was made."

Santana wanted to beat the hell out of him. "How does Aziz plan to kill the president?"

Chandler gave a weak shrug. "I don't know."

"I've got to alert the Secret Service and Homeland Security," Gamboni said, removing her cell phone from her purse.

"No!" Chandler said. "Once Aziz discovers the president has been warned, he'll kill my daughter." He held his eyes on Santana. "Do your best to find her, Detective. I'm counting on you. I love her very much." It was the first genuine emotion Chandler had expressed.

"It might be too late for that now, Senator."

"I hope not," he said. "I really hope not."

Chapter 34

Santana steered the Crown Vic through a gauntlet of emergency vehicles and patrol cars clogging the streets around the Landmark Center, their red lights flashing in the cold night air. Diana Lee sat in the passenger seat beside him, her face tense, her seat belt strapped across her chest. Santana knew if he were going to figure out where Karim Aziz had taken Grace, he had to control the growing sense of panic that threatened to shut down his thinking.

"Gamboni will be angry when she discovers we've left," Lee said.

"I'll deal with it later."

"Where are we going?"

"To Grace Chandler's houseboat on the river."

Santana stepped on the accelerator as the Crown Vic cleared traffic around the Landmark Center and raced down Market Street past Rice Park and the St. Paul Library. The back tires squealed as the big sedan fishtailed left onto Kellogg Boulevard and then right onto the Wabasha Bridge. Santana gunned the car across the bridge and then hit the brakes and turned left onto Water Street and left again onto Levee Street.

They were in the second parking lot and out of the car and sprinting toward the boats on Harriet Island a minute later.

Santana punched in the security code when they reached Gate E, and they ran down the steps and along the dock to Grace Chandler's houseboat.

They stopped five yards short of the boat and drew their Glocks.

Santana's mind flashed back to Pao Yang's house and Kacie Hawkins lying wounded on the front lawn. "Stay close, Diana."

They each swung a leg over the rail and stepped onto the deck. The water lay still beneath them. The moon hid behind a cloud. A single lamp lit the interior of the cabin. Santana saw no one inside.

He pushed the handle and the unlocked glass door slid open. They followed their guns into the living room. Everything appeared undisturbed, just as Santana remembered it. "I'll check the bedroom."

He moved slowly down the narrow corridor to the left of the galley island, checked the bathroom and then the bedroom where city lights puddled the carpet. He remembered lying on the bed with Grace in his arms, remembered his nightmare in which he felt he was drowning. He felt as if he was living a nightmare now.

When he came into the living room again, Lee said, "The code at the gate and the bedroom in back. You've been here before, John."

Santana saw no point in denying it. "I have."

"Then this is more than just a kidnapping."

"Much more."

He put his Glock back on his hip, sat down on the couch.

"How long have you known Grace Chandler?" Lee asked.

"Not long enough."

"So what do we do now?"

Santana had no idea, no clue. He pictured an hourglass in his mind, the sand flowing from top to bottom like blood draining from a wound. "We need to search this place."

"If it's like Hassan's house," Lee said, "it'll be clean. This Aziz, or whoever he is, wherever he came from, knows what he's doing."

Santana leaned forward and placed his elbows on his knees. Adrenaline-fueled energy had awakened the demon inside him. Stay calm, he told himself. Think. "Aziz left something."

"All we found in Hassan's house was the drawing," she said.

"What did you say?"

"The drawing. That's all we found."

"And the C-4 that appeared to be clay."

Lee looked at him and shook her head in confusion.

"I took the piece of clay I found in the basement to Jeff Jenkins in ODU. It wasn't clay. It was C-4. I think Aziz was making it in the lab in Hassan's basement."

"So he's planning to blowup something?"

Santana thought about it. "Hassan was an environmental engineer. He was investigating polluted ground water. What carries water?"

"Pipes?" she said.

"And where would you find water pipes?"

"Underground?"

"Exactly. The drawing you found in Hassan's garbage wasn't a maze, Diana. It was of tunnels below a building."

"The Landmark Center!" Lee said. "Aziz is going to blowup the Landmark Center and kill the president!"

* * *

"Maybe we should wait for Gamboni and someone from the bomb squad," Diana Lee said.

She and Santana were standing beside the rectangular table in the Homicide Unit where Rita Gamboni conducted her murder meetings with the detectives. A large map of the underground water system lay open on the table.

Daren Ritchie from the city water and sewer department stood next to Santana. Ritchie was a heavy-set man with large features and a ready smile.

"I don't want all kinds of cops in the tunnel alerting Aziz that we're coming for him," Santana said. "And I don't have time to convince Gamboni that Grace Chandler and Aziz are in the tunnels underneath the Landmark Center."

"But if Air Force One doesn't land at the airport, the press will know something's up," Lee said. "If Aziz has a radio, he'll hear the announcement. He'll blow the building when he discovers the president isn't coming."

"That's why we don't have time to wait for backup. We've got to move now."

"You lookin' for a terrorist, Detective Santana?"

Santana looked at Ritchie. "I believe so."

"No shit?"

"Tell me about the tunnel system, Daren."

"Well," he said, pointing at the map with a shaky index finger, "we've got over fifteen miles of multi-level, interconnecting tunnels underneath the street. The tunnels were dug mostly through raw sandstone, although in some places there are brick or cinderblock walls. The tunnels that carried power lines for the old streetcars are abandoned. But there are tunnels that carry gas and electric lines, telephone lines, sewer and water."

"What's the shallowest tunnel system? The one closest to the street?"

"That'd be the main water lines. They run just beneath the street grid. There's about two and a half miles of 'em. They carry fiber optic trunk cables and water to the buildings and fire hydrants. We use the tunnels so we don't disrupt traffic when we do maintenance and repair work. The primary water line runs along Wabasha Street."

"Would we need flashlights or headlamps?"

"Wouldn't hurt to carry flashlights. But all the tunnels are equipped with florescent lights. We usually keep about a fourth of them on. I can make sure you got plenty of light."

Santana thought that lights might work to his advantage. He imagined it would be easier for Aziz to see a flashlight beam cutting through the darkness. Then again, Aziz could probably spot someone coming toward him from a distance in a florescent-lit pipe.

"Diana," Santana said. "Give Daren your phone. Do you know how to use the walkie-talkie, Daren?"

"You betcha," he said.

"Good. How do we get into the tunnels?"

"One way is through the courthouse."

Santana recalled the drawing they had found in Hassan's house and how much the building above the maze resembled the city hall. He wondered if Hassan had made the drawing for Karim Aziz when he went to Pakistan and before Aziz or someone else killed him.

"How far is the walk to the Landmark Center?"

"No more than five minutes above ground. No more than ten minutes through the tunnels. And all the major intersections in the tunnels are marked with street signs. Here, I'll show you."

Ritchie used a black marker to trace the path on the map. "First, you go west to St. Peter. Then north. You'll see a sign at Fourth Street. You go west again until you reach Washington. Take the tunnel heading north. It'll take you directly under the Landmark Center."

As Santana looked at Lee, he recalled Hawkins's warning again. He wondered if Lee really had no clear shot at the Mazda, or if she just couldn't bring herself to pull the trigger and take a life. Then he remembered how he had lost his last partner and nearly lost Kacie Hawkins. "No need for you to come along, Diana."

"You need back up."

Santana knew he needed a partner in the tunnel that wouldn't hesitate to take a shot or put her life on the line. He wasn't certain if he could trust Lee. But he knew if he left her here and went into the tunnel alone, it might permanently damage her standing in the department, especially if something happened to him. Then again, he would probably be dead and Lee's standing in the department would be a moot point as far as he was concerned. "You've got your Kevlar?"

She nodded.

Santana did a mental checklist. He had his Kevlar body armor and two extra clips. His G-27 backup Glock fit snugly in the ankle holster on his left leg. He was ready. "Then let's do it," he said.

* * *

The Saint Paul City Hall and Ramsey County Courthouse, located on Kellogg Boulevard, was a twenty-one-story, Art Deco skyscraper built out of limestone during the Great Depression. The vertical rows of windows were linked by plain, flat, black spandrels. The building's woodwork was fashioned out of twenty-three different species of wood. There were murals and bronze stair railings, bronze door handles and locks, and six bronze elevator doors. Santana and Lee followed Daren Ritchie through Memorial Hall with its white marble floor and three-story black marble piers leading to a gold-leaf ceiling. At the end of the hall was the thirty-eight-foot white onyx Indian God of Peace. Darin unlocked a utility door, swung it open and flicked on a light switch.

224

The three of them entered a large, empty storage closet. Daren Ritchie grabbed a ringbolt in the floor and lifted open a trap door.

"What time do you have?" Santana asked.

"Goin' on eleven," Ritchie said.

Santana handed him a business card. "If we're not back in an hour, you notify SPPD Homicide. Ask to speak with Commander Gamboni. Tell her what you know."

"One thing that might help, Detective Santana. You'll come across a small office near the Landmark Center. The crews use it for breaks, but they're off for two days. Budget cuts. The guy you're lookin' for may be holed up there."

"Thanks for the tip, Daren. Keep the cell phone ready."

"I will. You be careful now, detectives."

Santana needed both hands free as he climbed down a fifteen-foot iron ladder into the tunnel. His holstered Glock would be of no use if Aziz were waiting for him. Halfway down the ladder he jumped. As his feet hit the ground, he crouched, drew his gun and looked both ways.

Nothing.

Daren Ritchie was correct. Bright fluorescent bulbs were fitted to a four-inch diameter pipe. The pipe was attached to the wall midway between the floor and ceiling. The lights were placed every ten yards. Shadows darkened the ground and walls between the lights. The arching sandstone walls were four feet wide by six feet tall. Santana had to duck slightly to avoid bumping his head. A water pipe ran along the ground on the left side of the tunnel. It was three-feet in diameter and left a narrow one-foot clear path. The air was cool and damp and smelled like wet sand.

Santana waited until Lee reached the ground and drew her Glock. "This way," he said, heading in a westerly direction. Lee followed close behind.

Santana moved slowly, holding his gun in his right hand. He saw no graffiti, only the pockmarks of laborers' tools in the walls and ceilings. Occasionally, he heard the rumble of traffic overhead.

They walked for three minutes before they came to an intersection with a brick arch and a sign bolted to a fuse box. An arrow pointed in the direction of St. Peter Street to his right. A second sign bolted below the first indicated that the tunnel to the left was a dead end. They kept moving until they reached Fourth Street where they turned west again.

The water pipe was smaller along this stretch of tunnel and the extra walking space allowed them to move quicker. Santana's Kevlar vest seemed heavier than usual under his leather jacket, and he was sweating even though the air remained cool and damp. They moved past small piles of sand and a narrow vertical shaft that he presumed led to a fire hydrant.

When they reached the intersection of Washington and Fourth, he stopped and sat on the water pipe. He motioned for Lee to do the same.

In the shadows of the tunnel under Fourth Street, he saw two red eyes staring at him. Then the eyes moved into a beam of light, and Santana saw they belonged to a rat the size of a small cat. It moved slowly away from them, down the tunnel, and disappeared into the deepening shadows.

"Daren Ritchie said there was a break room along the Washington stretch of pipe," Lee said. "It's near the Landmark. Maybe Aziz is there."

"Listen," Santana said. "What do you hear?"

Lee closed her eyes and held her breath and listened. "A radio. Turned down low."

"Aziz is in the break room. Right where Daren Ritchie thought he might be."

Chapter 35

Santana knew that if Karim Aziz was holding Grace hostage in the break room, he could easily kill her once he spotted the two detectives approaching from the Washington tunnel entrance. But that scenario assumed that Grace was still alive. Santana had no doubt Aziz would kill her once he heard the president had cancelled his visit. He figured if she were alive, he would have only one chance to get Aziz and save Grace.

He stood up and peered around the corner. A consistent pattern of rectangular, white light and black shadows marked the tunnel floor for twenty yards. Then a splash of pale light spilled out from a space in the wall on the right. Santana could hear the radio more clearly now. It was tuned to a news station.

He looked at Lee who gave him a tight smile. He could see that she was struggling to hold herself together, to remain calm. He would have no time to worry about her safety once they began moving again, no time to worry whether she was up to the task. He considered leaving her there.

Then she stood up, took a deep breath and let it out. "What's the plan?"

Santana thought about his limited options one more time before he responded. "The break room is about twenty yards down the tunnel on the right. The tunnel isn't wide enough for both of us to move side by side. Besides, that would leave both of us vulnerable. So I'll go first. You stay about five yards back. We've got to take Aziz by surprise."

Lee nodded but said nothing.

Santana stepped into the Washington tunnel and moved slowly and quietly forward, bent at the waist, offering Aziz less of target. He could sense Lee behind him, but she was moving silently over sand that muffled their footsteps.

After ten yards Santana stopped and listened. He imagined Aziz bursting into the pale light with his gun spitting fire and death. Hearing nothing but the newscaster's voice coming from a radio, Santana moved forward again, thankful that the radio was camouflaging their movement.

He stopped just before the break room and squatted in a shadow behind a beam of ghostly light that streamed out an open wooden door.

Lee squatted three yards behind him.

Santana could see that the open door swung into the room from the right. As he peered through the narrow space between the doorframe and hinges, a burst of adrenaline kicked his heartbeat up a notch. Grace Chandler was seated in a card table chair, her chin resting on her chest, her hands bound behind her, duct tape across her mouth. He couldn't tell if she was resting or unconscious, but he could see her chest rise and fall and knew that she was alive.

A small television sat on a wooden table behind her and a black phone hung on the wall. He saw no sign of Aziz within his limited vision. He was either on the other side of the room or not in the room at all.

Santana put an index finger to his lips and then waved Lee forward with his gun. When she was beside him, he pointed to her and then to the left side of the room. She nodded, indicating she understood that he wanted her to move left as she entered the room behind him.

Santana stood and stepped out of the shadow and charged through the doorway behind his Glock. He felt Lee come in behind him. He saw immediately that Grace was alone in the room.

"Cover the door," he said to Lee.

He went to Grace and cupped his hand under her chin and raised her head off her chest. Her left cheek was swollen and streaked with blood and her eyes were glassy as though she had been drugged. A feeling of relief and joy flowed through his body as if a warm liquid had been poured into his veins. "This might hurt a little," he said, using his fingers to slowly peel off the tape covering her mouth. Then he bent down and untied her hands and feet. "Can you stand?" he asked, touching her cheek gently.

She kissed his hand and stood and wrapped her arms tightly around his waist and held him close. "How did you find me?"

Santana saw Lee look at him. He contemplated telling Grace about her father but quickly dismissed the idea. "I'm a detective. It's what I do. Where's Aziz?"

Grace held him for a moment longer before she stepped back and looked into his eyes. "I don't know. But we've got to go before he returns."

Santana's eyes shifted to the workbench and to the strip of gray material that appeared to be modeling clay. It was a larger batch of the same substance he had found in Rashid Hassan's house. The same substance Jim Jenkins had identified as C-4.

Besides a radio and a portable television, the break room contained a workbench on which were a microwave, an oscillating fan, and a coffee maker. There were four card table chairs in the room, including the one Grace had been sitting on. A map of the tunnel system covered the wall behind the workbench.

"Grace, you're going with Detective Lee," Santana said.

"What about you?"

"I'm going after Aziz."

"No, John," she said with a firm shake of her head. "No. You're coming with us."

"I can't do that, Grace."

She opened her mouth as if to protest and then appeared to realize it was pointless. "I don't want to lose you."

He put his hands on her shoulders. "You won't. Just do as I say. Go with Detective Lee." He turned toward Lee. "You see anything, Diana?"

"No. You think he's under the Landmark Center?"

"That would be my guess."

"You need back up," Lee said.

"Getting Ms. Chandler out of here safely is more important right now. Go," he said to Grace. "I'll see you soon."

Her gaze was steady, as if she were memorizing his every feature. "You better not disappoint me, John Santana."

He smiled. "I won't."

Grace turned reluctantly away and followed Lee out into the tunnel and back toward the main entrance.

Santana watched them until they made a left turn into the Fourth Street tunnel and disappeared from sight. He checked the map on the wall, reconfirming his current position and then contacted Daren Ritchie.

"Daren. It's Detective Santana. I'm in the break room and about to head for the Landmark Center. I believe the suspect may be in the tunnel under the building."

"Roger that."

Apparently, Daren had been watching crime shows.

Santana smiled and put the phone in his jacket pocket. Then he stepped out of the light and into a shadow, moving in a northerly direction, away from Grace and Diana Lee, and toward a rendezvous with Karim Aziz.

Chapter 36

As Santana moved through light and darkness in the tunnel, he saw the image of Grace's bruised face in his mind's eye. That image melted away like a wax figure too close to a flame, and was replaced by the charred body of Hassan's daughter, Safia. Santana knew that his motives for insisting that Diana Lee take Grace to safety were anything but altruistic. No amount of rationalizing could disguise the darkness in his heart. He had his cell phone and could easily have called for back up. Instead, he had chosen to take Aziz alone, and he knew exactly why.

The break room was a short distance from the Landmark Center. Santana crept cautiously along the wall opposite the water pipe. He gripped the Glock in his right hand, waited in the long shadows between the lights and peered down the tunnel, hoping to catch a glimpse of Aziz before the terrorist spotted him.

There were footprints in the patches of dirt on the tunnel floor, but maintenance workers could have made those. Traffic sounds were louder now, and he could no longer hear the radio.

He was just about to step out of the shadow when he saw movement in the lights up ahead. He crouched low, leaned a shoulder against the cool tunnel wall and watched as Karim Aziz picked up something from atop the water line and then walked in the opposite direction heading north.

Santana waited until Aziz turned right into an intersecting tunnel and then he followed. As he hurried past the water pipe where Aziz had been standing, Santana saw two rectangular, gray bricks of C-4, each about twelve inches long, on the water pipe.

Santana stopped at the intersection five yards beyond the C-4 and looked slowly around the corner. He saw nothing at first. Then Aziz walked out of a shadow and into a beam of light about thirty yards ahead. A sign bolted to a cable pipe directly in front of Santana indicated that Aziz was on Fifth Street, heading east.

Santana followed at a distance, keeping pace with Aziz. He considered taking a shot, but the light was poor and the distance long. He needed to get closer.

When he passed Market Street, Santana realized that Aziz was planting the explosives somewhere other than the Landmark Center, which stood between Washington and Market.

The Federal Building. The president would be touring the Federal Building tomorrow.

A tenth of a mile separated most downtown blocks, though Washington and Market were closer. Santana calculated the distance he traveled by counting blocks or, in this case, tunnels. He crossed the intersecting tunnel at St. Peter Street and then Wabasha where the main water line was twice the diameter of any pipe he had previously seen. He followed Aziz past Cedar and Minnesota. The city map in his mind told him that he had traveled about four tenths of a mile.

Santana was halfway between blocks when he saw Aziz turn right at Robert. He picked up his pace until he arrived at the intersection. Then he carefully peered around the corner.

A water line ran along the center of the Robert Street tunnel. Twenty yards ahead and to his left Santana could see an opening in the tunnel wall. He made his way to it and listened. Hearing nothing, he extended his head and peered into the opening. It was a clean, steel pipe about four feet in diameter that would eventually attach to the water line in the Robert Street tunnel behind him.

Santana removed a flashlight from his jacket pocket, held it in his left hand, the Glock in his right, and ducked into the pipe.

He moved slowly along, bent over at the waist, his back occasionally brushing the top of the pipe. He could see nothing directly ahead of him, only a speck of light in the distance.

After a minute of walking, Santana squatted and wiped sweat away from his eyes with his jacket sleeve. He considered using the flashlight but decided against it. The light up ahead was growing brighter. He realized it was coming from outside rather than inside the pipe. He focused on it and started moving again. Soon, he could hear the rumble of a gas-powered generator.

He passed a connecting pipe on his left that was the same size as the pipe he was walking in, but it had a large water valve covering the opening. Just above him was a guillotine-like gate that slid down, stopping the flow of water through this section of pipe. There was a thick steel lever below the gate.

He crept forward until he had nearly reached the end of the pipe and sat on his heels in the shadows. Directly ahead Santana could see two fluorescent extension lights with hinged hooks hung along the underside of the building floor six feet overhead. Fifteen yards beyond his current position, a second section of open pipe ran along the ground and then turned upward at a ninety-degree angle and entered the bottom of the building. A similar pipe entered the building floor from the opposite side of the site.

He could see Karim Aziz in the soft glow of the lights attaching C-4 to concrete pillars and then stringing detonation lines from the plastic explosive. Santana was no demolition expert, but he figured there were enough explosives to bring down the whole building.

He moved deep inside the water pipe again and used his Nextel walkie-talkie. "Daren?"

"John, it's Diana."

"Where's Daren?"

"He's here. So is Grace. Where are you?"

"Underneath the Federal Courthouse. Aziz is planning to bring it down and not the Landmark Center."

"My god."

"Contact Gamboni," he said. "Let her know we're going to need ODU to disarm the C-4."

"Get out of there, John."

"We don't have much time. I've got to stop him."

Santana clicked off. He had taken two steps toward the construction site when the light up ahead suddenly went dark and then light again.

Aziz was returning for the remaining C-4. A flashlight beam hit Santana in the face and then quickly went out. He blinked, but all he could see were spots in front of his eyes.

Instinctively, he dove forward into a prone position and fired three quick shots. The sound of gunfire inside the steel pipe was deafening and left his ears ringing. Santana wasn't sure if he had hit Aziz so he lay flat in the pipe, listening and waiting for possible return fire.

He kept blinking until the spots in front of his eyes disappeared and he could see the opening up ahead again. Then he heard what sounded like a metal door slide shut and the light vanished, throwing the pipe into pitch darkness.

Suddenly there was a burst of white light and heat flashed outward. Santana cupped his hands over his ears and closed his eyes. A shock wave sucked the oxygen out of the air and slammed into his body. Pieces of sand blew through the air stinging his hands and face. He realized he could hear nothing now, and he wondered if the blast had blown out his eardrums.

He flicked on the flashlight and pointed the beam in the direction of the construction site. To his horror he saw a wall of water rushing toward him. He inhaled a deep breath of air just before the wave hit him.

Immediately, he felt as though he had been dragged to the bottom of the sea in a cold undertow. He quickly lost all sense of up and down as water carried him along like a bullet hurtling through the barrel of a gun. The Kevlar vest was as heavy as an anchor. Water pressure crushed his chest. His lungs burned. Air trickled out his mouth.

He knew he was drowning just as the dream had predicted.

He clamped his teeth and lips together tightly and fought a growing sense of panic. He saw no way out now, no way to survive unless he reached the end of the water pipe soon. For an instant, he thought how easy it would be to open his mouth and give up the fight.

"You're almost there, Juan."

He heard the voice clearly though it seemed to be inside his head rather than outside his body.

"Hold on."

The ghostly image of a woman materialized in the water above him. He recognized Natalia instantly, though she was no longer a child, but a beautiful, young woman. A tender smile graced her lips. She held out a hand. He felt it brush his shoulder.

Something he could only describe as total peace and tranquility enveloped him then. It was as if he were in his mother's womb, floating in amniotic fluid. Maybe this is what death is like, he thought. When the brain is screaming for oxygen, fighting for survival, just before the black minute.

As he reached out for his sister, Santana realized he still held the flashlight in his left hand. He looked at it, then up again and saw nothing but an arc of light from the beam. Then a rush of air hit him as he burst out of the pipe like a disgorged bone. He was momentarily airborne before he landed hard on his back.

Water poured over him and he rolled away from it and struggled to his feet. He wobbled and nearly collapsed in the pool swirling around his ankles. He staggered to the tunnel wall and leaned against it and gulped fresh air into his burning lungs.

It took a minute before his breathing returned to normal and he realized he was back in the Robert Street tunnel. He could hear a constant humming in his ears, as if they were filled with a nest of angry bees.

Water flowing out of the pipe to his right had become a trickle now. Santana wondered if someone had closed another gate or a shut off a valve. He wondered if his bullets had found their target and if Aziz had blown down the building. He wondered if the image he had seen in the pipe was real or if it was caused by a lack of oxygen in his brain. Regardless, he believed Natalia had saved his life.

His head felt as if it was being squeezed in a vice. Nausea roiled his stomach and the tunnel wall tilted abruptly. His legs felt as stable as two streams of water. Chills shook his body. He stripped off his jacket and Kevlar vest and sat down and waited until the nausea finally subsided. Then he searched his jacket pockets for his cell phone and his Glock, but they were gone. He considered looking for them in the water pipe but decided against it.

Ten yards to his left he saw a vertical shaft and ladder leading to the street. He hoped he could climb the ladder and have enough strength to lift the manhole cover if it wasn't sealed. He got his legs firmly under him, stood and leaned against the wall. He took a few more breaths to clear his head. His ears still buzzed but he could hear the sound of his breathing now. He took a few unsteady steps toward the ladder. Then he felt a shift in the air behind him.

Santana spun to his right and saw Karim Aziz lunging toward him, a long-handled pickaxe in his hands, his eyes filled with rage. Aziz let out a yell and swung the axe at Santana's head as though he were swinging a bat at a baseball.

Santana ducked underneath it and stumbled back. Aziz reversed his grip on the handle and grunted with effort as he adjusted his angle and swung the axe the other way. Santana knew he couldn't get underneath it this time and threw his right arm up to protect his head. The impact of the axe handle against the muscle of his forearm sent a current of pain rocketing up his arm and neck and into his brain. Then he lost all feeling and movement in the arm. Before Aziz could take another swing, Santana hooked him in the mouth hard with his left fist. The punch split Aziz's upper lip against his teeth. His eyeballs rolled up in his head and he stepped back and sank to his knees.

Then a second wave of nausea overwhelmed Santana. It was stronger than the first, brought on by the exertion of the fight. He wanted to take Aziz now, finish him, but he had no sense of balance, no strength. He staggered away and leaned against the tunnel wall for support.

Aziz shook off the punch and slowly rose to his feet, a glint of cruelty in his eyes. A maniacal grin sliced his face as he bent over, wrapped both hands around the handle, and lifted the pickaxe off the ground.

Santana quit thinking and instinctively reacted to the scene moving in slow motion now. He dropped to his right knee. Reached down with his left hand and pulled up his left pant's leg.

Ten feet away, Aziz started toward him.

Santana unlatched the leather strap on his ankle holster.

Aziz stumbled forward. He was within five feet.

Santana wrapped his left hand around the grip and yanked the Glock out of the holster.

Aziz lifted the axe into a striking position.

In that moment, Santana knew he was a second too slow. There wasn't enough time to aim and fire.

He wasn't going to make it.

Then a single shot exploded in the tunnel and a red spot appeared in the center of Aziz's chest. He stopped moving. The axe fell from his hand. He watched it hit the ground with a mixture of surprise and perplexity. The red spot on his chest quickly expanded like ripples in a pool of water.

A second shot rang out. It blew off a chunk of Aziz's face and knocked him off his feet.

Santana looked to his left. Saw Diana Lee halfway down the ladder hanging onto a rung with one hand, her Glock held steady in the other.

Chapter 37

DAY ELEVEN

A nurse at Regions Hospital kept Santana awake all night as a precaution because he had suffered a mild concussion. He had a deep bruise on his right forearm but no break. Fortunately, his hearing had suffered no permanent damage.

He spoke on the phone with Kacie Hawkins who had been released. A doctor came into his room early in the morning and declared Santana "a very lucky man" and fit enough to go home.

As the doctor left the room, Rita Gamboni walked in carrying a fresh change of his clothes.

"I just was thinking about how unpleasant it would be to wear dirty clothes," Santana said.

"You left a change of clothes in your locker."

"Thanks."

He pushed back the covers and sat up on the edge of the bed. The room spun momentarily and then stopped. He no longer heard buzzing in his ears, but his head still ached and his skin tingled, as though his nerve endings were vibrating from the explosion.

Gamboni tossed the clothes and a clean jacket on the bed. "We located your cell phone and gun in the water pipe. Did you get another Glock from the OIS team and another cell phone?"

"Yes. Thanks."

"How's your head?"

"Hard."

She crossed her arms, let out a frustrated sigh. "You should have it examined again while you're here. See if there's a brain in it."

"You're not happy with me?"

"You and Lee weren't supposed to leave the Landmark Center. Get dressed. I'm driving you home and you're staying there until you've fully recovered."

* * *

Gitana was eager to see him but more eager to be fed. Rita obliged and sent Santana to bed. He fell immediately into a deep, dreamless sleep.

When he awoke he saw Rita sitting on the corner of the bed. Gitana was seated on the floor next to her, watching him intently. The radio clock on his nightstand read 5:09 p.m. He had slept for eight hours.

"Hey," he said. His tongue felt dry and heavy, the sound of his voice strange.

Gitana stood on all fours and wagged her tail when he spoke.

"Sleep well?" Gamboni asked.

"Like the dead," he said, relieved that his head no longer ached.

"Are you hungry?"

"Starving."

"Steak and baked potatoes sound all right?"

"Wonderful."

"I can bring dinner up to you."

"No," he said, slowly sitting up. The room spun once in front of his eyes and then his vision cleared. "I need a shower."

"And clean sheets," she said.

"Good idea."

Rita held his arm as he stood. "Okay?"

His legs felt steady under him. "Okay."

He shampooed his hair twice and used a body scrub to cleanse his skin. Then he shaved and put on a pair of jeans, a black cotton sweater and a pair of deck shoes. When he came downstairs, he smelled logs burning in the fireplace.

"I made you some hot chocolate, John. Sit down and I'll serve you."

"No wine?"

"No alcohol for two days."

Santana pulled up a chair and sat.

Rita was dressed in white socks, blue jeans and a red turtleneck pullover. Her lipstick was fresh and her face pink from the heat in the kitchen.

"Diana Lee called. I let your voice mail answer."

Santana sipped hot chocolate and wondered why Rita was here. "I appreciate you helping me out."

"Dinner's almost ready. We can talk while we eat."

When they were dating, Santana always looked forward to eating whatever Rita prepared. She took pride in her culinary skills though her job left her little time to use them.

"I went back to headquarters after you fell asleep," she said. "We're working with the feds. Trying to convince the news media and citizens that terrorists haven't overrun the city."

"Having any luck?"

"Some."

Rita had grilled the tenderloin steaks medium rare, just the way Santana liked his. The dinner would have been perfect had he been able to drink some red wine.

"Were you able to talk with the Officer Involved Shooting team last night, John?"

"Briefly. I gave them a statement. They want a more detailed interview at headquarters once I'm back to work."

"Lee won't have any problem proving the shooting was justified."

Santana nodded. He hadn't realized how hungry he was. "So is the Federal Courthouse still standing?"

"It is."

"You can thank me now if you'd like, Rita."

She hid her smile by taking a drink of coffee.

"Why blow up the Federal Courthouse and not the Landmark Center? In either scenario, the president probably would've been killed."

"The city just renovated the courthouse. Aziz no doubt saw it as a symbol of the U.S. government." She sipped more coffee and held the cup in both hands before speaking again. "It appears that Aziz killed Farah Hassan and her daughter, Safia. Aziz was driving Hassan's car. He had a passport and driver's license with Hassan's name but his own photo. Rashid Hassan was probably killed when he arrived in Pakistan. Aziz then assumed his identity. The feds are investigating."

"What about David Chandler?"

"He's a U.S. Senator."

"So his part in this gets swept under the rug."

"Eat your food before it gets cold."

Santana ate some steak and potatoes. Drank some hot chocolate. Then he thought of something. "What about the general?"

"The feds are questioning him as we speak."

"And his son, Kou?"

"Despite the general's denials, the feds believe that he and his son were up to their eyeballs in the plot to overthrow the government in Laos. General Yang conspired with Karim Aziz to smuggle heroin into the country. The general used his son's connections with the Asian Crips to sell the heroin and split the profits with the ACs. He planned to use his share of the profits to buy weapons and recruit mercenaries. But everything went to hell when Pao killed the general's daughter. That's why I'm thinking Kou Yang killed Pao and his two cousins."

"I think the general told me the truth, Rita. I think he's had his fill of war."

"He's going to have to convince the feds of that, not us."

"And why would Pao Yang kill Mai? He loved her?"

"Maybe he didn't mean to, John. Maybe he gave her an overdose of GHB."

"The seat on the Mazda was way back when it was towed into the impound lot, Rita. Whoever drove the car last was much taller than Kou Yang."

"That's thin."

"I think it's important. So is the fact that Tanabe believes Pao Yang's killer was left-handed."

"Is the general left-handed?"

"Yes."

Gamboni shrugged. "So maybe he killed Pao Yang and Yang's two cousins. The general is certainly skilled enough. After the feds make their case against the general and his son in the Laotian plot, we'll pursue murder charges."

"It just doesn't wash with me, Rita."

"Look, John, I'll admit I was wrong about David Chandler. But unless you've got solid evidence to the contrary, we'll go to the grand jury with the evidence we've got when and if the time comes."

They finished dinner, cleared away the dishes and sat in living room, she on the leather couch and he on a leather chair opposite her. Birch logs crackled in the stone fireplace, and Gitana stretched out on the floor in front of it, soaking up the heat. It was only seven-thirty but darkness had fallen over the landscape.

Rita set her mug on the coffee table, leaned forward, but kept her eyes focused on his. "Seems you have a bullet hole in the sheetrock upstairs."

"Really?" he said, stalling for time.

"Looks like a rifle shot."

Santana knew damn well she wouldn't believe he had accidentally fired a rifle bullet into his wall. "You know how those deer hunters are, Rita."

"No," she said. "I don't. Maybe you can explain it to me."

"Sometimes hunters are real careless."

"Did you report the incident?"

"I considered it. But whoever fired the bullet doesn't know where it landed." He gave her an ingratiating grin, hoping it would cover the lie. But he could see the disappointment in her lowered eyelids and mouth and the way she cast her eyes down.

"Please don't take me for an idiot, John. You recently had the glass replaced in your slider."

"You were busy while I was asleep."

"I'm still a detective as well as your commander."

"Meaning?"

"I want the truth."

"The truth is, Rita, I don't know who fired the shot or why."

"I do," she said.

"You want to fill me in?"

She drank more coffee before she spoke again. "We found a Winchester Model 70 rifle with a scope in Hassan's car trunk. Aziz probably fired the bullet."

"That's probably true. I did see Aziz in Jenna Jones's apartment, Rita. I could identify him. Jenna Jones saw him, too. She was a loose end in the case. It would make sense if Aziz killed her and then tried to take me out as well."

"I'll discuss it with Pete Canfield."

Santana was reluctant to reveal that Tony Novak had taken impressions of the shoe prints Santana had found near the river. Gamboni would have Novak's hide. But if Novak could match the impressions with Aziz's shoes, it would provide more evidence that he was responsible for the attempt on Santana's life.

"I found some prints in the sand near the beach the morning after the shooting, Rita. I asked Novak to take some photos and impressions."

She rolled her eyes, "That's terrific. So my forensic specialist and one of my homicide detectives are collecting evidence in a murder attempt and not sharing the information with me."

"I figured Aziz might've taken the shot. But I wasn't certain."

"You thought it was the Colombians again."

"It was a likely possibility."

Rita shook her head in obvious frustration. "You ask me time and time again to show my trust in you, John. And I do. Yet you continue to demonstrate by your actions or, in this case, inaction, that you don't trust me."

"What do you want me to say, Rita?"

"How about admitting I'm right?"

"That's important to you?"

"I wouldn't be asking if it wasn't."

"I told you about the impression evidence."

"That's a start."

"And I'm trusting you'll go easy on Novak."

"How about trusting me as much as you trust Novak?" she said.

"Okay."

"Good."

The wind rattled a pane in a window. Santana could hear it whistling in the chimney. "Is there any evidence that Jared Chandler was involved? He runs the company that could supply tactical gear."

"He's being questioned," she said.

Santana thought about his next question before asking it. "Isn't Grace Chandler wondering why she was kidnapped?"

Gamboni's faced reddened and she gazed downward for a second. When she looked at Santana again she had a controlled smile on her face. "David Chandler discovered that Aziz was planning to assassinate the president. Aziz kidnapped his daughter to keep him quiet."

"Come on, Rita. You're not swallowing that bullshit story from the feds. We both know what Chandler told us. Lee knows it, too."

"You and I just discussed trust, John. I'm trusting that you'll keep your confidence about David Chandler's involvement."

"And Lee?"

"I've already spoken with her. I believe she understands that there's much more at stake here."

"Like what? The C.I.A.'s reputation? Chandler's? Or is everyone afraid to admit that government officials mistakenly let a terrorist into the country? A terrorist who nearly killed the president."

"I believe at some point, David Chandler will resign from his senate seat."

"So General Yang and his son are going to take the fall. And our government screws the Hmong again."

"Let it go, John. Take a few days. Make sure you're okay. Then come back to work. You want to partner with Diana Lee until Kacie Hawkins recovers, fine. You want to work alone, done."

"How come?"

"I owe you. If you hadn't kept after it, Aziz might've taken down the Federal Courthouse and killed the president. As it stands now, our department is looking good as far as the FBI and Homeland Security is concerned."

"And you're looking good, too."

She smiled. "Do you mean that literally or figuratively?"

"Both."

She studied the fire for a long while. "You were right about us, too."

He said nothing and let her continue.

"If we weren't working together, if I wasn't your superior." She shrugged.

"You want children, Rita."

"Things change."

"Yes, they do."

"Have they changed for you?"

Santana knew she wasn't talking about children. She was talking about his relationship with Grace Chandler. "Yes."

"Are you in love with her?"

"I don't think we've reached that point yet."

"Yet sounds to me like you think you could."

"I guess we'll see."

She gave a tight, little smile and stood up. "Grace Chandler is at Regions. You can call her there."

He walked Rita to the door and helped her on with her coat.

"You should've stayed in the hospital, too, John."

"I'll let you know if I have any problems." He opened the door.

"Make sure that you do. I'd like you to stay alive."

"Thanks, Rita. For everything."

* * *

After she left, Santana got an ice bag out of the freezer and placed it on his right forearm that was badly bruised and slightly swollen from the axe handle blow. The ice quickly numbed the throbbing pain. Then he phoned Grace.

"How are you feeling?"

"Better," she said in answer to his question. "I've been listening to the news, John. You could've been killed!"

Santana assured her that he only had a mild concussion. He purposely left out any mention of Rita Gamboni. "How did Aziz take you?"

"He hit me as I was getting out of my car in the parking lot on Harriet Island. When I woke up, I was in the tunnel."

"Did Aziz talk with you at all?"

"No. And I couldn't talk with him because he'd duct taped my mouth."

Santana saw no point in telling her what he knew about her father. Still, he was angry about the government's sanitized version of the truth. "The bruise will heal."

"I'm hoping they'll release me tomorrow."

"I'll pick you up."

"Is the case closed now?" she asked.

"Karim Aziz is dead."

"You do that a lot, you know."

"Do what?"

"Avoid answering the question that's asked."

"It's more habit than intention."

"I can work with that," she said.

Chapter 38

Early the next morning, Santana took Gitana for a run under a gray, misty sky. Wet leaves squished under his shoes and headlights shone like specters in the tar road. He ran farther and longer than usual, pushing his body hard, waiting for a negative reaction. A germ of doubt had burrowed its way into his mind, and it was difficult to shake the uneasy feeling that the explosion had done serious damage.

Gitana's tongue was lolling when they finally returned home. She drank a full bowl of water and then lay down on the kitchen floor with a heavy sigh and closed her eyes.

Santana pummeled the heavy and speed bags and lifted weights in his exercise room until his muscles burned. His forearm was still sore and he had some difficulty punching the bags with his right hand and gripping the heavy bar, but he wrapped his forearm with athletic tape and worked through the pain.

After a shower and shave, he made some *changua* soup out of eggs, potatoes, cilantro, and salt. It was a soup made by the Chibcha Indians in Colombia. His mother used to make it without potatoes. But when he wanted a heavier soup in the cold fall and winter in Minnesota, Santana preferred to add potatoes to the mix.

He read the morning paper as he ate breakfast. It was loaded with stories of Karim Aziz and his failed attempt to blow up the Federal Building and kill the president.

There was little concrete information about Aziz and no mention of any relationship between Aziz and David Chandler according to the journalistic spin provided to the media by the feds and the SPPD. Santana saw no mention of General Yang and his son, Kou, either. Maybe the feds were still putting their case together, no matter how weak Santana thought it might be.

He suspected Chandler and Aziz's paths had crossed in Iraq in the late eighties when Chandler worked for the CIA. Perhaps they had even worked together and with others in attempting to assassinate Saddam Hussein. Chandler had many contacts in and out of government. It wouldn't surprise Santana if Aziz had remained one of them. But he figured he would never know. And neither would anyone else outside the CIA and the highest levels of government.

Santana and Diana Lee's names appeared prominently in the articles along with a photo he thought didn't do him justice. He was surprised and pleased to read that Chief Ashford had recommended him and Lee for Medals of Valor.

When he finished reading the paper, he cleaned both his Glocks, loaded them and chambered a round. Then he completed his reports, updated his case files and checked in with Diana Lee. She was on administrative leave pending the OIS investigation. He had already thanked her once for saving his life, but he thanked her a second time.

"You would've done the same for me, John."

"Are you feeling okay about the shooting?"

"Yes," she said. "I'm okay."

"I know a good psychologist."

"Thanks, John. I'll see you soon."

Santana had just hung up when his cell phone rang. He didn't recognize the name or number but answered anyway. "Santana."

"Detective Santana. This is Patricia Lewis. I'm a forensic entomologist at the University of Minnesota. Reiko Tanabe asked me to give you a call. I have some information regarding the postmortem interval on the body you found on Harriet Island."

"Is it Doctor Lewis?"

"Please, call me Patricia."

"All right."

"As you may know, Detective, in order to calculate the postmortem interval I have to account for the differences in temperature between controlled studies that establish developmental times of different insect species and the fact that the temperature at the crime scene fluctuates."

"Yes. I'm aware of that."

"Well, blowflies quit flying below fifty-five degrees but the weather was unusually warm for a late September weekend. The mean temperature was sixty-two degrees. The maggots Reiko collected were nearing the end of their first instar, which generally requires about forty-four hours. When I calculated the ADH or accumulated degree hours and divided by the average temperature, I got PMI of midnight on Saturday, September 26th. I can't say that's the actual time of death, but it's the minimum period of time that could have elapsed between death and the collection of insects."

"I appreciate your time, Patricia."

"And I appreciate yours, Detective Santana. Thank you for stopping the terrorist."

"You're welcome." He was beginning to feel like a minor celebrity and it made him uncomfortable.

Later, he ate a lunch of black beans and rice. Then he called Grace again. "How's the cheek?"

"A specialist is coming in later today to have a look at it. It's very black and blue. But ice has reduced the swelling." She sounded less optimistic and upbeat than she had the day before.

"So you won't be released today?"

"Tomorrow. I miss you, John."

"Have you heard from your father?"

"He stopped by yesterday. Jared did, too." She sounded surprised. "The FBI was here as well, questioning me about the terrorist. I couldn't tell them much."

"Let me know if there's anything I can do, Grace."

"If you feel up to it, you could come by and see me."

"Okay."

"It's my brother's birthday tomorrow. We haven't been that close for quite a while. Maybe there's a chance to reestablish my relationship with Jared and my father. Some of Jared's friends from work have organized a party at his house. I'd like to go. You could come with me if you'd like."

Santana had no desire to see David Chandler again, but he didn't want to disappoint Grace. "Where does your brother live?"

"In Mounds Park."

A chill ran through Santana, as if he had just been given an IV of ice water. Mounds Park was where Kou Yang had driven after hearing the news that his sister, Mai, had been murdered. Yang claimed he had gone there to think. Santana had doubted that explanation. He wondered now if Yang had driven to Mounds Park to meet Jared Chandler. "Your brother lives in Mounds Park?"

"Yes. Not far from the overlook."

It could be just a coincidence, Santana thought. Then again, it could be much more.

"John? Are you still there?"

"Yes. But I need to make another call."

"Okay," she said.

He could hear the disappointment in her voice. "I'll come by and see you later."

"All right."

He broke the connection and poured a shot of *aguardiente*, ignoring the doctor's suggestion to wait two days before drinking any alcohol. He knocked it back and poured another. He took the full shot glass into the living room and sat on the couch. His notebook was on the coffee table. He opened it and read through his notes about Katherine Chandler's death. Then he drank the *aguardiente* and called Detective Matt Colburn in Arlington, Virginia.

"What can I do for you, Santana?"

"When we last spoke on the phone, you mentioned Jared Chandler was out with a friend the night his mother was murdered."

"That's right."

"How solid was his alibi?"

"Well, we questioned his friend. He backed up Chandler's story."

"You wouldn't happen to have the friend's name?"

"Give me a minute. The Chandler file is still on my desk from the other day."

Santana waited.

"All right. Let's see. Yeah, here it is. The kid's name was Mark Stiles."

Santana recognized the name but where had he heard it before? Then he remembered. Mark Stiles was Jared Chandler's secretary. "What time was the nine-one-one call?" Santana could hear Colburn shuffling through pages.

"Grace Chandler called at 12:23 a.m."

"Hey, thanks, Colburn. You've been a big help."

"Something breaks on this, you let me know."

"Definitely," Santana said. He closed his cell phone and glanced at the clock. 3:00 p.m. He had no headache. He really shouldn't leave the house until he was certain he was fully recovered. But shouldn't was a word he often ignored.

Chapter 39

Santana drove to the Tactical Systems plant and showed his badge to the security guard in the gate kiosk. The guard recognized him and waved him through.

Then he sat in the parking lot where he had a clear view of the front entrance and waited. At 4:47 p.m., Mark Stiles walked out of the main entrance. Santana got out of his SUV and met Stiles before he got to his car. "Mark Stiles."

"Yes?"

Santana showed him his badge wallet. "Detective Santana. St. Paul PD. I was here the other day."

Stiles's eyes narrowed. "Yeah. I remember. I already spoke to the feds. I don't know anything. I just work here."

"How 'bout I buy you a beer?"

"Now?"

"Now would be good."

Stiles studied Santana without speaking for a time. "I saw your picture on the news. You're one of the cops that killed that terrorist the other day."

"I am."

"How 'bout I buy you a beer, Detective?"

Santana followed Mark Stiles to a sports bar on Lexington Avenue. Santana ordered a Sam Adams, Stiles two bottles of Budweiser and a basket of popcorn.

The bar was filling rapidly with a young after-work crowd that talked loudly and laughed even louder. Televisions were turned to sports shows with talking heads reviewing replays of last weekend's college and pro games.

When the drinks and popcorn arrived, Stiles lifted a bottle in a toast. "Here's to the end of terrorism."

They drank.

"What do you want to talk to me about, Detective?" Stiles said cautiously.

"You're a friend of Jared Chandler."

"That's right."

"Known him a long time?"

"Since we were kids back in Arlington, Virginia."

"What was Jared like as a kid?"

"Smart."

"How smart?"

"Smarter than anyone I ever met."

Santana could hear both admiration and envy in Stiles's voice. "What do you and Jared do for kicks?"

"We like to play poker. Pick up women. Jared's a real chick magnet."

"Women like him."

"No. They love him. Especially the Asian women."

"Jared likes Asian women?"

"Well, he likes all women but Asians in particular. It's great being his wingman. 'Cept I always got to settle for second best."

"How does he treat them?"

"What do you mean?"

"I mean, does he ever hit them?"

Stiles thought about it. "I've only seen him do it twice. But I've never seen him really hurt a woman. They were just a light slaps, you know?"

"Uh-huh."

"I guess Jared has a temper. I think it motivates him in the mixed martial arts ring. You ever see him fight?"

"Briefly."

"Well, he's good."

"How often does Jared play poker?"

"Once or twice a week."

"Does he mostly win or lose?"

"Some of both."

"How's your poker game?"

"Not good. I don't play much anymore."

"Did Jared lose a lot of money recently?"

Stiles drank some beer. "Yeah. He lost a bundle."

"To whom?"

Stiles shook his head. His right eye blinked. "I don't know."

Santana wondered if the blink was a tell indicating he was lying. And if the gamblers he played poker with had picked up on it. "So if Jared needed money, where would he get it?"

"From his father's business, I suppose."

"Would his father know?"

"Jared pretty much runs the company now."

"Does Jared have a lot of close friends?"

"I'm his friend."

"Anyone else you know of?"

"Not really."

"He a good friend to you?"

Stiles held up his damaged hand. "He gave me a job even though I can use only one hand."

"Tell me something. Is Jared left-handed?"

"Yeah. And so am I . . . now."

"So, Jared's been a good friend to you through the years."

"Sure, he's been a friend."

Santana noted that Stiles had left out the word good when describing his friendship with Jared. Santana wondered if the real reason Jared Chandler gave Stiles a job was to keep him close and keep him quiet. "Was Chandler a good soldier?"

"If by good you mean someone who kills the enemy, then yeah."

"Killing ever bother you?"

"Sure," Stiles said.

"Killing ever bother Jared?"

Stiles turned his eyes to one of the TV monitors, ate some popcorn. "I don't believe it ever did."

"Was Jared a good shot?"

"Damn good."

"You served together in Afghanistan?"

His eyes came back to Santana's face again. "I did two tours. Well, I didn't quite finish my second tour." He held up his damaged right hand once more.

"Jared told me he did two tours."

Stiles gave a small laugh. "Jared likes to tell everyone that. Truth is, he barely made one."

"Why is that?"

"He's always had a problem with authority figures. I was surprised he ever enlisted."

"Why do think he decided to enlist?"

"Well, it was shortly after his mother died. His father encouraged him to. I believe he thought the Army would discipline Jared and maybe give him some structure. But it didn't work. Wasn't for his old man, Jared would've had a dishonorable discharge." The sarcasm in his voice was obvious.

"So, how did Jared's father get him out of the service?"

"He got him a medical discharge."

"Jared was wounded?"

"No."

"Do you know what the diagnosis was?"

Stiles's right eye blinked. He looked away and shook his head.

Santana sensed that Stiles's friendship with Jared Chandler was a house of cards. He thought if he pushed hard enough, it would collapse, and Stiles would tell him what he wanted to know.

Stiles finished off the first bottle, gave Santana a puzzled look. "What exactly is it you want to know about Jared, Detective Santana? Like I told the feds, if Jared was into something, I don't know anything about it."

"I understand he was with you the night his mother died."

The blood drained from Stiles's face. He sat motionless for a time, his left elbow on the table, the Budweiser held stiffly in his good hand. "How'd you know that?"

"I'm a cop."

"Yeah," he said, and drank from the bottle.

Santana took out his notebook, flipped it open and found the page he was searching for. "According to the police report, Grace Chandler called nine-one-one at 12:23 a.m. right after she found her mother's body. You claimed you were with Jared at the time."

"That's right." His gaze began moving around the room.

"I don't think you were."

His breathing appeared to stop as his eyes refocused on Santana. Then he gave a half-grin and exhaled a breath of air. "You don't?"

"No."

Stiles ate some popcorn. Glanced at a TV monitor. Drank more beer. "The Arlington police already cleared Jared. His mother committed suicide."

Santana took a chance. "I have evidence that says otherwise."

Stiles's eyes widened in shock and disbelief before he regained control. "Then give the evidence to the Arlington police."

"I will. But I thought I'd offer you a chance to come clean. Before you're charged with being an accessory in Katherine Chandler's murder."

Stiles started to rise, but Santana clamped a hand tightly over his forearm. "Leaving isn't a good idea."

Stiles hesitated. Then sat again and signaled the waitress. "You want another?"

"I'm fine."

He held up an index finger.

Santana drank some Sam Adams and mentally mapped out his next series of questions. "What time did you last see Jared the night his mother died?"

"That's a long time ago, man."

"You remember."

Stiles finished off his second bottle. Thought about it. "I last saw him at about eleven forty-five."

"And where were you when you last saw him?"

"At a bar."

"How long would it have taken Jared to drive home from the bar?"

"Maybe fifteen minutes."

"Why did you lie to the police, Mark?"

"'Cause Jared asked me to."

"And you've always done what he asked you to do. Like enlisting in the Army."

"Yeah," he said. "What a stupid fuckin' idea. Cost me two fingers and the use of my right hand."

Santana wondered if Jared Chandler had wished that his good friend Mark Stiles had lost more than the use of his right hand. He wondered if Chandler wished Stiles had lost his life. "Did Jared have difficulty with authority figures as a kid?"

"Well, he occasionally got kicked out of school for mouthing off to teachers and principals."

"How 'bout problems with the police?"

"Just once."

"What was that?"

"They accused him of burning down an abandoned warehouse. But they couldn't prove it. I think his mother intervened."

"How was Jared around animals?"

"What'd you mean?"

"I mean how did he treat them?"

Stiles stared at Santana. His eyes were watery and red. "He could be kinda cruel."

"Cruel like in killing them."

"Yeah. Like in killing them." Stiles picked at the label on the beer bottle as if it were a bandage covering an old wound. "You believe Jared actually killed his mother, don't you, Detective Santana?"

"Yes," Santana said. "And you do, too."

Stiles shook his head in resignation. "Yeah, I guess I do. I guess I always did."

"Any reason why Jared would want to kill his mother?"

"He hated her."

"Why?"

Stiles looked at Santana for a long time. "It's no excuse. But she was a real cold woman. Not like a mother."

"What about Jared's father?"

"His old man was gone most of the time. Jared was pretty much on his own."

"I could try and cut you a deal with the Arlington P.D. if you'd be willing to testify against him."

"And if I won't?"

"Jared's going down for his mother's murder," Santana said. "And probably for four others."

"Hey, man. I don't know anything about four other murders."

"Right now you could be charged as an accessory in his mother's murder."

Stiles kept his eyes on Santana as he continued picking at the label on the empty beer bottle. "You a religious man, Detective Santana?"

"Not really."

"Well, lying for Jared has bothered me for a long time. I took some risks during the war. Trying to make up for what I did . . . and didn't do." He lifted his deformed right hand off the table. "I think my wound is maybe God's punishment. Kind of a reminder of what I did wrong. But the past is the past. You can't change it."

"Maybe you can't change it," Santana said. "But now you have a chance to do what's right. Don't waste it."

* * *

"I've been reading about you in the paper, Detective Santana," Karen Wong said. "How are you feeling?"

"I'm fine."

"That's good to hear."

"Sorry to call you after hours," Santana said, "but I need some information for a case I'm working on."

"No problem. What would you like to know?"

"Suppose someone has difficulty with authority figures. Had problems with the law as a kid. Tells lies. Is promiscuous. Has a temper. Likes to gamble and fight."

"I'd say you're describing someone with symptoms of anti-social personality disorder."

"Like a sociopath?"

"Yes."

"Can you give me some background?"

"Well, the majority of convicted criminals have some form of APD. It's really an adult version of juvenile conduct disorder. People with APD generally have complete disregard for the rights of others and the rules of society. They lack remorse, shame, or guilt. They're narcissistic, charming, manipulative, superficial and often impulsive."

"What about friends?"

"Their friends are really just victims or unwitting accomplices. The same with their lovers."

"How do you treat APD?"

"There's really no effective treatment other than locking them up in a secure facility."

"What about a diagnosis?"

"You can't diagnose it before the age of fifteen although bedwetting, animal abuse, and pyromania are markers of the disorder. Also, there would have to be evidence of a conduct disorder. We don't know the number of children who exhibit these signs and grow up to develop APD, but these are often the traits of diagnosed adults."

"Does it run in families?"

"Some research suggests a connection between APD and maternal deprivation in the first five years of life. Mothers of children who developed the disorder usually didn't discipline their children and showed little affection toward them."

"Thanks, doctor," Santana said. "You've been most helpful."

Chapter 40

Santana called General Yang the following morning and told him he had evidence that might clear his son. The general was reluctant to let Santana see Kou at first, but Santana pressed him.

That same afternoon, Santana was seated in a wing chair in General Yang's study.

Clouds had darkened the sky and the room glowed with a dim light from a small desk lamp. The general stood in the shadows in a corner opposite the desk, his son sat on a chair opposite Santana.

Santana took out his notebook and pen and directed his first question at Kou Yang. "When you left the house after I told you your sister was dead, you were angry. You went to see Pao Yang because you thought he killed her."

"Yes," Kou said. "But Pao wouldn't see me."

"So you knew he was dating her."

"I did. But I didn't know Mai loved him until you showed me the photo of her he had in his wallet."

"What did you do when Pao refused to see you?"

"Jared Chandler called me. He'd heard about Mai's death and wanted to talk. We met at the overlook. He told me he believed Pao Yang murdered my sister."

"Why did Jared think that?"

"He'd taken Mai out a couple of times and said Pao was jealous."

Santana thought the opposite was true. Jared was jealous of Pao. "Jared only dated Mai twice?"

"As far as I know. After that, she had started seeing Pao."

"Tell me about your relationship with Pao Yang."

"I met him at the Myth."

"You're a college kid with a bright future. What made you decide to join the Crips?"

He lowered his head. "I wanted to get the Mono Boys who raped my sister. The Crips helped me find them. We messed them up pretty good."

Santana stopped writing in his notebook and looked at the general and then at Kou again. "What's the connection between you and Jared Chandler?"

Kou lifted his head. "My sister and I met Jared a year ago at the Myth."

"Did you introduce Jared to Pao Yang?"

"Yes. Jared told me he wanted to meet him."

"Do you know why?"

"No."

"Did Jared ever mention anything about heroin?"

Kou shook his head.

Santana figured that Jared knew about the heroin and had served as his father's contact with the Crips after Kou introduced him to Pao Yang. But Jared wanted it to pay off his gambling debts. "Why didn't you tell me any of this before?"

Kou hesitated and then looked at his father.

The general gave him a nearly imperceptible nod. "He was protecting me." General Yang moved across the room as though he were floating and lowered himself lightly into a wing chair. "My son assumed Pao Yang had killed Mai, and that I, in turn, had killed Pao Yang and his two cousins. I did not like Pao Yang, Detective Santana. I did not want him dating my daughter. But I did not kill him. And I did not kill Benny Vue or Kevin Xiong. My son believes that now."

Santana concentrated his attention on Kou. "Why didn't you tell me that you'd met Jared at the overlook?"

"Jared told me our fathers were planning a coup in Laos. He said if the police started investigating, then it might all come out. But my father told me today that he wasn't involved, that Jared was lying."

"Did Jared Chandler ever show you a butterfly knife and a Taurus 85 .38 Special double action revolver?"

"He showed me a butterfly knife and a gun, but I'm not sure of the make or model."

"It had a two-inch barrel, stainless finish, and rosewood grips."

"Yes. That's the gun."

"You touched them both?"

"I guess I must have because Jared framed me for the murders, didn't he?"

"I believe he did," Santana said. "He followed you after you left the overlook and stole your car when you stopped at Malina's for a drink. But I'm going to need your help to prove that he framed you."

"Anything my son agrees to must be cleared with his attorney," the general said.

"Fine," Santana said. "I'll explain what I want him to do and then you can contact your son's attorney."

* * *

Santana drove to Grace Chandler's houseboat and took the photo of Jared from the frame. Then he called Brittany Hayden, the young woman he had met at the Myth nightclub, the woman who reminded him of his mother and sister. She had to work later that evening but agreed to look at the photo.

The drive from Harriet Island to Brittany Hayden's townhouse took twenty minutes.

Santana could feel the adrenaline pumping through his veins now. But he felt no joy, no victory in knowing that Grace's brother was a sociopath and murderer. It was all about justice.

"Sorry for the last minute call," Santana said, as Brittany Hayden opened the front door. She was dressed in black pants and a plain, white, long-sleeve blouse that Santana figured she wore for work.

"No problem. I've got some time before I leave."

She led him into the living room where he sat down on the couch. She sat in a rocking chair across from him. The townhouse was furnished simply but tastefully like an IKEA showroom. "You said on the phone that you wanted me to look at a photo, Detective Santana."

He removed the photo of Jared Chandler from his briefcase and handed it to her. "Is this the man you saw with Mai Yang the night she was murdered?"

Brittany peered intently at the photo. "It's hard to say for sure. But he looks like the man I saw that night. In fact," she said, gazing at Santana, "he looks exactly like a guy who fights at the mixed martial arts matches at the club."

"Would you be willing to identify him in court?"

"Did he murder Mai Yang?"

"I believe he did."

She looked at the photo again and then at Santana. "Yes. I would identify him in court."

Chapter 41

Jared Chandler's small Victorian house was located on a dead end street near the Native American burial mounds, about a quarter mile from the overlook. From the front yard, Santana could see an empty lot across the street and the Beacon Tower near the burial mounds. To the west he could see Holman Field and its three runways nestled in the valley between the Mississippi River and Dayton's Bluff.

After meeting with Brittany Hayden, Santana had picked up Grace at Regions Hospital and had driven her to her houseboat on the Mississippi River where she had showered and changed into a pair of jeans, a bright-blue cotton turtleneck and suede jacket. Her damp hair hung loose over her ears and rested on her shoulders. She wore no makeup or lipstick but she didn't need any. She looked beautiful and natural and vulnerable.

Santana could tell by her reticence and cool attitude that she was upset because he hadn't stopped by the hospital the previous day as he had promised. But Santana was more concerned that her brother was the primary suspect in five murders.

A thin layer of clouds veiled the late afternoon sun that was sinking toward the western horizon as Santana followed Grace along the sidewalk and through a cyclone-fenced gate behind Jared's house. Two-dozen people were gathered in the backyard where scattered leaves had fallen on the grass like dead dreams. Smoke rising from hamburgers sizzling on a gas grill carried a scent that reminded Santana of the pit behind Rashid Hassan's house.

David Chandler stood near the grill next to his wife and son, Jared. He wore a chef's hat and an apron that read: NUMBER ONE COOK. He smiled and waved a spatula in greeting.

Jared Chandler wore a navy-blue sweater, tan khakis, and Dockers that matched his pants. A muscled Rottweiler sat beside him. The dog had a black coat with tan markings on his muzzle, cheeks, chest, and legs.

Santana hadn't seen the Rottweiler before and yet he remembered him. It was the dog in the dream he'd had four days ago, the dog that was dragging him by his leg off a large rock. He wondered now if the rock in his dream was the limestone one he had stood on when he sidestepped down the steep incline below the overlook in Indian Mounds Park.

"Good to see you two," David Chandler said, shaking Santana's hand. He leaned over and kissed Grace on the cheek. "I'm glad you both could make it."

Santana saw no guilt or embarrassment in David Chandler's eyes or expression, nothing that would indicate he had been involved with mercenaries and with Karim Aziz and that Santana knew it. Maybe, Santana thought, Chandler had shaded the truth so often in his life that he no longer recognized what was real and what was imagined. But Santana could no more ignore the truth than he could a stone in his shoe.

"Happy Birthday, Jared," Grace said, handing him a card she had taken out of her purse. Her tone of voice suggested she meant it.

Jared glanced at the envelope but didn't open it. "Thank you, Grace. It was nice of you to come."

David Chandler's gaze lingered on Santana. "I want to express my appreciation once again for saving my daughter's life. We owe you a great deal."

Santana figured the compliment would be the last one he would receive from the Chandler family.

"Could I get you two something to drink?" Jared said. "I have wine, beer and something stronger if you'd like."

"Beer is fine," Santana said.

"Make that two," Grace said.

Card table chairs were set up around a long rectangular table covered with a checkerboard tablecloth. On top the table were plastic squeeze bottles of mustard and ketchup, paper plates and plastic silverware, bowls of chips and potato salad, two cookie sheets filled with hamburger patties, a half dozen bottles of red and white wine, a large birthday cake and basket filled with cards. Underneath the table were three coolers filled with ice and cans of beer.

Jared took two cans of Michelob Golden Draft from a cooler, popped the tabs and handed a cold can to his sister and one to Santana.

"Drink up," he said.

Because Santana cared about Grace, he did his best to mask his feelings of contempt for both David and Jared Chandler. He wanted both men to go down for their crimes. But the feds were protecting David Chandler, and Santana knew that before he could arrest Jared Chandler he needed evidence of Jared's guilt beyond Mark Stiles's testimony. Santana saw no sign of Stiles among those gathered in the yard, and he wondered if Stiles had decided to skip the party.

Santana drank his beer while Grace made small talk with her family. When Jared turned his attention to some new arrivals, Santana excused himself and went into the house on the pretext of using the bathroom.

He took a moment to get his bearings before he walked through the kitchen that opened into a dining room. To his right he saw the living room and a stairway. He paused and listened for any sounds coming from inside the house. Then he took the stairs up to the second floor.

The first door on his left opened into a bedroom that was empty save for a half dozen unopened boxes stacked in a corner.

Santana headed down the hallway and found the bathroom. A bath towel and hand towel were neatly folded over separate towel racks. The shower and tub were shiny and smelled liked pine. Inside the medicine cabinet over the sink he found a throwaway razor, shaving cream, toothpaste, and a toothbrush.

Jared Chandler's bedroom was directly across the hall. Santana doubted he could convince a judge to issue a search warrant for Chandler's house. And any evidence he found would be poisoned fruit and inadmissible in court. But he needed something that would confirm his suspicions that he was on the right track. He figured he had no more than ten minutes before Grace or Jared would come looking for him. He weighed the risks of getting caught. Then he slipped on a pair of latex gloves, walked into Jared's bedroom and closed the door behind him.

The bedroom was sparsely furnished with a double bed and large, mahogany dresser. A rectangular mirror hung on the wall above the dresser. Mixed martial arts posters covered the remaining open wall spaces. He went quickly through the nightstand and the dresser and found nothing but shirts, socks, and underwear. Everything was neatly folded and arranged, as if Chandler was still in the service.

On the floor of a walk-in closet, Santana found a padlocked military trunk. He took a leather pouch from a jacket pocket and a pair of padlock shims out of the leather pouch. He pressed his thumb against the pivot side of the lock shackle to increase the clearance between the shackle diameter and the hole. He inserted a shim into the clearance on the outside of the shackle and pushed it down as far as it would go. Then he rotated the shim until the wings were pointing outwards away from the lock. He did the same with the other shackle until the lock sprung. He pulled open the lock, removed it from the hasp and opened the trunk.

There were two small trays inside the trunk containing four six-by-nine manila cushioned mailers. The mailers were filled with photos of Jared Chandler and his Army buddies. Some were taken on Army bases; others, Santana guessed, were taken in Afghanistan. Santana quickly leafed through the photos but stopped when he came across one that showed Jared Chandler manipulating a butterfly knife. He put the photos back in the mailers and lifted the trays out of the trunk. Underneath a neatly folded dress uniform, Santana found a half dozen women's watches. One was a gold Rolex. For Katherine was inscribed on the back.

* * *

While Grace made two cups of hot chocolate with whipped cream, Santana laid a fire and immediately felt the flames cutting the chill in the air. Then he sat on the couch and considered how he was going to tell Grace that he believed her brother was responsible for five murders, including her mother's. The more Santana played out the scenario in his mind, the less confident he felt. Not in Jared's guilt, but in Grace's acceptance of it.

She brought the cups of hot chocolate into the living room and sat next to him on the couch.

"Does your cheek still hurt?" Santana asked.

The bruising appeared more yellow than purple now, but there was less swelling.

"A little."

She held the coffee mug in one hand and his hand in the other. "Are you all right, John? You've been a little distant all afternoon."

"I'm fine."

She squeezed his hand and smiled. "Thanks for coming with me to Jared's birthday party. My father wants all of us to spend some time together. He even asked if I'd go flying with him."

Santana knew that what he was about to tell Grace about her brother would hurt her even though she and Jared hadn't been close in recent years. He saw no reason to compound the hurt by telling Grace about her father's involvement in the scheme to overthrow the Laotian government and his connection with the terrorist, Karim Aziz. Yet, Santana saw the secret as a virus that would infect their relationship and eventually cause the death of it if she ever discovered that he had withheld the truth from her. He imagined that David Chandler's relationship with his daughter would suffer the same fate if Grace ever found out that her father had lied to her.

"I don't know if our family can repair our damaged relationships," she said, "but I think the party was a start."

Telling Grace now that he believed her brother was guilty of first-degree murder was like kicking a helpless animal. Santana considered not saying anything. And then in his mind's eye he saw Mai Yang lying in the weeds on Harriet Island as maggots chewed off her face. He saw Pao Yang with his throat slit and Benny Vue and Kevin Xiong with their brains cored out by .38 slugs. He saw Kacie Hawkins lying in a hospital bed, her face twisted with pain from the wound in her shoulder. "Did you know your brother got a medical discharge from the Army?" he asked.

The smile died on her face. "Who told you that?"

"Mark Stiles."

"Mark?"

"Yes. He works for your brother. Do you know him?"

"I remember his family and ours were neighbors in Arlington." She let go of Santana's hand. Sat up straighter on the couch. "Why the sudden interest in my brother and his friend, John?"

Santana could hear the concern in her voice. He drank some hot chocolate and set the mug on the ship's wheel coffee table. "Your mother always kept a gun in her nightstand and the patio doors locked. But on the night she killed herself the patio doors were unlocked. That doesn't fit her pattern."

Grace studied him for a long while before speaking. "Did Detective Colburn tell you this?"

"Yes."

"But why? My mother's been dead for ten years."

Santana ignored her question. "I think someone used a key to open the patio doors and murder your mother. He just forgot to lock them on his way out."

"He?"

There was no going back now. He couldn't change who he was and always would be. A cop. "The military wasn't the only reason that you and your brother grew apart, was it, Grace?"

She paled, set her coffee cup on the table. "Please, John. Don't do this."

Santana knew he couldn't let it go even if it meant letting Grace go. "There is a Colombian saying. *Entre cielo y tierra no hay nada oculto.* Between heaven and earth there is nothing you can hide."

"Are you suggesting that my brother had something to do with my mother's death? Because he wasn't even home the night she died."

"But you were. And Jared knew you and your mother didn't get along. He knew that you'd be a likely suspect."

"What makes you think Jared could do something like that?"

Santana heard no anger in her voice now, only apprehension. "A lot of things. But mostly because I found your mother's watch in Jared's house."

The light in her eyes faded. Her mouth moved, but no words, no sound came out. Finally she said, "You went to the party with me this afternoon looking for evidence so you could charge Jared with my mother's murder."

It was an accusation he could not deny. "Not just your mother's murder, Grace. I believe your brother killed Mai Yang and at least three other people."

"I don't want to hear anymore." Her voice was devoid of any emotion, as though she were in a trance.

"Jared met Mai Yang at the Myth nightclub. He dated her a couple of times, but she was in love with Pao Yang. Jared didn't like rejection. He drugged her and then raped her. Mai died from a drug overdose. The ME collected tissue samples. I'm going to ask your brother to submit to a DNA test. Whether Jared intended to kill her is beside the point. To cover up her murder, he killed a gang member named Pao Yang and Yang's two cousins. Then he framed Kou Yang, Mai's brother, for the murders."

Grace said nothing. She just stared at him as though she didn't recognize the person in front of her.

"Your brother is a sociopath, Grace. You've suspected it ever since he killed your cat. Your mother's death confirmed it. I think your father knew it, too. He persuaded Jared to enlist in the Army, hoping it would help. But Jared had problems in the Army as well. So your father got him a medical discharge and let him run his company."

She gave a little shake of her head and sat silent for a time, her pale-blue eyes glistening in the soft light.

"You need to go now, John." Her eyes held no hope, only regret.

Santana searched his mind for something he could say, something that would close the distance between them. But he knew there was nothing he could say or do now. Grace would have to decide if their relationship was worth saving.

Chapter 42

We need a warrant for Jared Chandler's house," Pete Canfield, the Ramsey County attorney said. "But right now, all we have is circumstantial evidence of his involvement in Mai Yang's murder." He looked at Santana and then at Rita Gamboni.

The Saturday morning meeting was in Gamboni's office. Santana had spent the last thirty minutes convincing Gamboni and Canfield that Jared Chandler had murdered Mai Yang, Pao Yang and his two cousins and Katherine Chandler. He left out any mention of breaking into Jared Chandler's military trunk.

"Chandler may have murdered his mother," Canfield said. "But proving it will be up to the Virginia authorities. At least they have no statute of limitations for murder."

"We're getting ahead of ourselves," Gamboni said. "We have no probable cause to arrest Jared Chandler."

"And I can't file murder charges with what I've got," Canfield said. "We need to match his DNA with the tissue sample Tanabe found on Mai Yang's body. But under Minnesota law, he's under no obligation to provide a DNA sample unless he's convicted."

"We could tail Jared Chandler," Gamboni said. "Maybe collect a beverage cup he uses from a fast food restaurant. Something we could swab for a DNA sample."

"That could take time," Santana said. "What if we got Chandler to admit he killed Mai Yang?"

Gamboni turned her eyes on him. "How do you propose to do that?"

"We set up a meeting with Chandler and Kou Yang. Get Yang to wire up."

"That might work," Canfield said. "If Yang could help us prove Jared Chandler murdered Mai Yang, we'd obviously agree to drop the charges against him. But I'd have to clear it with Kou Yang's attorney."

"I already did," Santana said. "And Yang will do it."

Gamboni looked at him steadily. "Why would Jared Chandler admit to killing Kou Yang's sister?"

"Ego. Chandler's a sociopath, Rita. He knows Kou Yang can't do anything about it even if he confesses."

"It's risky."

"If we don't get anything on tape, we can go with plan B. Tail him and see if we can get a DNA sample off a cup or something else he uses."

Rita considered it. "Where do you suggest we set up the meet?"

"At the overlook in Indian Mounds Park. They've met there before. We have Kou Yang talk with Chandler inside the car where it's quiet."

"If Chandler makes us," Gamboni said, "things could get hot."

"We bring in a few female undercover officers. We pair them with men so we have a few couples sitting in cars. It'll look more natural."

"We should have undercover officers sitting on the benches or walking along the sidewalk," Gamboni said. "I want good disguises. And everyone wears body armor."

"We use a minidisk recorder with an external microphone," Santana said. "That'll give us seventy-five minutes, which should be plenty of time."

Canfield said, "Kou Yang needs to get Jared Chandler to admit he killed Mai Yang. Otherwise, he walks."

* * *

Santana made sure the minidisk recorder had fresh batteries. He ran the microphone wire under Kou Yang's shirt and positioned it as high as possible for maximum pickup of speech. He did a test recording so Yang would be familiar with the controls and location of the recorder and microphone. Santana played it back and checked the sound. He had Yang record his name, the date and time, where he was and whom he was about to meet. Then he had Yang put the recorder in his pocket.

Rita Gamboni, General Yang, and Alvarado Vega, Kou Yang's attorney, were with Santana in Vega's expensively furnished downtown law office. With his glasses, thick dark hair and mustache, and penchant for publicity, Vega reminded Santana of Geraldo Rivera. Vega made an excellent living defending wealthy clients accused of murder. But he also took cases *pro bono* if he thought an injustice had been committed and the accused couldn't afford his services. Vega was the last guy Santana wanted to see in a courtroom defending a scumbag accused of murder, and the first guy he would call if he were in trouble.

"Make sure the car radio is off," Santana said to Kou Yang. "Speak clearly. But don't talk any louder than normal. The microphone will be able to pick up your conversation. Repeat any important facts if you can. Once the meeting is over, I'll have you record a postscript with the time you turn off the machine. I'll open the record-protect window slide and listen to the tape to confirm that it was recorded properly."

Santana could see nervous sweat forming on Kou Yang's brow, but he also saw determination in the kid's eyes. Yang wanted Chandler to go down for his sister's murder and he was willing to do anything to make it happen. Santana understood the motivational power of revenge. But he also understood that it could lead to risky behavior and stupid mistakes.

Santana handed Kou Yang a small cigarette lighter. "Put this in your other pocket. It's a listening device. I'll have a receiver in my SUV. We'll be able to hear everything that's being said. Stick to the script we rehearsed. Don't get cute. Chandler's smart. If he's unwilling to admit anything, you just back off. We'll go after him another way at another time. You understand?"

Yang nodded.

Santana liked the audio bugs' portability. If Jared Chandler wanted to talk with Kou Yang in his car or take a walk, Santana could still hear their conversation, although it might not be as clear outside as inside the car.

"You sure you're okay with this?" Vega asked.

"I'm fine. But this vest is heavy."

"It's for your own protection," Santana said. "Just keep your jacket zipped."

Kou Yang's eyes flicked sideways toward his father who was standing like a statue against the wall.

Santana saw something pass between them.

Kou Yang stood up. "I'm ready."

Santana checked his watch. "We have thirty minutes to get to the over-look lot. You drive your father's car. Commander Gamboni and I will follow. Other police officers are already in position."

General Yang said something to his son in Hmong and walked out the door.

They were the only words he had spoken.

Chapter 43

A web of low, gray clouds hung in the sky. Dry, dead leaves blowing across the overlook parking lot sounded like fingernails clawing at coffin lids. A light wind blowing out of the north had lowered the late afternoon temperature to fifty degrees. Thanks to the unseasonable chilly temperature, eight of the twelve people in cars or on park benches were police officers in disguise rather than civilians.

Santana sat in driver's seat of his SUV, Rita Gamboni in the passenger seat. He wore a sweatshirt and jean jacket over his Kevlar and a Minnesota Twins baseball cap on his head. Gamboni wore a sweater and black windbreaker over her vest. A small receiver rested on the console between them.

The driver's-side window was a quarter of the way open and Santana closed it now and drank from a cup of hot chocolate.

Gamboni checked her watch. "Chandler should be here any minute."

They were parked four spaces to the left of Kou Yang, who was sitting in the driver's seat of his father's black Cadillac Escalade.

"Kind of like old times, huh, John?" Gamboni said.

He gave her a sidelong glance. "We spent some days like this."

"And nights," she said.

"You ever wish you were out of the office and back on the street?"

"Sometimes."

275

"But you're happy being commander of the Homicide Unit."

"Happy isn't how I'd describe it. More like satisfied."

"You worked hard to put yourself in the position, Rita. You deserve it."

"Thanks," she said.

He could see in her eyes that she was about to ask him a question. He knew what it was. "I'm not complimenting you because we were partners or lovers," he said. "You know what you're doing and deserve to be in command."

"You think the other detectives would say the same about me?"

"Yes, Rita. I believe they would."

"You ever see yourself in this position, John?"

Santana thought about the compromises Rita had to make, compromises that anyone in her position would have to make to satisfy the powers that ran the bureaucracies and the world. "No, Rita," he said. "Running the department is not what I want or what I do best."

They waited quietly for a time until Gamboni said, "Did you say anything to Grace Chandler?"

"Yes."

"That could compromise the whole situation, John."

"She needed to know."

"But if she warned her brother that he's a murder suspect."

"She didn't."

"You'd better hope you're right for Kou Yang's sake."

And for my own, Santana thought.

At 6:22, Jared Chandler's black Hummer entered the overlook lot and parked midway between Santana's SUV and Yang's Escalade.

Kou Yang rolled down his window and motioned to Chandler. "Let's sit in my car."

Santana could clearly hear Kou Yang's voice over the receiver.

Chandler got out of the Hummer and into the passenger seat of the Cadillac. "What was so urgent we needed to meet? I'm a busy guy." His irritation was clearly evident in his voice.

"They're going to charge me with four murders, Jared."

"Hey, I can appreciate your concern. But what can I do about it?"

"I told the cops I stopped here after I heard about my sister's death. I didn't tell them I met with you."

"There's no crime in that."

"I think you framed me for Pao Yang's murder and for the murders of his two cousins."

"Hey," Chandler said with a small laugh. "You need to get a grip. I'm real sorry about your sister. But I had nothing to do with it."

"You were jealous because Mai was in love with Pao Yang and had quit going out with you. You saw her at the Myth, put GHB in her drink and then took her to Harriet Island where you raped her."

Silence.

Gamboni looked at Santana. He held up his index finger indicating that he wanted to wait. Yang was doing a good job.

"What gave you the idea that she took GHB?" Chandler asked.

"The autopsy report. The cops told me Mai died from an overdose of GHB. And she would never willingly take any drug, Jared. I knew my sister."

More silence.

Finally Chandler spoke again. "Pao Yang was her boyfriend. He probably gave it to her."

"Pao loved her. And she loved him."

"You're way off base."

"I don't think so. But you can tell your story to the cops. I'm going to tell mine."

"Wait a minute."

Santana heard a rustle of clothing, like maybe Chandler had grabbed Kou by his coat. This was the critical point in a conversation that had gone pretty much as Santana expected it would. Chandler was either going to confess, walk away or do something real stupid.

Santana pulled his Glock from its holster. Gamboni pulled hers.

"Look," Chandler said. "I'm a business man. I've already got a shit load of problems to deal with. I don't need any more. What do you want?"

"For what?"

"For keeping my name out of this."

"I don't want anything except the truth. Did you kill my sister?"

"Why would I confess to something I didn't do?"

"The police found DNA on Mai's body, Jared. When I tell them I think you're responsible for her murder, they'll want a DNA sample from you. I think it'll be a match. What do you think?"

Santana was hoping that Chandler didn't know Minnesota law and was unaware he couldn't be forced to provide a sample.

"I think you should keep your mouth shut," Chandler said.

"Put the knife away, Jared."

"We should take him," Gamboni said.

"Chandler hasn't confessed to anything," Santana said. "Listen."

"You can't go to the cops," Chandler said.

"You killed Mai. Didn't you?"

"It was an accident."

"No matter. You killed her."

"She was a hooker."

"You killed Pao Yang and his cousins, too."

"Three useless gangbangers. The cops should give me a medal."

"You framed me, Jared!"

"Let's go," Santana said.

He and Gamboni were out of the SUV and moving toward the Escalade in a heartbeat. As they ran toward it Santana yelled, "DROP THE KNIFE, CHANDLER, AND STEP OUT OF THE CAR WITH YOUR HANDS UP!"

Gamboni pointed toward the Escalade. "John! Look!"

Santana saw a shadow rise up from the backseat. It was General Yang.

There was a crack of gunfire. Jared Chandler's head jerked and a rose of blood blossomed on the windshield.

Epilogue

The moon was full and the stars were out in force as Santana jogged on the road that ran parallel to the St. Croix River. He wore a stocking cap, leather gloves, and a lightweight ski jacket over his running suit. His cheeks were glazed with sweat and he could see his breath frosting the air. His compact Glock was tucked firmly in a kidney holster. Gitana loped easily along beside him.

Houses and spruce trees were strung with Christmas lights. Yards were lit with nativity scenes, snowmen, sleighs, and reindeer. One house in the neighborhood pumped Christmas music through outdoor speakers. Families and friends would soon be gathering to celebrate the holiday.

As Santana listened to the rhythmic thumping of his running shoes against the hard-packed snow, he remembered the late October day when he and Diana Lee were given Medals of Valor at a ceremony hosted by the mayor, city council members, and the police chief, Carl Ashford. A large crowd of local and national radio, television and newspaper reporters, as well as politicians and citizens had assembled at city hall, anxious to honor the two detectives who had prevented a terrorist attack from wrecking havoc on the city and the country.

The chief, a large African American man and ex-Minnesota Gopher football player, stood on a stage behind a podium that was awash in light. "The medals," Ashford said, "recognized personal bravery in the face of imminently dangerous or life-threatening situations."

Standing on the stage, awaiting the presentation of his award, Santana felt as uncomfortable with the accolades and attention as Diana Lee looked. Their eyes met and she gave him a tentative smile. Her parents had flown in from California, and Santana had met them before the ceremony. She had been cleared of any wrongdoing in the shooting death of Karim Aziz.

Santana tuned out the chief's speech and instead focused his thoughts on the limestone relief near the Kellogg Street entrance to city hall in which a goddess held a staff with two entwined serpents. The serpents represented civic government. In her other hand she held balanced scales inscribed with the words law and order. The symbolism reminded him of the challenges the country faced in maintaining a balance between law and order, between dictatorship and anarchy, between fear and freedom.

As he surveyed the crowd sitting in rows of folding chairs, Santana wondered how governments and laws and cops could stop men like Karim Aziz, terrorists bent on self-destruction, who willingly sacrificed their own lives in the reckless pursuit of some twisted vision of a world run by ideology and hate. And how could he stop men like David Chandler? Men who believed that soldiers and not policeman were the solution to the conflicts plaguing the world. And what about men like General Yang? Men, Santana thought, who killed for revenge or for justice, men who operated under their own moral code, men like himself?

The general had been arrested and booked for killing Jared Chandler. He made bail and was later arraigned on first-degree murder charges. His attorney, Alvarado Vega, argued that General Yang had killed Jared Chandler only after Chandler admitted he had murdered the general's daughter. Vega planned to use the heat of passion defense during the upcoming trial, but negotiations to plea-bargain the first-degree murder charge down to voluntary manslaughter were ongoing. If General Yang were found guilty of voluntary manslaughter, the judge would likely sentence him to ten years in prison. With good behavior, he could be out in seven. Apparently satisfied with General Yang's sentence and unable to find solid evidence connecting him with the plot to overthrow the Laotian government, the feds never filed charges.

Pete Canfield, the Ramsey County Attorney, dropped all murder charges against the general's son, Kou. Jared Chandler was cited for having committed the murders of Mai Yang, Pao Yang, Benny Vue, and Kevin Xiong. Santana had called Arlington Detective Matt Colburn and given him his theory on Katherine Chandler's death and Jared's involvement in it. But Santana knew that Jared Chandler had committed other murders, that there were more innocent victims buried along the psychopathic trail of Chandler's short but deadly life. Hopefully the watches found in Chandler's military trunk would lead investigators to other victims.

David Chandler announced that he would soon be leaving the Senate, citing the trauma of his son's death and the need to spend more time with his daughter.

Santana saw Kacie Hawkins sitting in the second row. She had recovered from her wound and would soon return to work as his partner. His gaze shifted to the back of the room where he hoped he might see Grace Chandler seated in one of the aisles. He had gone to her houseboat on the afternoon of her brother's death to deliver the news and had stayed with her until her father arrived. David Chandler had already been to the morgue where he had confirmed the identity of the body. Grace soldiered through her brother's funeral, as if Jared was a stranger she had barely known. And perhaps, Santana thought, he was. But how well could you know anyone? How much could you trust anyone?

After the awards presentation concluded, Santana and Lee answered questions from the press and posed for photographs. Santana looked one last time for Grace, thinking that she might be waiting for him in the corridor outside the ceremony room, but all he saw were the faces of strangers.

She had said she needed some time to put the past behind her. But time had never healed the wounds that had fractured Santana's soul and broken his heart. The Cali cartel would not let him forget his past. He would always have a target on his back, and so would anyone close to him.

He could smell wood smoke as he ran now, see snow crystals blowing off the top of a high drift lining the road. The blowing snow stung his skin and teared his eyes. The numbing cold and snow had arrived well before Christmas. He knew it would be a long, hard winter.

THE END

ACKNOWLEDGMENTS

This book could not have been written without the help and kindness of many people who gave me the benefit of their knowledge and experience. I am grateful to Sgt. Kevin Navara of the Metro Gang Strike Force and to Sgt. Rich Straka of the SPPD for the information on Hmong gangs. I would like to thank Sgt. Dan Malmgren of the SPPD for the OIS seminar and for the information on SPPD range qualifying. Thanks to Sgt. Phil Chelstrom of the Ramsey County Sheriff's Department and Officer Bill Krause of the SPPD for the great contacts, and to Officer Layne Lodmill of the SPPD for the wonderful tour of the Law Enforcement Center and for answering my questions regarding forensics.

The following individuals also provided valuable information and contributed to the writing of this novel. Many thanks to Paul Xiongpachay and Gao Nou Xiong for their suggestions and insights on Hmong culture; to John Johnston for the detailed information on duct tape; to Dick Streeper for the 3M tour; to George Anderson for answering my questions about Stillwater Prison; to Bob McAdam for talking with me about Hmong funerals; and to David Knudson for the information on handguns and target range shooting. Any errors are purely the fault of the author.

Finally, I would like to thank Deb and Lyle Taipale for the boat rides and for the connection to Bob. Also, Linda Donaldson, Lorrie Holmgren, Peg Wagensteen, and Jenifer LeClair for their help with the manuscript and for their friendship. Most of all, I'm indebted to my wife, Martha, for her belief, inspiration, and love.

AN INVITATION TO READING GROUPS/BOOK CLUBS

I would like to extend an invitation to reading groups/book clubs across the country. Invite me to your group and I'll be happy to participate in your discussion. I'm available to join your discussion either in person or via the telephone. (Reading groups should have a speakerphone.) You can arrange a date and time by e-mailing me at cjvalen@comcast.net. I look forward to hearing from you.